Praise for Or...

"I'm a huge fan of Amy's writing and I read One More Lie pretty much overnight. This is another incredible book from Amy.... I found it gripping, intriguing, sinister and it really had me hooked from the first page! I will definitely be recommending it to everyone!"

—Karen Hamilton, author of *The Perfect Girlfriend*

"A chilling, tragic story that feels like you're reading behind the scenes in a real criminal case."

—Araminta Hall, author of *Our Kind of Cruelty*

"I read it in a day. Superb. I'll be thinking of this for ages to come. An absolute masterclass in suspenseful storytelling."

—Jo Spain, author of *The Confession*

"Wow! What a compulsive, chilling novel. Both Charlotte and Sean are so thoughtfully and believably drawn, I felt almost as if I was intruding on their most private of thoughts—it makes it a really sinister and yet ultimately tragic story. I will definitely be recommending it."

—Phoebe Locke, author of *The Tall Man*

"Dark, chilling and totally gripping.... What I loved about this one is how skillfully Lloyd builds up an almost unbearable dread."

—Catherine Ryan Howard, author of *Distress Signals* and *The Liar's Girl*

ONE MORE LIE

Also by Amy Lloyd

The Innocent Wife

ONE MORE LIE

A NOVEL

AMY LLOYD

HANOVER
SQUARE
PRESS

**HANOVER
SQUARE
PRESS™**

Recycling programs
for this product may
not exist in your area.

ISBN-13: 978-1-335-62902-9

One More Lie

First published in 2019. This edition published in 2021.
Copyright © 2019 by Amy Lloyd

This edition published by arrangement with Harlequin Books S.A.

Hanover Square Press
22 Adelaide St. West, 40th Floor
Toronto, Ontario M5H 4E3, Canada
HanoverSqPress.com
BookClubbish.com

Printed in Spain

For Mum and Dad

ONE MORE MORE LIE

EVIL DUO RELEASED FROM PRISON

Pair given new identities, cosmetic surgery and full benefits costing the taxpayer over £1,000,000...

Mother of victim says she is "horrified"...

Public anger at resources spent on ensuring the pair remain protected...

Together they abducted their disabled classmate Luke Marchant...

Police involved in the investigation say justice has not been done...

ONE

Her: Now

There is a child staring at me from across the aisle. I turn to face the window and enjoy the warmth of the sun on my face until we pause at a bus stop and the light is blocked. When I look back, the child is still staring, and I blush. For a second I imagine doing something cute, something like sticking my tongue out at him or crossing my eyes, but I know that when I do these things they are not cute and can even come across as sinister. Maybe it is my shyness. Maybe I cannot pull it off because I am shy or maybe people can sense that there is something missing in me, that I am broken.

"Excuse me," someone is saying. They don't say it in a nice way. When I look up there is an old lady who smells a little like lavender and like her coat has been tucked away for a long time over the summer and she has only just taken it out. I don't know what she wants.

"What?" I say. It comes out wrong. I think about what Dr. Isherwood said about appearing abrupt, cold. I smile with 70 percent of my teeth showing and then relax my face.

"Is anyone sitting there?" she asks.

There isn't anybody sitting there. It's just my bag. Then I realize what she means and I put my bag on my lap, and she sits down with a tut and a sigh. I don't know why people don't just say what they mean. Why she doesn't say, *Please can you move your things so I can sit down?*

I look back to the child, but now it is the mother who's staring at me. It looks like others are, too, and that they are all wondering what is wrong with me and why I made the old lady stand for so long without moving my bag.

Now my stomach is trembling. I wasn't worried about my first day of work until all this happened. Two more stops and we'll be on Walters Road. Get off the bus, walk towards the traffic lights, take the next left. I need to go to Customer Services and say, *Hello my name is Charlotte and I'm starting here today.* I need to ask for Mr. Buckley, the manager.

I can picture all of this in my head as Sarah and I did a dummy run last week before I left the unit for good. But still I think that I'm remembering wrong and I feel nervous. Sarah said it was fine to feel nervous, that this was a big step and she knew I could do it. Because Sarah normally works with teenagers and children, she talks to me like I'm also a child. Dr. Isherwood says Sarah means well and she's just trying to put me at ease. Secretly I think Sarah believes I am mentally disabled and not just a little strange. She doesn't know who I am, or my real name, or why I am twenty-eight and need help to catch the bus. If Sarah knew who I am, I know she wouldn't be smiling so widely. With 80 percent of her teeth and intense eye contact.

My ankle itches. I bend down and squeeze a finger underneath my tag. Under the tag it is always moist and I can't scratch it properly no matter how much I try. I snap back up, frustrated. Without thinking I bring my finger to my nose to sniff. Sometimes, if water gets trapped behind the tag when I shower, it starts to smell a little cheesy. The woman next to me hunches her shoulder away from me. I realize she has been watching and she is making a show of being disgusted. She needn't be; my finger smells of nothing today.

My stop. I press the bell a long time before I really need to and I squeeze past the old lady and stagger down the bus, holding the bars as I go. When I look back the old lady has moved into the window seat and rested her large handbag on the space next to her. *That's rich*, I think. I'll tell Dr. Isherwood about her tomorrow.

When I step off the bus I have a moment of panic. Nothing looks as I remember it. I'm worried I'll get lost and be late. If I'm late they will change their minds about hiring me and if I don't have a job they'll send me back to secure care and— I take a breath. I look at the watch they gave me: I am forty minutes early. The walk there will take less than ten minutes. I want to be at least ten minutes early. Even if I am lost for twenty minutes, I will still be there on time.

This soothes me and when I look at the road ahead of me it looks just as it did last week: the traffic lights and the railway bridge behind them. Further ahead will be the supermarket where I will work part-time, some mornings and some afternoons, for as long as I am told to. Maybe this will be forever. I walk slowly because I have time. Too much time, I realize, as I turn left. I'm glad I brought a book.

Inside the supermarket is a Costa coffee shop. When I arrive I have enough time to get a coffee, but when I look at the menu behind the counter, I can't believe how expensive it is. The man at the till asks me what I'd like and I pretend to look at my watch, then tell him I'm just waiting for my friend. I walk away as if I'm looking around for someone and my cheeks burn. What if he sees me working later and he knows I was lying?

I wonder what it's like to meet a friend for coffee. I'm imagining the type of friend I might have, someone quiet, a woman—obviously—who wears glasses and puts her hair up in one of those claw clips. Someone who likes to read and hates loud places. I'm walking around in my own world, as Dr. Isherwood says I am prone to, when I see something that I can't ignore, even though I want to.

It is today's newspaper. A headline: "EVIL DUO RE-LEASED FROM PRISON."

For a second I think this can't be about me. The article says I've had cosmetic surgery but I haven't had anything like that. So I unfold one from the shelf to see the rest of the article. As I read it I have to resist the urge to talk to it, to tell it that it's lying. To shout that I'm not evil and to beg it to stop talking about it, that it doesn't understand and it just makes people mad.

Then I read a paragraph. Then I reread the headline and I realize the worst part. They said "duo." Two. Not just me, but Sean is out, as well.

TWO

Her: Then

There are no windows in the van and it's dark. I'm sitting facing sideways, which always felt like fun until now. Each bump and turn makes me lean onto one of the policemen on either side of me. Whenever I lean on Constable Hartley, he pushes me back and his nose wrinkles like he smelled something bad. Constable Adams is kinder. He says things like "Whoopsie-daisy!" and he smiles to try to make me feel better. It doesn't really work, though.

I feel sick but not carsick. It's worse because I can't see where we're going and I don't know how close we are to the court. The policeman who's driving says something to his radio and the radio says something back. I try to hear what it is but the engine is too loud so I can't.

The policemen start to act differently. They sit straighter

and they roll their shoulders and this is how I know we're getting close.

"Shit," says the one who's driving, and Constable Hartley stands, bent over so he doesn't hit his head on the roof, and slides the hatch between us and the driver open a little further.

"What is it?" I ask Constable Adams. My lip is already wobbling because I can hear the noise of the people outside. Adams pats my knee and smiles.

"Nothing to worry about," he says, lying to me.

The noise is deep and angry. The kind of sound the earth makes before it cracks apart.

"I don't like it," I'm saying. I can't catch my breath. The shouting is getting louder and louder and the van has slowed to a crawl.

"There's fucking hundreds of them," Constable Hartley says as he sits back down.

"Lee," Constable Adams says quietly. The kind of voice someone uses when they're warning someone they're about to tell them off.

"What?" Hartley says. He's pretending he doesn't know that I'm scared. He likes to do that; he does it a lot.

There's a bang. Something against the metal at my back. It hits the van so hard that I can feel it. I scream.

"Quiet," Hartley snaps.

"It's okay," Adams says, holding my hand in both of his. "Don't worry."

"Some bastard threw a brick," the driver calls back. I cry. I can't help it, even though I know it will make Hartley angry.

There's more banging, coming from the outside the van.

"Don't let them in," I sob.

The van has stopped completely and people are pushing

and slapping the sides. We begin to rock and the noise gets so loud that I cover my ears with my hands and I'm crying so much my body is shaking.

Hartley takes my wrists and pulls my arms down. From the outside I can hear people screaming: "Evil!" "Monster!" "LIAR!"

"You listen to it," Hartley says. "Listen to how much they hate you."

"Lee! What the hell is wrong with you? She's only ten!"

"So was Luke," Hartley says, and the name makes me scream and try to wrench my hands free.

Luke. I can hear his voice. Feel his warm hand in mine.

The crowd outside is slapping their palms against the van like a drumroll. I cover my ears again and close my eyes. Then I take one of my plaits and put the end in my mouth and suck on it. Miss told me not to do that but she isn't here and so I do. I like the way it feels on my tongue, between my teeth.

Before the van came to pick me up, Miss sat on a chair behind me and pulled my hair into two plaits so I'd look smart for my first day of court. I was crying like I had been all night and all through breakfast.

"Tell me all the things you're afraid of," Miss said. "Tell me everything and we'll see how to make it better."

I told her about the people who shout and about Constable Hartley. I told her about having to stand up and say my name in front of everyone in the court. I told her how I didn't like it when people talked about what had happened. How I didn't want to hear them say what we'd done because I couldn't remember what happened and I didn't know if they were telling the truth.

"Is that all?" she asked. I shook my head. "What else?"

I didn't want to say it at first. She smoothed my hair and told me I'd feel better if I said it.

"I don't want to see Sean," I said. She held me and it was so warm, her woolly jumper so soft, that I didn't want to let go even after I'd stopped crying.

"Sean won't be there, sweetheart. Remember? Sean has already been in court. You don't need to worry. You'll never see Sean again."

The van starts to move again and Constable Adams gently pulls my plait from my mouth.

"You don't want to do that, love," he says. "Yuck. If you chew your hair you'll get big hair balls in your tummy, like a cat. And then you know what will happen?"

I shake my head but his face is making me smile so I think I know what he's going to say.

"One day it'll start to come up again, like this," and he starts to pretend to throw up, like a cat, and it's so funny that I laugh. Then he pats my head. "That's better," he says.

Suddenly Constable Hartley stands and thrusts open the doors and there's a million flashes and the roar starts all at once. Constable Adams hangs a blanket over my head but it's too late, I know they've already seen me. The crowd swarms in and I don't want to get out of the van. Adams tries to pull me out and he's telling me it's okay, but I know it isn't. People are shouting my name.

"Enough," Hartley says, and he grabs my legs and puts one hand under my arm and carries me on his shoulder. The blanket falls on the ground and I want him to let go so I thump his back with my fists as hard as I can.

My face is all screwed up from crying but they're still taking pictures. They don't stop; they never stop.

THREE

Her: Now

"Stop!" I say out loud. *Stop thinking about it!* I look around, remembering I am in a supermarket, in front of the newsstand. A pretty blonde TV presenter smiles at me from the loud cover of a gossip magazine. For a second I can't remember where I am or how I got here. These memories are so real that I can feel Constable Hartley's shoulder digging into my stomach, taste the salt of my tears on my lips.

Dr. Isherwood tells me these are "intrusive thoughts," memories that I suppress but that come back when they're triggered. Perhaps I shouldn't have looked at the paper.

I don't recognize myself in the girl in the picture. She is smiling, one baby tooth at the front of her mouth that didn't fall out until she was almost twelve. The caption reads: "CHILLING SMILE AT FIRST COURT APPEARANCE."

Her hair is so blond it's nearly white. After the sentencing it grew out mud brown, as if whatever evil was inside her spilled out and tainted the surface.

She is so small. Almost eleven years old but looks eight. Can we really be the same person? I'm not even sure. I am new now: new name, new history, new life. I can't tell what the old me is thinking in this picture, what she was ever thinking, before…

I fold the paper and take it to the counter, then I grab a packet of mints and pay for them both with a five-pound note.

I need to get some fresh air. I try not to think about Sean and where he might be, what he might be doing. I try not to think about whether he is thinking about me.

"Don't think of a pink elephant," Dr. Isherwood said once. I smiled like I understood. "Do you see what I mean? If you tell yourself not to think of something, you'll think about it anyway. Let's try some exercises to help you when you get trapped in these memories."

I put a mint in my mouth and bite hard.

"Concentrate on your breathing. Breathe in for five, out for seven," Dr. Isherwood said.

This helps. This always helps.

I close my eyes and count. Soon my heart rate is slower and Sean's face disappears from my mind.

"Charlotte."

I take another mint out of the packet and place it on my tongue.

"Charlotte?"

When I open my eyes there's a man standing over me, one hand holding on to the strap of his bag and the other stretched out in my direction.

"I'm Neil? Mr. Buckley? We met at the interview? I'm

your manager." He smiles and waits before pulling his hand back and adjusting his bag on his shoulder.

"Hi," I say. The collar of his shirt is dotted with flakes of skin. One of his top front teeth is trying to push past the other one.

"Do you want to come in with me now and I can show you where the staff room is?"

I look at my watch.

"But I don't start for twenty-two minutes yet," I say. The mint I tucked into my cheek is starting to melt but it's rude to chew when people are talking to you. Neil stares at me, smiling. I try not to look at his tooth.

"Quite right," he says after a moment. "Of course. I just mean that you're welcome to spend time in the staff room if you want to get out of the cold? Perhaps a good opportunity to meet some of your new colleagues, if you like?"

"No, thank you," I say. I smile. He smiles.

"Well," he says, but doesn't continue. "I suppose I shall see you again in twenty-two minutes."

Twenty-one, I think, minus the five minutes I'll take to speak to Customer Services and find him. If you aren't five minutes early, you're late. They told us that in Life Skills at the center.

"Nice to meet you again, Charlotte," Neil says before he leaves.

I resist the urge to look at the paper again as I don't want to lose track of time, but I feel it next to me, the hate it's radiating. For a second I think of leaving, for anywhere, taking the bus to the seaside and reading on the pier, a bag of chips hot in my lap. But this is my first day and Dr. Isherwood said I must at least try. So many people would be disappointed, she told me. "We all want you to succeed."

When it is time I make my way to the Customer Services desk and I introduce myself.

"Hello," I say. "I am Charlotte Donaldson."

Am I? I wonder. It feels uncomfortable, like a blazer that's too tight on the shoulders. The police had come to the center and slid my new passport across the table towards me. I looked at the picture and I saw myself: the too-short hair and the thin lips held straight. The name didn't match.

"Charlotte," I said out loud. "Donaldson. Charlotte Donaldson."

I tried to make the name match the picture. I imagined a friendly voice calling, "Charlotte, Charlie, Sharl." *Sharl.* That is what people say when you're called Charlotte. It sounded like the noise a trapped animal might make.

"Are there any other names?" I asked the police officers. "I don't know if I am a *Charlotte.*"

They shared a look. It's a look a lot of people share when I've said the wrong thing, or I've said exactly the right thing but it turns out it's not okay to say it.

"Love," one started, leaning in. "Have you ever heard the phrase, 'Beggars can't be choosers'?"

Sometimes people ask questions that they don't really want you to answer. Now I am Charlotte.

"I need to see Neil, the manager," I say now. "It's my first day."

"Yeah, no worries, you can just go round if you like," the girl at the desk says. I remain where I am, unsure what she means. "The doors?" she says. "Behind me?" She turns and points and I make my way around the long counter, through the doors and into the staff area.

Inside there are lockers and round white tables with coffee stains and crumbs on them. The people bent over their mobile phones look up briefly to see who has come in, but when they realize I'm a stranger they look back down and say nothing. They seem young, teenagers, perhaps twenty-one-or twenty-two-year-olds. I realize, suddenly, that I am lonely. I realize how much I had hoped that I would make new friends at work but now I can see that I don't fit in here, either. I take a seat in the corner, no phone to stare at, and feel stupid for expecting anything to change.

"Charlotte," Neil calls as he comes in, the doors swinging behind him. "I hope you're ready to get started?"

Neil pairs me with a woman named Dawn. Dawn has worked here for fifteen years. She has two terriers called Pepper and Frank and she had to go back to work when her husband got cancer. She has brown hair with gray roots and her shoes look like they are designed for comfort rather than style. Dawn is too old to be a friend. Perhaps I am being unkind but it's true. What could we ever talk about, me and Dawn? Besides, in the hour in which we rotate the stock in the poultry station, she asks me only two questions about myself.

Not that I could tell her about me, anyway. I couldn't say, "Well, Dawn, the truth is that I have spent eighteen years in secure institutions, I have a new name and a new history, and this is the first day of my new future, and so far I don't like it at all." I couldn't say, "I wonder if I am a monster, like they say, or if really I am a normal person who did a bad thing like others say."

No. I'd have to tell her about Charlotte, the new me. The story I practiced and repeated until it came out halfway natural. The kind of story people forget. Not like the real one.

"Now we take this lot back and mark it as reduced," Dawn tells me, nodding towards the piles of chicken we found that are on their sell-by dates. "When we bring them back out, you watch. Vultures."

I smile like I understand.

We go back into the cold warehouse-type area and Dawn shows me how to use the sticker gun. This is the kind of task I enjoy: repetitive, rhythmic, soothing. Dawn is talking about how her husband worked for fifty years, never missed a day, and how his employers won't help him now he's sick. He's not "entitled" to anything, she says. I like the click of the gun, the mounting pile of reduced chickens to my side.

"Meanwhile, you've got people who never worked a day in their lives and they get everything handed to them on a plate. The system is broken. Work doesn't pay anymore."

I nod, even though it feels as though she is talking about people like me.

We wheel the trolley back into the shop but we are barely out of the doors when people start to push and shove past each other, grabbing whatever they can.

"At least let us get out of the doors! Move back!" Dawn is yelling. She shouts like she's annoyed but she looks like she enjoys it.

I don't. The trolley pushes against my stomach and soon it feels like I can't breathe. Someone shoves me with their shoulder and people are stumbling and staggering as they fight for the reduced chickens. I let go of the trolley and go back through the doors, into the cool. I hear the crash as the trolley topples to the floor. At least in here it's cold and I can breathe; it's dark, I'm alone.

"I warned you," Dawn says when she comes back through. "Animals. They're worse than animals."

At the end of my shift I take my bag from the locker

and I'm rooting through it as I head for the door. Neil is suddenly in front of me, his arm a barrier between me and the exit.

"Could you step aside for a minute, Charlotte?" he says. His smile doesn't go with his eyes. The direction he guides me in ends with a security guard, a fat one whose jaw works on a piece of chewing gum the way a cow chews grass. Because his mouth is occupied he breathes through his nose and every now and then he makes a noise like a snorer. He looks everywhere but at me, his hands clasped behind his back.

"The way we do things here, Charlotte, is that every day we select random members of staff to have their bags checked as they leave," Neil explains.

"All right?" the security guard says, as if he's only just noticed we're there.

I pull my bag further onto my shoulder and wait for Neil to say more.

"It's only a cursory look, always by myself or one of our boys from security. It doesn't mean we're accusing you of anything." Neil laughs. "But we've had some issues in the past, so in the interest of not singling anybody out, we just perform random checks. Is that okay with you?"

I nod. Neil knows I've been in care, I think. He doesn't know who I am, but he knows where I have come from.

"So if you pass your bag to Dan..." Neil says.

I pass my bag to the security officer. He pulls out the newspaper I bought earlier and a sanitary towel falls to the floor. Quickly, I bend to the floor and pick it up, squeezing it in my palm. My face must turn red because Neil is talking again, laughing in a way even I recognize as uncomfortable.

"You don't need to worry about any feminine items! Dan's seen it all before, haven't you, Dan?"

"And worse," Dan says, his thick fingers rifling through my few possessions. When he's finished he hands me back the bag. He almost seems disappointed.

"We'll see you next time then, Charlotte. Thanks for all your hard work today," Neil says. We shake hands and I leave, feeling their eyes on my back.

On the bus back to the house I look at the streets of the town I've been sent to. On the high street we pass a hairdresser's, a Poundstretcher, a charity shop. The stores are already closed for the night and the unlit windows look depressing. The place where I live is close to the city but still feels like a whole different world. I think they call it *suburban*: streets lined with oak trees, a park with a lake and a café and paddleboats that look like swans. My support worker, Sarah, and I walked around the lake the first time we came here.

"Aren't you lucky," she said. "All this right on your doorstep!"

I didn't say anything. The thing about nice places is that they're much nicer when you've got someone to share them with.

I told Dr. Isherwood that I didn't want to leave the institution. I didn't want to be alone again.

"You have to try new things," she said, trying to sound encouraging. "You'll make new friends, eventually."

"Like last time?" I asked. I was being sarcastic and she knew this.

"You know better this time," she said.

So instead of my own flat, my own house, like last time, they put me in a shared home. A halfway house. I think they thought I wouldn't feel as lonely, but here the other women are either the kind who keep to themselves, or the kind who should but don't. Some are escaping from abusive relationships, or have been evicted from their homes, while others, like me, have been released from rehab centers, prisons, and institutions, and have nowhere else to go.

Being surrounded by people doesn't make you any less alone. I know this now. That isn't why I felt better at the institution. I felt better there because I was me. Or at least, if not me, I wasn't Charlotte. There wasn't a life I never lived that I had to remember. If there had been, no one would even ask. Inside, people simply were. They didn't need to explain why they were who they were and they didn't ask it of you.

At the home I'm in now (the *the* is important, it is not our home, it doesn't belong to us; rather, we belong to it), women watch and they wonder. They ask questions and try to work you out. I can tell them all about Charlotte, about where she grew up and when she left school and how she ended up homeless after a bad relationship. I've been given enough detail to avoid suspicion, not enough to trip myself up.

But there's not enough of Charlotte to fill me up. There's still me, trapped inside. I feel me shaking in the hot core of myself and there's nowhere for me to go. I want to forget it, I want to forget me, but no matter what I try, I'm still there.

FOUR

Her: Then

The first time I left the institution I was only eighteen. They gave me my own house and I didn't have to work. Or they thought that I couldn't work because I lacked certain social skills and didn't do well on my exams.

All this was okay at first and I was happy, kind of, with my own TV and my visits to Dr. Isherwood, who moved so we could continue the therapy. But then there were long nights and days where I didn't see or speak to anyone and the loneliness was like screaming in my ears that kept me awake and drowned out music and books and TV and every other thought in my head.

I started to drink but the drinking only made me want to talk more. In the silence of my empty house I said things out loud to no one and the words seemed to hang in the air and fall down like layers of dust disturbed by the wind.

So I drank and I went out. I went to bars and looked over at the groups of friends who laughed and spoke so easily together. How did you get in? How did you become one of them?

A man touched my shoulder and asked if I wanted a drink. His face was red from alcohol and his hot beer breath felt clammy against my cheek. I nodded. The man asked me questions and I answered them and each time I asked him the same question he'd asked and it felt like learning to ride a bike, at first so frightening and new and impossible but then like second nature. He kept buying me drinks.

When I felt the dizzy sickness of too much vodka I told him that I wanted to go home and he offered to come with me. I felt too stupid to say no. How had I not realized that this was why he was speaking to me? Not friendship but sex. It seemed so obvious then. On our way out I looked again at the group of friends and one of the women looked up and smiled and I smiled back before the man opened the door and the cold air outside hit my face and cooled my red-hot cheeks.

It went on like this, for years. When I was lonely I went out and the men bought me drinks and we talked and then we would sleep together because that was the unspoken deal. For a while I would feel less alone but somehow still lonely, still barely there at all.

One morning, the morning of my twenty-fifth birthday, I woke up with that familiar taste in my mouth: old alcohol, the tongue and skin of a stranger still lingering in my saliva. I felt a weight beside me shifting on the bed and saw a man I did not recognize. I realized I was naked and quickly rubbed a hand between my legs to see if I had been careful or not. My hand came away dry and when I smelled my fingers I recognized the scent of a condom. Relief washed over me.

I got out of bed slowly, trying not to wake him. I wasn't ready to talk yet. I wasn't sure I ever wanted to. On my way to the bathroom I grabbed yesterday's clothes off the floor and slipped silently out of the room. It was summer, a heat wave, and the small house was stuffy and stifling. When I moved, the hangover became worse than I had thought. My legs shook as I walked to the bathroom and I thought I might faint. I had to drop to my knees and crawl to the bathroom, where I vomited as soon as I reached the toilet, closing the door behind me with my foot.

When there was nothing left inside me I flushed and ran the cold tap, splashing my face, holding my mouth open beneath the water and letting it run over my dry tongue. I didn't brush my teeth. Not then. I didn't want the man to kiss me, so I left myself sour and dirty.

Before I went downstairs I peered into my bedroom where the man was lying flat on his back, his head to one side, a leg emerging from the sheets. By then there had been many men, many mornings just like this, and yet it would be this one that stuck so vividly in my mind.

I never told Dr. Isherwood about the men, or the drinking, or the times I'd nearly said too much about who I really was. Sometimes it was as if I was standing on the edge of a cliff, moving one foot closer to the precipice, daring myself to jump.

Downstairs, memories of the previous night came back to me all at once. A powder wrapped in torn toilet paper, swallowed with Red Bull and vodka. A man with brown hair and tight jeans whose hand kept crawling underneath my shirt.

"It's my birthday tomorrow," I had said, pushing his hand away. "Not my birthday. My *real* birthday."

Jump, I told myself.

He wasn't listening. His hand squeezed into my jeans, pressing against my bladder.

"I'm not who you think I am," I told him. "I did something bad but I'm not really a bad person." *Jump and it will be over.*

"You can be bad," he said, pushing me against the wall. We were under a bridge; the railway above us was quiet and dark. The light flickered and it smelled of dried piss.

"I don't want to be bad," I said. I pushed him away and when he stepped back he started to undo his belt. The feeling faded and I stepped away from the ledge. "Can we just talk? Can we lie down in the grass and talk?" My skin felt hot and the breeze was so good and my blood rushed through me faster than I knew it could flow.

"Now?" he asked but I was already walking away, searching for more music, more sensations. When I looked back he was peeing against some graffiti.

I must have met the man in my bed sometime after I had left but the memory was lost to blackness.

In the kitchen I got a cold can of Coke from the fridge and ran it over my forehead, my cheeks. For a second my headache stopped; but then it came back, along with the ache in my jaw from grinding my teeth.

My phone buzzed on the counter. I almost didn't answer because the screen read No Caller ID, which usually meant it was my parole officer or a social worker. But I felt a fluttering in my stomach, like the possibility of something unexpected. These are the moments that make me believe in something magical, something more than what there is, because somehow I just knew that this was a moment that would change things.

I answered. There was just silence, the type of silence that only exists between two people. I waited. It felt like someone was pulling me through the air towards them. I don't know how long the silence lasted before they finally spoke.

"Happy birthday, Petal," the voice said.

I realized I had been holding my breath. When I exhaled I tilted my face away from the phone so he couldn't hear. I didn't want him to know that I felt anything. I could hear him smiling. I could hear his lips against a cigarette while he inhaled. It was him and I already knew it.

"Are you surprised?" Sean asked. "You shouldn't be. We'll always find each other, won't we, Petal?"

FIVE

Her: Now

I look up and realize I've missed my stop. I press the bell and walk down the aisle, swaying like a sailor on a ship in rough seas. It takes ages for the bus to stop and when it does, nothing looks familiar and I'm not sure how to get back to the home.

Across the street there's a little Tesco and I press the button at the crossing and wait for the green man. Outside the shop is a group of teens, rowdy, and I wish they weren't there. A girl shrieks and jumps backwards as a boy sprays something at her from a bottle, and when we almost collide she apologizes. One of the boys says, "Sorry, love," and they all giggle but I don't know if it's at me or something else. *Love.* Like he's a middle-aged man.

Inside, the fluorescent lights make everything look more appealing: all the colors, the crisp packets and the chocolate bars and the cans in the glass-front fridges. I pick up a basket and choose three chocolate bars for one pound twenty—a peanut butter KitKat, a Double Decker, and a Twirl. I get thick-cut white bread, a block of cheddar cheese, and a tin of beans.

At the counter, while I pack my things into a plastic bag, I ask the man the best way to get back to the area I'm living in. "I'm not from here," I add, unnecessarily. "I'm only visiting."

"Left at the end of the road, through the underpass. There are signs from there. About five, ten minutes' walk."

My stomach sinks.

"Underpass? Is there another way?"

"No," he says abruptly. "Unless you want to go way, way out of the way." He laughs.

"I don't mind," I say. "I could do with a walk."

"You'll have to ask someone else, love," he says, bored of me. "I wouldn't know."

"Thanks," I say, taking my bag as I leave.

Back outside I almost ask the teenagers but I change my mind at the last second and turn away. Behind me, I can hear their noise as I walk away. It is the kind of noise that says they are free, that they don't feel the eyes of the world on their backs like I do.

Following instructions, I turn left at the end of the road. It's not dark yet but it's trying. When I see the concrete steps leading down to the underpass, I stop. Why do they all look the same? The handles of the plastic bag dig into my palm.

The underpass, open like a screaming mouth. *Stop.*

I breathe; I count the seconds. Still my legs don't move. I try to think of a way out, watching the traffic on the four lanes, try to time it so I can cross, but there's never a gap long enough. Then I think of turning back, of following the road as far as it goes and crossing when I can, but the fading light reminds me of my curfew, and that the tag on my ankle is always watching. Not enough money for a taxi, no sign of the bus stop on this side.

I take one step at a time, slowly so that I don't slip on my shaking legs. The lights inside the tunnel are on and they flicker like it's winking at me, willing me in, a dare. When I'm at the bottom I look back and feel like I am leaving the world behind me. There's no one else inside. The walls are covered in overlapping graffiti, some beautiful, most not.

The slap of my shoes on the concrete; the way the sound bounces back off the walls.

Luke, the way he laughed at the echo, his laugh echoing back, laughing more.

I walk more softly, careful not to make a sound. A wind upsets the litter and leaves that line the path. They chatter like teeth. Above me, the world carries on, as if I'm not there.

It feels as though I will never make it. The end stretches away from me; a painted face leers at me from the wall. I sense something behind me but I don't turn. I don't want to know.

I walk forward, heel toe, heel toe, no echo, no laughter. The sounds of the world above get a little louder; the lights seem to buzz, like they're angry, like they've seen who I am and what I'm doing.

Luke, laughing. Luke, asking, "Where are we going?"

Heel toe, heel toe. I feel something creeping up on me, I move faster. Then my feet are slapping but I don't care. The feeling is creeping up on me, the sickness; I am angry and scared of myself, at myself. I am disgusted. I run until I am out of the underpass and I am spit out. I run up the steps and my legs ache but I don't stop until I'm at the top and I'm out of breath but I'm free. The roar of the traffic replaces the roar in my ears. Suddenly, I know exactly where I am.

As I approach the home I see the group of smokers. There is no smoking on the premises, so they gather at the gates in the hours before curfew, their tribe blocking the pavement and flicking their butts into the road. They are not supposed to do this but no one seems to stop them. Often they are in their pajamas and dressing gowns. At first I thought this was a little strange but now I am almost used to anything. When I turn to go in the gates they part and their conversation stops. I look at the ground, at one woman's slippers, the bottoms of them all gray with dirt they've dragged up from the street outside.

"All right?" one of them asks.

"Yes," I say, and keep moving. Behind me I hear a giggle, a whisper. I know it is about me; it always is. It always hurts.

Inside I go straight to the shared kitchen. Suddenly I'm very hungry. Empty stomach, dizzy-headed. My feet ache from a day of standing. The shoes they bought me for work are that stiff new leather. When I slide them off and peel down my socks I see curled skin where they have rubbed on my heels. I leave them both under the table and enjoy the cool of the tiled floor on my hot soles.

The sink is full of others' dirty pans, which is not a surprise but is still a disappointment. I eat my KitKat to calm the rumble in my stomach and then I start to wash everything in the sink. There are rules: that we wash up after ourselves, that we leave things as we found them. But no one ever seems to wash up and so everything is always left as it was found: a mess. Crumbs that bring in lines of ants, the rancid smell of the bin that's always overflowing.

When I've finished, I put a clean pan on the stove and tip in the beans I bought from Tesco. I put two slices of white bread in the toaster and I grate some cheese. On the long table behind me I unfold the paper and open it to my story. "Tomorrow's chip paper," my auntie Fay always said. Not anymore. I am glad I don't have a phone because it is much worse online, always.

The toast pops. I open the fridge to get my butter but when I lift it it's strangely light. Inside I see that the butter has gone, scraped to the sides, and I am so angry that I almost scream but I don't. This is something I should have guessed would happen. Why wouldn't it?

There's another butter in the fridge that isn't really butter but something made of olives. I'm about to take it when someone comes in, the sound of her flip-flops sucking on the bottoms of her feet as she walks. She's one of the loud ones, and a smoker, too, from the smell that accompanies her.

"All right..." She searches for my name, though I don't think I've ever told her.

"Charlotte," I say, putting the olive spread back in the fridge.

She's sitting at the table, one foot up on the chair, knee under her chin. She reads the paper upside down. I turn away, red-hot, hoping she doesn't recognize something in me from the grainy picture she's looking at. I stir the beans, hearing the crinkle of the pages as she turns it to face her.

"Fucking terrible, innit?" she says, but I pretend not hear. "A million pounds! If you ask me they should've thrown away the key. If you can do that when you're a *child*..."

I turn off the stove and tip the beans onto my dry toast.

It was a mistake to bring the paper back here. The hot pan sinks into the soapy water with a hiss. We're not supposed to take food to our rooms but if no one else is following the rules then they may as well not exist.

"I heard," she says, looking up at me, "that *she's* working in a petrol station by Colton industrial estate."

At this I smile. It is funny the things people make up.

"How do you know that?" I ask.

She shrugs. "Mate told me."

"I don't really know anything about it," I say. I turn to leave.

"Perverts," she says. "Both of them. Evil. But *her* especially."

I try to stop the plate shaking in my hands as I walk away from the kitchen.

"It was all *her* idea," she adds, stabbing at my picture with a finger. "She was the ringleader. Manipulative. A sociopath."

SIX

Her: Then

"Please." I'm on my knees like he told me to. "Pleee-aaaaaase can I borrow it?" I put my prayer hands together. "You are the best cousin in the world, pleeeeeaaaaaaase can I borrow it for one hour?"

Ryan laughs. "Will you clean my football boots?"

"Anything!" I am lying. I will not clean his football boots. They smell like old cheese.

"One hour," he says, tipping the BMX towards me. "But if you scratch it, you're dead."

Ryan thinks he can tell me what to do because he is ten and I am only eight.

"Yes! Thank you!" I stumble trying to get on the bike and he laughs. The handles are soft and squish in my hands. As I pedal away the bike wobbles side to side but I start to pick up speed and it feels good, standing because the seat is too high.

"Don't tell my mum!" he shouts behind me but I am already gone and I wouldn't tell Auntie Fay anyway because she'd only tell me I'm too small for Ryan's bike.

Soon I am flying. I steer into the speed bumps, the bike taking off and thumping down after each one. Lawn mowers and barbecue smells and paddling-pool splashes. The bike is a horse and I ride him to the end of the estate, loop around the flats and over the gravel, skidding and sliding around the corners, and ride back to the green where I pull on his reins, *Whoa, boy*, and settle him on the grass for a break, minding the dog poo, in the shade of a tree.

There are other kids that I recognize from school. Older kids: year fives and even some year sixes. I shrink when they see me, wishing I could sink into the shade and slip away like a shadow. I pick up the bike and roll it away but I hear them call to me. "Hey! Hey! Wait a minute!" They are smiling when I look at them and so I stop. I rest the bike against the tree and roll a stone under my shoe.

"What's your name again?" they ask me. I don't know why. I tell them but it comes out like a baby in my small voice. They laugh so I laugh.

"Do you go to St. Peter's?" the biggest boy asks me. His name is Liam Marchant and everyone knows who he is.

I nod.

"I knew I knew you. Is that your bike?"

I chew my lip. I think, *No.* I say, "Yes."

They all look at the bike and then Liam says, "Can I have a go, then? I'll ride it once around the green. I'll show you how to do tricks," he says.

"I can't," I say. "My auntie Fay made me promise not to let anyone else have a go."

"Your auntie Fay?" he says. They all laugh again so I try to laugh, too, but my stomach is jitterbugging.

"Oh, I know who she is now!" one boy says.

"Go on, let me have a go. I know your auntie Fay. She thinks I'm all right," Liam says.

"I can't," I say. "I have to go." I hold the bike handle but he is holding the seat.

"How come you live with your aunt?" a boy at the back says. They're still laughing.

"I don't," I say. I don't know why I say this.

"Yes, you do. Why are you lying?"

"Sorry," I say. "I have to go home because I promised I would come home soon."

"Is it really your bike?" one of the other boys asks.

"Yeah."

"She's lying."

"Did you nick it?" another says.

"Yeah," I say. Then, "No, I didn't."

"Oh my God, she's such a liar," Liam says.

When I try to pull the bike away from him he just holds it tighter.

"Tell us it isn't your bike and where you got it and we'll let you go," he says.

"It's my cousin's bike," I say, my cheeks hot like fresh sunburn.

"Why do you live with your aunt?"

"Can I go now?"

"Is it true your dad killed your mum?" the first boy asks. A girl slaps his arm but she giggles, too. My eyes fill with tears, warm like bathwater.

"You said I could go," I say.

"My dad told me about it," Liam says. "That your house burned down and your dad did it because he was mental."

"Shut up!" I shout. I pull the bike again but he pulls back harder.

"And that's why you're so weird and you lie all the time. You probably nicked this bike."

"I didn't," I say.

"We should call the police."

"I have to go home," I say, and my voice is shaking as much as my legs.

"Let her go," the girl says. She sounds bored. The boy releases the bike and I start to wheel it away because I am shaking so much I can't get on yet.

"How come you don't have any friends?" Liam says, and the sound of them all sniggering makes my brain roar and I turn around and I'm shouting before I can stop myself.

"Well, my auntie Fay says your dad's ripping people off and someone should report him to the council."

"What did she say?" Liam says. He sounds shocked. I don't know what "ripping people off" means but I know it is bad because of the way Auntie Fay's voice curled when she said it. And now they are all walking towards me and I have to force myself to climb on the bike to get away. "Oy," he shouts. "Come back and say that to my face!"

I'm pushing on the pedals and the bike is as wobbly as me but when they start running I pedal faster and faster. I wish I hadn't said it. They chase me but the bike is quicker and I look back from the end of the street and see they are far behind but then a gold car is suddenly right in front of me and I have to brake, the tires scraping the tarmac, the man in the car using his horn to scream.

I blink at him through the window and see him shouting but I can barely hear it. His whole face is angry even though I'm the one he nearly ran over and I feel my mouth hanging open but no words come out of it. Then I hear the boys laughing at me from back down the road.

As I ride away the tears tickle my neck and dry in the breeze and I don't want to go back home, I want to go nowhere, to not exist. I ride further than I'm allowed to go, past the rec club and to the playing fields. I ignore the park and the swings and the people and I ride over the soft grass even though it will make the wheels dirty and Ryan will make me clean them later. I ride to the end of the playing field, where the grass slopes down into the hedges at the backs of the houses. I leave the bike on the slope and climb down. There is a space in the hedges where you can hide, where the fences that fell down are on the ground and you can sit. You can hear the people in the park but they can't see you.

I look for the break in the hedges and I go through. But there's someone there, someone else who's crying. I know it's a boy because his orange hair is shaved close to his head. He hugs his knees and his head rests on his arms and every now and again he sniffs or huffs. He has on a denim jacket that's too big for him by miles.

"Hello?" I say. It makes him jump and when his head comes up I can see there are no tears on his face.

"Fuck!" he says. The sound of the word is like a slap. Ryan once told Auntie Fay I said the *F* word but I didn't and I didn't even know what it was then. I found out at school and I said it aloud in the bathroom, watched my face in the mirror as I said it, and it made me feel ashamed even though I was alone.

"You shouldn't say the *F* word," I tell the boy now.

He laughs.

"I thought you were crying," I say.

He shakes his head. Then he holds up a lighter and he flicks it twice, sparks jumping.

"You're not allowed to play with fire, either," I say, shaking my head.

"I'll show you something cool," he says. When he says it he smiles and it lights up his eyes with trouble. "Watch this," he says. He takes a deodorant can and shakes it, then he sprays it all over the leg of his jeans. He grins and flicks the lighter, holding the flame against his leg. The flame grows and suddenly it covers his whole leg. I stumble backwards, the heat of it on my eyelashes. Then he pats his leg and it's gone, like nothing happened. He's laughing. I lean forward and look at his jeans but they aren't burned at all.

"How did you do that?" I ask.

"Do you want a go?" he asks. I shake my head. "I'm Sean," he says, flicking the lighter again but not letting it flame.

"How old are you?" I ask.

"Nine," he says.

"How come you have a lighter if you're only nine?"

He shrugs. "Found it. Do you go to St. Peter's?" he asks.

"Yeah," I say. "But I'm in year three."

"How old are you?"

"Eight."

"You don't look like a year three," he says. "Are you really eight?"

I nod. He shrugs again.

"Oh, wait," he says. "Your mum's dead, isn't she?"

I feel my lip wobble and I hate it so I turn to leave even though this is my place.

"Wait," he says. "I didn't mean it like that. I don't have a mum, either, but she isn't dead."

At the top of the slope I grab the bike and decide I might

as well go back home. Sean is saying something but I ignore him and walk with my head down so no one can see me cry.

"Hey," someone ahead says. I look up. I see Liam and the group of year fives and sixes from earlier and it's too late to hide because they are coming towards me really fast like they might smash right through me. I drop the bike and I scream but it's the park and loads of kids are screaming so no one notices me. I cross my arms over my face and screw up my eyes tight and wish I could disappear.

"Say it to my face," Liam says. "Look at her, she's mental."

They're laughing and I'm crying. I keep my face hidden so they can't see me. Then from behind me I hear someone yelling, like a roar, and Liam and his friends start to scream so I look up. They're running away and Sean is chasing them; the whole front of his jacket is on fire and he's waving his arms around. The older boys keep running but they're shouting back that we're mental and Sean says, "I am mental! I'm mental!" And it makes me laugh and he drops on the floor and rolls around until the fire has gone out and the mums are looking from the benches and they all have open mouths and it makes me laugh more and more until the laughing feels almost like crying and I realize that they are the same, laughing and crying, the same. Like a release. Like I'm a bottle of pop that's been shaken and shaken and now I'm fizzing over and I can't stop; it will last forever.

SEVEN

Her: Now

I spend a sleepless night thinking about Sean, wondering if the woman in the kitchen was right, if it had all been my fault, right from the start. I try to make sense of everything and put it in order, to remember who had started it and who had been the one to bring it all to an end.

But my memories are all twisted and tangled and by the time the sun comes up I have a headache from trying to keep my eyes closed and I feel something strange, new. It's like I miss him. Sean. Miss the way my stomach cramped from laughing and that feeling like I was free-falling, the terror and the fun of it.

I pull my chair to the window and look out. A pigeon limps on the fire escape; a plastic bag trembles in a tree; the rooftops of the houses are gray and moss grows in their drainpipes. I am lonely. I'm so lonely I want to die.

Before the others can get up I take my towel to the shared bathroom and I wash. The water is tepid but when I turn up the heat the pipes groan like an old giant turning in his sleep and then the water is boiling, so hot I leap forward and the dingy shower curtain clings to my skin. I can barely reach back under the stream to turn the temperature down but when I do the cold feels like medicine.

Though my appointment with Dr. Isherwood is still four hours away I decide to leave before all the others get up. I stop in the kitchen to get rid of last night's uneaten dinner and when I look there's a woman at the end of the long table, a cup of coffee in front of her, a balled-up paper towel in her fist. We look at one another; she sniffs. I run my empty plate under the tap and feel tingles up my spine from her presence behind me. When I leave I look back and see she has her face in her hands.

Outside, I walk without purpose, knowing only that I want to avoid the underpass. The roads are quiet and the shops won't be open for ages. I find myself at the lake; the swans are sleeping with their heads tucked under wing. I sit on a bench and watch the water, the surface dead still. A man picking up litter says good morning but doesn't smile. Soon, the dog walkers begin to pass, throwing chewed-up tennis balls down the path; Labradors slosh in the shallows. I have always wanted a dog.

I get up and start to walk towards the high street, passing cyclists on their way to work and vans unloading boxes onto the pavement. Hungry, I look for a café amongst the hairdressers and the Chinese takeaways, ignoring the coffee chains that are too expensive. I can smell the café before I can see it: bacon and fried bread. Kelly's, the sign says. The window is covered in fluorescent cards advertising breakfast and lunch specials. Inside, there are men in overalls and paint-splattered jeans, who eat with one hand while they turn the pages of newspapers with the other. I scan to see if anyone is reading about me, but it doesn't look like it.

The woman at the counter (Kelly?) takes my order and asks me where I'm sitting.

"Um," I say. I am not yet sitting anywhere. "Can I sit... by the window?" I point to the free table by the window, four yellow seats and a tomato-shaped sauce bottle in the middle.

"If you're on your own, can you sit at a smaller table." It's a question but it doesn't sound like one.

"Oh," I say. I look around. By the toilets there is an awkward table meant for two people. "There?" I point, uncertainly.

"Table nine," she says. She rips the ticket off the top of the pad with my order and disappears behind a beaded curtain.

When I sit down my face is hot and I'm wishing I hadn't ordered anything so I could just leave. The radio is playing tinny-sounding pop music and a man laughs loudly in the corner at something his friend has said. Sometimes I feel like everyone is looking at me, or thinking about me, or laughing at me. I feel it now. As if every time I look up they have just looked away. What are they reading? And what if—

"Tea," Kelly says, putting down a metal teapot and a mug with a blue rim. "Breakfast will be out in five."

"Thanks," I say to her back as she leaves.

Two sugars. Maybe my blood sugar is low, because I shake as I hold the spoon, little white granules scattering on the table like hail. We have talked about this, Dr. Isherwood and I, how a healthy body is a healthy mind. All those mornings that I woke up with a head thick with drink, too sick to eat, trembling and weak. Three meals a day, exercise, no alcohol. I promised I would try.

Breakfast arrives after five minutes, just like Kelly had promised. I eat quickly, though it's too hot and I burn my tongue. When I'm finished I order some bread and butter so I can mop up the yolk and the beans left on the plate. A man returning from the counter stops at my table and says, "I wish I could eat like that and stay so thin!" He pats his round stomach like a shopping center Santa Claus and shakes his head, laughing. By the time I finish my second slice of bread the plate is as clean as if it has been washed.

Kelly doesn't ask if I'm finished. As soon as I rest my knife next to my fork she takes my plate away and returns with a cloth to wipe the table. I leave what's left of my tea and thank her.

There is nothing left to do except walk. I walk around the lake a few times, stopping to sit and watch the people go by.

Bored, I decide I will make my way to Dr. Isherwood's office early. The whole street is big Victorian town houses that have been converted to solicitors' offices and dentists' and dermatologists'. I sit on the low wall outside her building, next to the burgundy sign that reads: Glennwood House, Dr. Evelyn Isherwood (MRCPsych, MD), Child and Adolescent Consultant Psychiatrist.

I'm even earlier than expected and I kick my heels against the wall and imagine what I will say to Dr. Isherwood today. That I am lonely, that I do not like living in the halfway house, that the intrusive thoughts are back and they are strong and I do not have time to breathe before they happen. They come quickly, like a bag thrown over my head, and I'm unable to think of anything else.

I hear someone say hello. I look up and down the pavement but a hand touches my shoulder from behind and I jump. "I didn't mean to scare you," Dr. Isherwood says, her face kind. "You're here early, even for you."

"I didn't have anything else to do," I say. I wish she would leave her hand on my shoulder but she takes it away.

"Do you want to come in?"

"Don't you have another appointment?"

"I thought you might be early," she says. She smiles and looks at me over the top of her black-framed glasses. "I kept my morning free just in case. Come in."

I can feel the tears in my eyes and when I blink they roll down my cheeks. I catch one with my tongue, salty and hot, and my nose tingles like I just jumped into deep water. Dr. Isherwood walks ahead of me up the stairs to her office. The carpet looks as if it used to be salmon pink but now it's grayed and patchy. I push a finger into the patterned wallpaper that bubbles and peels behind the bannister.

"This isn't as nice as your old office," I tell her.

"It's a work in progress," she says. At the top of the stairs she turns. "I mean, I'm decorating. We're still getting everything moved in."

We go into her consulting room and she slides the sign on the door to say Occupied.

"Right," she says. She always says this, always. I smile. "How have you been?"

I sit on the high-back armchair. Around us, there are still boxes full of her books that she hasn't put on the shelves. It doesn't look like there are enough shelves for them all.

"Okay," I say. I am not okay. She knows this. Even after all these years it is not easy to say what I am when we start.

"I'm just trying to find…" she says, moving things around on her desk. I look at the backs of the photo frames on her desk and as usual I long to flip them around, to see who she keeps with her all day. "Ah! Here it is." She waves a file. My file. "Now, we saw each other back at the unit before you moved into the home, and at the time we discussed that, though you were nervous, you also felt quite positive about the steps you were taking. How have your first two days been?"

I clear my throat. "Um," I say. I clear my throat again because it feels like there's a hand around it, getting tighter.

"Oh dear," she says. She sits down on the chair opposite, crosses her legs, and tugs her bright flower-print skirt below her knee. "Let's start from the beginning. Are you all moved in?"

"Yeah," I say, thinking of the single suitcase that contains everything I own.

"Tell me how you spent your first evening in the home," she says, patiently.

"I unpacked. Sarah was there; she helped. Then after I'd unpacked she took me shopping."

"And you feel comfortable enough to travel to the shops by yourself?"

"Yeah," I say. "Well…"

"Well?"

"It's not really the traveling," I say. "It's more…when I get there."

"Can you explain?"

"You know," I say, because she does. "I feel like everyone is looking at me. Like they think I shouldn't be there." My cheeks are hot again. I look at the window.

"But you know—"

"It's not true. I know. But it's what I feel."

"Do you remember how you overcame this before?" she says.

Drinking. Drugs. Only leaving the house after dark, in

the hours when everyone became somebody else, so that I could be whoever I wanted, too.

"No," I say.

"It's hard to remember now," she says. "But you felt this the first time you were released. It took months but eventually the feelings subsided. At the time we discussed..." She licks a finger and flicks through pages of my file, back to when I was first released. Dr. Isherwood knows me better than I know myself. "First, we discussed that your desire for independence outweighed your anxiety in those scenarios. Is this still true?"

I nod.

"Good, I'm glad. We decided that in these situations you would break your outings down into tasks. So walking to the bus stop would be the first task, the bus journey would be the second part, entering the supermarket would be the third part, et cetera. Now, at each of these points we decided to rate your anxiety on a scale of one to ten..."

Now I do remember. Those endless routines and exercises that calm the mind. I remember the day I realized it was no more than a trick, a distraction, and it stopped working the same way it does when you see an optical illusion clearly for the first time.

"It helped for a while but then it stopped," I say.

"Oh," she says. She seems hurt and I regret saying anything. "Okay, well, shall we talk about the home? We decided that last time you were released, when you lived alone, you felt a little lonely and you missed the company of the unit. How has living in shared accommodation been?" I feel my nose wrinkle and she starts to talk again, quicker than before. "It's not a permanent solution! But we wanted to start you somewhere you could feel safe and with other women who are...starting afresh."

I can't help smiling. There is a sweetness and an opti-
mism that has never worn down in Dr. Isherwood, even
after eighteen years with me. I remember her at the beginning when she assessed me before the trial. I remember how she smiled and the smile didn't end when Miss
closed the door behind her. I remember a rough green carpet and a pile of toys in the corner. When she caught me
looking she told me I could just play if I liked, whatever
I wanted to do. I had heard this before, with social workers who knelt on the floor next to me as I brushed the hair
of a doll that had seen too many sad children. They never
wanted to play, only to talk, and to ask trick questions that
made you say things that they used later to tell the story
they wanted to hear.

So back then I didn't play. I sat in my chair and she sat
in hers. I slid down and folded my arms and stared at the
wall. Dr. Isherwood didn't stop smiling, but it stopped being
a smile with her mouth and just became something in her
eyes, a softer face than I was used to by then. My eyes
filled with tears, then more tears came, because I knew
she would say what everyone else said: "Crocodile tears."
Or, "Here we go again."

Instead, Dr. Isherwood got out of her chair and her pen
rolled to the floor. She knelt on one knee and she rubbed
my arm and that made me cry more even though it felt good
and she got me tissues and made me blow my nose. When
she screwed up the tissue and threw it in the bin she grabbed
another and dabbed under her own eyes and I realized she
was crying a little bit, too, but not as much. She asked if I
was okay; I nodded. When I exhaled, a snot bubble grew
from my nostril and popped, and I looked at her and she
laughed, so I laughed, too, and it had been so long since I
laughed that it made my face ache.

Eighteen years, and all the places she's moved so she can "work with" me, as she says, from children's unit to adult unit to my first release to here. Eighteen years is longer than I have ever known anybody. She is all I have.

I've wondered whether she has family, or whether I am all she has, too. But I can only see the backs of the photographs and the face of the psychiatrist that she is with me. However close I feel to her, I have to remind myself that I am only as close as anyone can ever be to their doctor.

"And does it work?" she's saying now.

"Um," I say.

She laughs. "You weren't listening, were you?"

"No," I say. "Sorry."

"That's okay. What were you thinking about?"

"A memory," I say. "I'm getting them again. They're very…" I try to remember the word she uses. "…vivid. Sometimes I can lose track of everything around me. I missed my bus stop yesterday."

"Really?" she says, sitting higher in her chair. I know what she wants to ask, but she won't ask right away. "We said this might happen again. When you're in the unit they keep you busy, busy, busy. Morning till night. No time to think. But when you're on your own, your mind will wander, and the things you have suppressed…"

"I know," I say.

"What kind of memories?" she asks, adjusting her pen so she can write.

"About the trial, about the last time I was out. About Sean." I stop and think. I don't want to lie but I know what will happen if I say what else I remember. About the echoes and footsteps. "A little about Luke," I say eventually. Her eyes widen and she leans forward. I already know what she is about to ask me and I feel guilty because I know I won't be able to answer.

"Do you remember what happened?" she asks, trying not to sound too forceful.

"The underpass," I say quickly, knowing I have disappointed her. "Nothing after the underpass."

Her shoulders slump but she smiles that warm smile and her brown eyes are shining with forgiveness. She is beautiful, I think. Even more now than ever. The way the lines on her face show you how much time she has devoted to smiling, to being kind.

If I could remember what happened that day, I would tell her. I want more than anything to be able to tell her what she wants to hear: that it wasn't my fault, that it was Sean who... But what if it wasn't Sean? Maybe it's better to have forgotten.

"What about the job?" she asks. "Does that help take your mind off things a little? Last time, we felt that being unemployed contributed to negative feelings, and that a job might give you a sense of purpose and the opportunity to socialize. Has it helped?"

"Kind of," I say. "But...they made me work with someone old all day so I didn't get to make any friends."

"Someone old," she says back to me, laughing a little. "You're a very harsh critic! I dread to think of how you might describe me!"

I blush. "She's older than you. Lots older. And she was miserable, she moaned all day."

"But it was just your first day and you haven't met everyone yet. Perhaps you'll be working with someone else tomorrow. What about the women in the home?"

I wrinkle my nose and she laughs again.

"What's wrong with the women at the home, then?"

Everything, I want to say. *You name it.*

"They're just…" I start but I can't find the words. "I don't think any of them would be good friends."

"And what is a 'good friend'?" she asks.

I want to tell her about laughing until you fizz over, about falling and falling and never hitting the ground, about not having to think your own thoughts when they're with you. But I can't, because I'm not supposed to feel like that. Not about Sean.

"Do you think you ought to give people a chance before you judge them?" she says. "Maybe you'll find out things about someone that you would never have guessed until you talked to them."

But, I want to say, *how can I become friends with someone if I don't know who I am? How can they be friends with me if* they *don't know who I am? And what I am? And…*

I start to cry and, just as she first did eighteen years ago, she slides out of her chair and rests one knee on the floor. She does it slower now, lowering herself to my level, and something pops as she crouches, but she still puts her hand on my arm and rubs. My skin is cold. I wish she would hug me, I have always wished she would hug me, but she can't.

"It all feels too much right now," she says, her voice like honey and lemon. "It's only your first forty-eight hours. It's *so much* change and you're doing *great*! You are! I am *so proud* of you. Listen, can I tell you something?"

I nod. I accept a tissue when she reaches behind me and holds out the box.

"We all feel like this. We do. I do! This morning I had to register at a new dentist's and when I got there I'd forgotten to bring a letter as proof of address and the receptionist was *so rude* to me that when I got back in my car I started crying. It wasn't really the receptionist, or that I'd gone miles out of the way in school-run traffic, that made me cry. I just felt completely overwhelmed for a minute. I had to have a cry, get my frustration out, and get on with it. Do you see what I mean?"

She looks at me, wanting me to feel better, but I don't. Now I feel worse. That she has moved again, all to stay with me, and I have repaid her by being unhappy, ungrateful.

"We all have our moments," she says. Her knee cracks again as she stands. "It's about learning to deal with them, that's all. Give it a chance. Places don't feel like home until you've built some memories there."

But I have tons of memories and I have never felt at home. Anywhere.

EIGHT

Her: Then

We can see the shapes of two people behind the bendy glass. They knock again.

"Shit," Mum says. I put my hand over my mouth. "Sorry," she tells me and she brushes my head with her hand; my hairs float for a second as if they are reaching out and saying, *Don't go.*

She opens the door and they say her name, which is always weird because I only call her Mum. I am not supposed to listen because I am too little for grown-up conversations but I am six now and not a baby anymore, so I try to listen but I can only hear Mum because she is talking so much louder than the other person.

"Who called you this time? Well, it's my house and I don't have to let you in. Fine, call the police! Come back when you've got an order. I don't give a sh—" She slams the door and it's so loud it makes my eyes shut even though it's my ears that it hurts. "I'm sorry," she's saying. Her hands are on my cheeks and her thumbs wipe away the tears. "Mummy shouldn't have shouted, I'm sorry."

"Or slammed the door!" I tell her.

"Or slammed the door, you're right, I'm sorry. There we go, shh," she says, and it works because it always does. "Don't do that," she says. She takes my plait and pulls it out of my mouth, the hair all soaked with spit. "You have such beautiful hair," she says as she kisses my head. "If you chew it you'll get split ends."

"What are split ends?" I ask. She wiggles the end of her hair in my face and it tickles like I might sneeze.

"These," she says, but I can't see anything wrong with her hair.

"Your hair is beautiful, too," I tell her.

"Not as beautiful as yours," she says.

"You are beautiful," I tell her.

"No," she says. "I'm not." She sounds sad.

"But you are," I say and I feel almost desperate. "Except…" I put my finger to her purple eye but she jumps back like I'm going to hurt her. "I was going to be gentle! I promise!"

"I know," she says. "It's just that it hurts a lot and I got scared for a second."

I understand because before she puts the antiseptic on my cuts I always move my knee around because I can feel it hurting even before it really does.

"Why are the police coming?" I ask.

"They're not," she says.

"But you said to them—"

"They probably won't come. I just said that because I

don't feel like talking to any more bloody social workers right now."

"Mum," I say, but she's already apologizing for swearing and I can tell that I'm annoying her. "Is it…um…is it because of your eye?" I ask. We don't talk about him. We talk about the things that are there after he's gone. Like purple eyes and broken doors. Never him.

"It's our nosy neighbors," she says.

"Because of the banging?" I say.

"Did it wake you up?" she asks.

"No," I say. It wasn't the banging. It was when she closed the door and my room went dark. She turned the key and I knew he was here. But then I heard them, the shouting and the banging, the same as always.

"It won't happen again," she says like she always does. "I promise this time."

"I know," I lie, because sometimes lying is okay when you only want to make people feel better.

Then someone is knocking hard on the door and we both look at each other and I can tell she's scared. I grab her hand in case it's him and I don't want her to let him in even though he would probably kick the door in again anyway and that's even worse.

"Police," someone says, and Mum goes from scared to mad really quickly and she can't get to the door quickly enough.

"You got here fast. You're not this fast when I call you, though, are you? Come on then, come and do your inspection," she says, and she keeps talking and talking even while they try to speak.

The policeman is tall and takes off his hat in the hallway and tucks it under his arm. Behind him are a man and a woman who are both wearing smart clothes and holding clipboards. The woman looks at me and she smiles even though Mum is still shouting.

"Hello," she says. The policeman puts his free hand on my mum's shoulder and talks quietly until she stops shouting. "My name's Deborah and this is Gareth."

"'Ello!" says Gareth. I put my hair in my mouth because I want to hold Mum's hand but she's behind the policeman.

"Would it be okay with you if we just had a word with your mummy in the kitchen?" Deborah says.

I nod. I don't know why grown-ups ask things like this because they just do whatever they want anyway.

"One sec," Mum says to them. She picks me up even though she always says I'm too big to be picked up, and she puts me on the sofa in front of the TV. She kneels down and puts in a tape. It's already started because I was watching it earlier before she turned it off and told me I'd seen it too many times today.

"There," she says, and she turns to me and takes the hair out of my mouth again. I'm trying to see around her head because I love *Button Moon* and this is one of the best ones but she keeps moving her face so I have to look at her. "I'll be five minutes," she says. "Be good. Don't worry about me, okay?"

This makes me worry because I didn't know I was supposed to be worried until now. She kisses my head and closes the door after they all leave. I put my hair back in my mouth and crunch it between my teeth. Every now and again I can hear my mum's voice get louder but it fades again and it's like waves, in and out, in and out.

Then the door opens and my mum comes in and turns the telly off and I think I've done something wrong.

"It's okay," she says, like she can read my mind. "Deborah and Gareth just want to talk to you for a minute. On your own."

I turn and look at them and they are both smiling as if they don't mean it.

"Why?" I ask.

"They just want to make sure you're okay," she says.

"What do you mean?" I ask.

"It's all right," Deborah says. She comes closer to me. "We just want to have a little chat and find out more about you. We don't bite!" She laughs. I look at my mum to see why it's funny but it doesn't look like she gets it, either.

"Why can't my mum stay?" I ask.

"Because Mum needs to have a word with Sergeant Barnes for a minute, don't you, Mum?"

I look to Mum to find out why Deborah is calling her Mum and my mum shakes her head and squeezes my hand. "I'll be back in a minute. Just talk to them and then they'll be off and afterwards we can go to the video shop and choose something for tonight."

"And chips?" I say because I can tell she will say yes if I ask.

"Sausage and chips for my sausage," she says and we laugh. "Love you. Be polite."

Deborah and Gareth watch her leave the room and close the door before they look at me again.

"What are you watching?" Deborah asks. Her voice is all pushed out and loud.

"*Button Moon*," I say.

"And what's *Button Moon* about?" she asks me. I can't believe she has never seen it and I stare at her for a while until she asks me another question. "Is there a family in *Button Moon*?"

"Yeah," I say.

"And who's in the family?"

Her voice makes it sound like this is a trick.

"Is there a mummy in the family?" she asks. I nod. "Is there a little girl in the family?" she asks. I nod again. "Is it like your family?" I shake my head. "Why not?"

"Um," I say. I look at Gareth, who is nodding at nothing. "Because in *Button Moon* there's Mrs. Spoon and Tina Spoon but there's Mr. Spoon, too."

"Is Mr. Spoon the dad?" she asks. I nod again. "And your dad, does he live here?" I shake my head. "Does your dad ever come round here, even though he doesn't live here?" I stay still. Deborah nods to Gareth and he writes something down. "It's okay, we've spoken to Mummy and she says that sometimes he does come round."

"He's not supposed to," I say quickly.

"And why isn't he supposed to?" Deborah asks.

I shrug.

"Did Dad come round last night?" she asks.

"My dad?" I ask.

"Yes," she says. "Your dad. Did he?"

I stay still.

"It's okay for you to tell us," she says, leaning in closer to me. She smells like the hairdresser's. "Mum has already told us that Dad came over last night. Did you know he came over last night?"

I think about it and how I'm not supposed to lie and so I nod.

"What happens when Dad comes over?"

I shrug and they look at each other.

"You don't know? Or you don't want to tell us?"

"Um…" I wish my mum would come back in because I don't know what they want me to say. "When he comes here, then it's loud."

"Loud?"

I nod.

"Why is it loud?"

"Because of the shouting. Then the neighbors complain."

"Does Dad ever shout at you?"

I shake my head.

"No? Never?"

I shake my head again. "I stay in my room," I say.

"Why?"

"I'm supposed to," I say. "So Mum locks the door."

They both look at each other and I know straightaway I said something important but I don't know what it is.

"Does Dad come over a lot?"

"No," I say. "Sometimes."

"And when he does, does Mum lock the door to your room?"

I nod.

They talk to each other in quick voices. "Thank you," she says. "You've been very good. Do you mind if we just talk to Mum again quickly?"

I shrug. Gareth brings over a roll of stickers like they have at the dentist and he peels one off and holds it out to me. I take it and he ruffles my hair and when he goes I screw up the sticker and pull a chair to the mantelpiece so I can stand on it and see in the mirror. I lick my hands and pat my hair back to where it is supposed to be. Then I can hear Mum shouting at them again and it makes me jump so much that the chair wobbles and I have to hold on to the mantel or I'll fall off.

Mum's shouting gets louder as she stomps down the hall and I don't have time to get off the chair before she sees me and I'll be in trouble because I'm not supposed to do it.

"Sorry," I'm saying and my knees are shaking while I'm

trying to climb down. But it's like she hasn't even seen the chair and instead she picks me up and she holds my head against her shoulder so I can't see who she's shouting at behind me.

"If you would just do your bloody jobs," she's saying, "I wouldn't *have* to lock doors. I wouldn't have the bloody neighbors complaining to social bloody services because he'd be where he belongs!"

"Did you report him last night when he came over?" a man is saying. I grip handfuls of Mum's T-shirt and squeeze my eyes shut.

"No!" Her voice sounds louder with my ear on her shoulder, loud and booming. "Because it takes you half an hour to even turn up and it only makes things worse!"

"You shouldn't let him in," someone says and Mum makes a noise like a growl and she bobs me up and down and her hand swishes my back.

"If I don't let him in he just kicks the bloody door down! I'm sorry," she says with her breath in my hair. "I'm sorry."

"Until we can find a solution…" Deborah is saying and then Mum starts to cry.

"You're not taking her," Mum says. "She's fine. He won't bother her. I'd kill him if he even—"

"We are happy for her to stay with a relative if you have someone who can care for her, but we *need* to ensure that she's safe. I'm sure you can understand—"

"My sister," Mum says, still bobbing me like I'm baby, but it's too rough and my head bounces on her shoulder. "She can stay with my sister."

"No," I whine and Mum puts me on the sofa and sits with me. "I don't want to. You said we could watch a video and have chips."

"I know I did, I know, but…what if I ask Auntie Fay if she'll get you chips and let you watch a video?"

"Auntie Fay doesn't let me watch videos when I'm there," I cry. "And she watches boring things and you're not allowed to eat while you watch TV!" And she doesn't even let you have a drink in the TV room or talk or make any noise when she's watching something. "I hate Auntie Fay!"

"Mummy will ask her," Mum says. "I'll say it's a one-off. But you have to stay there. I don't want you to go, either, but—"

I cry more and Mum tells me it's not up for discussion and then she stands up and I let myself flop down, and I'm crying even though they've all left and it's just me and it's pointless because I'm going to Auntie Fay's anyway.

I'm in the back of the car with Mum, and Gareth is driving. Deborah is next to him in the front and no one is talking. I sit as close to the window as possible and stare out. I am ignoring Mum but she reaches out and squeezes my knee and this makes the lump in my chest go up into my throat and the tears come back.

"Auntie Fay says you can have chips," Mum says.

"Why can't you stay?" I ask.

"Because…" She sighs and goes quiet for a bit. "Because I have some things I need to sort out so that you can come back home."

I don't ask when because it's too scary. She packed my big case, the one that she packed when we went to the hostel.

"But I'll be coming over tomorrow," she says. "And every day, to see you."

"Then why am I going?" I ask.

"Because it's safer, sweetheart," she says. "For now."

Auntie Fay doesn't live far away, so we are already there before I have time to forgive Mum, and that makes me cry again. Mum hugs me, and when I look at the house I can see Auntie Fay looking through the net curtains, but she doesn't wave and neither do I. Next door's dog starts to bark and I cover my ears.

Gareth gets my bag out of the boot and he rolls it up to the door. Mum keeps telling me how she'll see me tomorrow, and when Auntie Fay opens the door even my mum starts crying and so I don't want to let go of her.

"Thanks for this, Fay," she's saying even though it doesn't sound like she's happy.

"What's he done to you now?" Auntie Fay is asking and then I'm squished between them as she hugs my mum. "The bastard," she says. "Utter bastard."

"It looks worse than it is," Mum says.

"Come on then, you," Auntie Fay says. It's her business voice that she only uses for me. "We're going to need to sort your bed out before tea, aren't we?"

I wrap my arms around Mum's waist and she says that she loves me in the voice that means she's leaving. Auntie Fay says, "I've got her," and her fingers start to unpick my fingers and she pulls my arms away and so I wrap my legs around Mum's legs and when she reaches to get my legs I grab Mum again with my free arm. "You're like a bloody octopus!" she says, out of breath, and Mum wriggles free and walks backwards towards the car and she's blowing kisses and I thrash and fight but Auntie Fay is strong and she turns me until I can't see Mum anymore and she takes me inside.

Auntie Fay's house is always quiet. It's so quiet you can hear the clocks ticking on the walls. They turn off the telly until there's something on that they want to watch and they circle all the things they want to watch in the magazine that comes with the Sunday paper. There are bowls of smelly dried flowers all over the place and everything is where it's supposed to be all the time, and I hate it.

My scream makes everything in the house shake and before she lets go of my wrist Auntie Fay slides the chain on the door because she knows I can't reach it so when I'm free and I run to the door I can't open it up. I can hear the car pull away and I panic and I dodge past her through the kitchen and to the back door and run down the garden to the gate at the back but the bolt is rusty and stuck and it takes me ages to open it and then I'm in the lane and I can't remember which way to go to get home because we never walk. Then Auntie Fay is there again and she's got me and she's taking me back in.

"Ooh, you're a little bugger sometimes," she's saying and her arms are tight on my tummy. "You'll be bloody seeing her tomorrow!" She lets me go in the kitchen and I know there's no point in trying to run away again so instead I crawl under the table and cry. The plastic table cover hangs down over the edges and I can see the pattern of the flowers through the back. Underneath it is darker and it makes me feel better so I lie in a ball and enjoy the texture of my hair on my tongue.

After a while Auntie Fay leans down and asks me what on earth I'm behaving like, but I pretend she's see-through and don't answer. I hear her run the tap and then she puts a glass of juice down under the table and my tummy turns because this is a nice thing to do and I'm being a little bugger.

"I'll go and make up your room then, shall I? Someone has to do it." She sighs and tuts to herself. "And Ryan was so looking forward to having someone to play with this evening. What a shame you'll be staying under the table."

Her voice gets quieter as she leaves but I still hear her talking about chips and sausages as she goes up the stairs. When it's quiet I sit up and drink Ribena but she's put too much water in or not enough Ribena so it doesn't taste like it does when Mum makes it. I know Auntie Fay is lying about Ryan wanting to play. Ryan calls me weird and tells me not to go into his room. But I do want chips and I do want sausage, even though Auntie Fay's house is scary and different.

Sometimes, when I get scared, Mum calls me her brave little soldier. I try to imagine her saying it, in the voice she always uses when she's trying to make me less afraid. I whisper it to myself: "Who's a brave little soldier?" I try to be brave.

NINE

Her: Now

All week I spend half my nights twisting and turning, trying to get to sleep, but the past keeps replaying itself behind my eyelids. The woman in the room above me talks on her phone, pacing the room, and I can hear the old floorboards creaking under her feet and the rise and fall of her voice. From another room on the floor above someone shouts, "SHUT UUUUUUP!" and slams their door, and after that the woman speaks more softly but still she paces back and forth, back and forth.

I try to remember my mother's voice. I try to forget that I never said goodbye.

Sometimes when I can't sleep I like to imagine killing myself. Jumping from a cliff, the lurch in my stomach when I am free-falling, the spray of the sea on my face for one, two seconds. Then nothing. It helps to think that I can do it if I need to. It makes me feel like I have some control when everything else is going wrong.

I'm already half-awake when my alarm goes off for work, so it should be easy to get up but it isn't. My body feels heavy, like I'm anchored to the bed, and even though my neck is stiff and I'm bored, I can't seem to throw the covers off and step out. I set the alarm for another ten minutes and just lie there waiting for it to go off but even then I can't make myself get up.

This is what Dr. Isherwood tells me is depression but it's more like...nothing. That I am empty. Or that someone has scooped out my insides and filled me with concrete, gray and solid and heavy. And way down deep inside is a little piece of me that's still there, trying to see and hear the world through the gray, but everything is far away and muted and so the good things don't make me feel good enough because I can barely see or hear them.

This makes me wish I had a phone. Dr. Isherwood said this would happen, that I would want to contact her and that I would need my own mobile phone to do so.

"You don't even need a smartphone," Dr. Isherwood said. "You could get an old-fashioned one without the internet and then you wouldn't have to worry about all of that nonsense."

But it wasn't really the internet I was worried about, even though it felt like I was always carrying around a hundred screaming people with me, angry and hateful. It was Sean. And I knew that so long as I had a phone, he would find me again.

The last time I was out, Dr. Isherwood had said that it would be impossible for Sean to find me. But there are things that Dr. Isherwood doesn't understand. How could I tell her that he had already found me, and that we had spoken for hours? I didn't know how to explain to her that I knew it was Sean before he had even spoken and that I had always known it would happen, that maybe I had even made it happen just by thinking of it.

I look at the clock again and know that I will be late if I don't get up straightaway. I count out loud, "One, two, three," and then throw the covers off in one go and swing out of bed. The air is cold, and as I grab my towel I feel my stomach sink again, thinking of getting in the shower. "One thing at a time," I say out loud to myself. "First, just brush your teeth."

I am not late when I get to work but I am only just on time, which is almost as bad. I have to throw my bag into my locker and rush straight to Neil's office because I'm not sure what to do or where to go. Every other day I've been with Dawn but this is her day off and so I'm lost.

"Charlotte!" he says, putting his hands in the air. "To what do I owe the pleasure?"

"What?" I say.

"How can I help you?" He picks up a pen and fiddles with it. I try to look at his face but my eyes keep going to the pen in his hand as he clicks it and clicks it and clicks it.

"I don't know where I'm supposed to be," I say.

"Join the club!" he says, laughing.

"Um," I say, not sure he's understood me.

"Come with me," he says as he pushes his chair back and stands. He gestures again. "Come, come."

We go back out into the store, which is quiet during the morning school rush, and he directs me to the front, where two pretty young girls are pinning Halloween decorations to the upper shelves. When they see me and Neil walking towards them, their expressions change and I blush because I know they hate Neil and it's my fault he's talking to them.

"Anita, Katie, this is Charlotte," he says.

"Hiiiii," they say. Their smiles look watery and weak.

"Can you both look after Charlotte for the morning and please share with her all your wisdom and knowledge from your time working with me."

They both laugh but not really. I smile in a way that I hope says, *I'm sorry*.

"You're in good hands, Charlotte! These two will tell you everything they know!" Anita and Katie force a laugh again and because Neil is enjoying the attention he goes on, "It won't take long!" He laughs at his own joke. As he walks away he whistles and Anita and Katie roll their eyes.

"Oh my *God*," Anita says.

"I know," Katie says.

"I'm sorry," I say. There's silence and I know I've said the wrong thing but then they both burst out laughing.

"He's a freak," Katie says.

"So creepy," Anita says.

"I don't even know what he's going on about half the time," I say, enjoying the feeling of unity we're having and wanting to be involved.

"I know!" they say together and then we all laugh.

"Anyway," Anita says. "We have to put all this shit up this morning but we're trying to drag it out so we don't have to go back on stock or checkout."

"So basically *don't* rush it because I seriously can't be bothered today," Katie says.

"Seriously," Anita says.

They both have shiny cheekbones and thick hair and there's something electric about them that makes me feel shy and excited and I don't want to mess up.

"Are you new?" Anita asks.

"Oh my God, she's obviously new," Katie says. They laugh so I do, too.

"I saw you the other day," Katie says. It makes me jump, as if she was accusing me of something, but she says it like she's bored. From her pocket she takes out a tin of lip balm and dips her finger in it and wipes it across her lips. "You were working with Dawn on the refrigerated meats. I felt *so* bad for you."

"We call her Dawn of the Dead," Anita says and we all laugh.

"Oh my God, she, like, kills me, you know?" Katie says. They both look at me and it feels like a test.

"She kept talking about her bunions," I say. They laugh and I am glowing because I know I made it happen. I don't want it to end but eventually their laughter fades and they look back to the stepladder and the shelves from which the Halloween bunting hangs to coil on the floor like snakes.

"Hold the ladder for me," Katie says to Anita.

She climbs and starts to fix the Halloween decorations along the top shelf. Every now and again she bites off more tape and sticks the bunting to the shelf.

"Oh my God, Katie, that looks properly shit," Anita says. Katie looks at me and I nod. She hasn't stuck it up evenly so that some parts hang lower than others and the string has twisted so that it isn't all facing the right way. It stresses me out to look at it, so I turn away.

"Who cares?" Katie says. Then, "Fine, you do it then." She climbs down the ladder and hands Anita the Sellotape.

"I can't!" Anita's voice squeaks like a child's.

"It isn't even that high," Katie says. "You are such a drama queen!"

"I hate ladders!" Anita says, covering her face with her hands.

"I'll do it," I tell them.

Katie hands me the tape and as she does her skin brushes against mine and I realize it's the first time anyone has touched me since my appointment with Dr. Isherwood.

"Yes, Charlotte!" Anita says. "My hero!"

I blush but I don't want them to see so I turn and start to climb. I put my foot on the third rung and my trouser leg rises, the cool air hitting my bare skin, except for where the ankle tag rests. I realize too late; my right foot is already off the ground. I take the next steps one at a time and when I get to the top I look back, hoping that they haven't seen, but I can tell from the way that they can't face me that they have. They aren't laughing or smiling anymore and I want to get down and leave but I can't because that would only make it worse.

I unpick the bunting and do it all over again. Beneath me I can hear them whisper something but by the time I look at them they've stopped. When I've finished I climb down and Anita tells me it looks good, but her voice is thin and her smile is weak at the edges.

They both pick up decorations and head to the end of the aisle to dangle cobwebs and stack the fun-size chocolate bars and bags of gummy sweets. I can see them still talking quietly and I know it's about me. Lost, I stand and wonder whether I will ever fit anywhere ever again.

Then there's an announcement over the loudspeakers: "Can Charlotte Donaldson please report to Customer Services. Can Charlotte Donaldson please report to Customer Services. Thank you."

Both Anita and Kate look at me and then back at the sweets. Even though I know that they can't possibly be calling me because of the ankle tag and that Neil knows I am on a release program for a crime that wasn't theft or sexually motivated, it feels like too much of a coincidence and my heart pounds and I start to sweat lightly.

At Customer Services, an older lady nods to the telephone and tells me there's a phone call for me.

"Hello?" I say. The voice that comes back is familiar and floods me with warmth.

"It's me," Dr. Isherwood says. "I've been trying to get hold of you. Didn't the reception at the home pass on my messages?"

"No," I say.

"I'm sorry," she says. "I've been trying to tell you that I have to cancel our appointment tomorrow."

I feel like I'm falling through the floor.

"I've had a bit of an emergency. I'm so sorry. You know that I hate to let you down," she says. I think hard and I can't remember a time that she ever has let me down. It is new and frightening. "And to make things worse, our computers are playing up. We can't get to half our patients' details. Our IT guy says it's a virus and we may not be able to recover... I'm sorry—you don't need to know this. I'm babbling."

"It's okay," I say, wanting her to keep talking, to stay as long as it takes.

"I know we discussed this before, but it would make me feel a lot better if you had your own phone. You could call me anytime. So long as I'm not with a patient I can always find time for you. Something to think about, maybe?"

"Maybe."

"Have a think. If you do need me tomorrow I'll be available on my mobile. You can always use the phone at the home, you know."

The phone is busy all the time: women spending hours on hold with the Department of Work and Pensions about their benefits money. Or else to the ex-boyfriends and ex-husbands that they aren't supposed to contact, apologizing, apologizing, apologizing.

"I know," I say.

"You can tell me if you're mad at me," Dr. Isherwood says. "It's okay if you are—we can talk about it."

Maybe I was mad, but now I feel bad because I can't think of any other time she has canceled an appointment. I've seen her when she'd lost her voice and had to hold up cards with questions on and we laughed through it all. I've seen her with migraines and panting out of breath because her car broke down and I have seen her stressed and distracted because a pipe burst in her house and the plumber could only come when our session was on and she didn't want to let me down. So it must be something more serious than has ever happened before and instead of worrying about that she's still worrying about me.

"I'm not," I say. "Are you okay?"

She pauses like she always does if I ask her something about herself. She is wondering how much is okay to share, how much I should know.

"Yes," she says. "Just a bit of a family emergency. That's all. It will be okay."

The word twists inside me. *Family.* She hasn't talked about family before. I think of the backs of the pictures on her desk, wonder whom she keeps with her all day, how lucky they are.

"Oh. Well, I hope it all works itself out in the end."

Dr. Isherwood laughs. "I'm sure it will. And thank you for being so understanding. Other patients haven't been as kind."

We say our goodbyes and I hang up the phone. I don't want to go back to the Halloween aisle with Anita and Katie so I go back to Neil's office.

"Charlotte!" he says again. "Everything okay?"

"I don't want to do the decorations," I say. "Can I do something else?"

Neil stares at me and I stare back.

"Has something happened?"

"I don't like heights," I say. "And I would rather work somewhere else so I can learn more."

Neil smiles. "We can make sure you get a chance to work in every section. Then we can see where your skills are best suited."

I wait for him to tell me where I'll be working but he just smiles. Slowly the smile fades, like disappearing ink.

"Okay," he says, suddenly clapping his hands together. "Come with me, we'll put you somewhere a little busier."

I follow him through the store, past the coffee shop and up the escalators to the clothing section. This time, Neil leaves me with a man called Thomas and a woman called Lisa who is about my age. I help them put out new stock and then they tell me to go around looking for stock that people have changed their minds about and dumped elsewhere.

I've never understood the way people leave things around shops. Since being here I've seen frozen food left on the shelves of the cereal aisle, a pack of steaks ditched alongside the DVDs, butter thrown in with the frozen chips. It all gets thrown away but I don't think they would care even if they knew that.

I feel some satisfaction from putting things back where they belong. It also gives me a chance to look around at all the things I can't afford. I look at a pair of ankle boots that are lined with fake fur and I love them but I know I don't have anything to wear with them anyway, so it's easy to walk away from them. It's harder to walk away from a soft cardigan that looks so warm and cozy I want to put it on right away. I look at the price tag: twenty-five pounds. There's no one around and I think about taking it. There's no security tag—I've noticed that they only put security tags on things priced forty pounds and up, unless they are the kind of things that people steal the most, like packs of tights and pants and children's clothes. The kinds of things that people need, so they have to steal them if they can't afford them.

Since I've been working here they have checked my bag as I left once. But since then, they have not. If I finish at the same time as Neil leaves—six o'clock—they will almost certainly check my bag. But today I finish at two and they have never checked my bag on this shift.

The cardigan looks too big to sneak out under my shirt but now I feel the prickle on the back of my neck and I know I have to take something. After everything that has gone wrong today I think I deserve to feel better. As I walk around looking for discarded items I also think about what I can get away with taking.

When I return a bra to the lingerie section I see a lace set in emerald green and I love it immediately. The bra doesn't have any underwire so it won't make awkward shapes under my shirt and it's so delicate and small I can hide it easily. Also, if they do search my bag, there's a chance they won't even question it because they'll be too embarrassed. I look through for my size and for a moment I worry that they've sold out but I find one right at the back. I check to make sure no one is close by and then I pull it out. As I do this I purposely knock off several sets at the front so that they all fall onto the floor. As I crouch and pretend to be untangling all the hangers, I undo the set I want and ball it up in my fist. I place the rest of the sets back onto the hook and as I stand I pretend to adjust my trousers while sticking the bra and knickers into my waistband. Finally I take one last look around, and when I'm sure no one was watching I go back to my job, tidying the rails and making sure everything is on the correct hanger.

After five minutes I find Lisa and Thomas and tell them that I'm going to take a break. I go to the locker room and get my bag and take it to the toilet, where I remove the set from my waistband and bury them beneath my book and my bus pass. I flush, lock my bag away, and return to work.

Instead of feeling bored I feel exhilarated; when customers ask me where things are I walk them over and I smile instead of just pointing and hoping they'll go away. There are butterflies, the kind you get when you're standing at the edge of a great height, knowing you could fall, or jump, if you wanted to.

I glance at the clock on the wall and at two o'clock I take a deep breath and my skin prickles with excitement. It is too late to change my mind and take the set back, so even though I suddenly think of Dr. Isherwood and feel a lurch inside me, I know I have to go through with it.

I go back downstairs and put on my coat. I take my time so people don't think I'm rushing. Neil isn't around, which is a good sign, and I peek inside my bag to check it isn't too obvious in case they do decide to search me. With another deep breath I walk towards the door. There's no security there but I hesitate momentarily and consider taking the lingerie out of my bag and sticking the items back into my waistband, just in case they do search my bag. But as I'm already almost at the door and other staff are coming and going I decide to just go on and get out quickly.

As I expected, no one stops me, and I am blinking at the light that comes in through the glass front of the building, zipping my coat against the crisp autumn afternoon air, when a hand falls on my shoulder. I stop.

"Sorry," the security guard says. "I was supposed to do a bag check but I got caught up on the way to the staff room."

He has gelled dark brown hair and really white teeth. He smells of aftershave and I have never seen him before. I readjust my bag on my shoulder.

"Oh?" I say.

"Can I just…" He gestures towards my bag.

"Here?" I say.

"In the staff room, then," he says.

I try to think of something but nothing comes. This is it. I have ruined everything. Again.

TEN

Her: Then

The church hall is cold like always and I sit on my hands to try to warm them up. Fiona is telling us about the Ten Commandments and what they mean. I look over my shoulder at the little children who don't have to do lessons during Sunday school. Instead they get to play with toys in the corner but because I am ten now I'm not allowed to play anymore. When I look back Fiona is handing out worksheets and putting the boxes full of pencils and crayons and felt tips on the tables.

"I want you to write down the Ten Commandments and draw a picture of each to illustrate what it means," Fiona says. Liam puts his hand up. "Yes?"

"Are we allowed to work in pairs?" he asks.

"Of course!" she says. There is a hissing noise when everyone starts saying *yesss* to their best friends. Sean doesn't have to go to church so I'm on my own. Fiona looks at me and then adds, "Work in groups, if you like! Make sure everyone is included."

I look around but the others are purposely trying not to look at me so I pretend I don't care and I grab a handful of pens and pencils and crayons out of the box and return to my seat.

I hate church. Mum never made me go to church because she hated it, too. Auntie Fay made me get baptized after Mum's funeral and I had to do it in front of everyone. Sean said only babies get baptized but I wasn't a baby when I got baptized. The vicar poured water on my head and all my hair stuck to my face. Then afterwards we had sandwiches and cake in the garden and people gave me presents but they were all rubbish things, like a tiny Bible and a silver cross necklace and a book token.

"Shall I help you?" Fiona says to me. She pulls up a chair that's too small for her. She's fat but pretty. Fiona is married to the vicar and I didn't know vicars were allowed wives until I met her. "Now, can you tell me one of the commandments?"

"Um," I say. I wasn't listening before and now all my thoughts have frozen up because she's close to me and I can smell her hair.

"What about the one about taking the Lord's name in vain? Do you know what that means?"

I shake my head.

"Yes, you do; we just talked about it, didn't we? What do people say sometimes when they're cross? They say, 'Oh, for God's sake!' Don't they?"

I nod.

"So shall we write that one down?"

I start to write, "Oh, for God's sake!" But Fiona stops me. She laughs.

"We need to write, 'Don't take the Lord's name in vain.'"

Fiona draws a funny picture of someone looking angry and in a speech bubble she's written, "GOD!"

"You tell me one now," she says.

"Don't...steal?" I say.

"Yes!" she says. She gives me a hug. "Well done!"

I know what to draw because sometimes Sean and I pinch things from the shops and so I draw a hand grabbing a load of sweets. It's not very good but Fiona acts like it's brilliant because she is trying to make me feel nice. It works even though I know what she's doing.

Fiona has to help me with most of the commandments and even then they don't make sense. The last one she tells me I can do myself but I can't remember what's missing.

"What's the very worst thing a person can do?" she asks.

"I don't know," I say.

"Yes, you do!" she says. "What is the most awful—" She stops and her face turns red. "Never mind," she says. "We'll leave that one. It's almost time to go into church anyway."

Before we go, Fiona hands us all a sheet with the Ten Commandments on there and I read through for the one we missed: "You must not kill."

When we walk into church, everyone is singing a hymn, a boring slow one, and people turn and smile at us all as we take our seats in the back. We all take a blessing and say some prayers, and then the vicar reads out the notices and we are finally allowed to go home.

In the car Auntie Fay makes me tell her about Sunday school and I show her my worksheet. Ryan complains that if I go to Sunday school he should be allowed to go and Auntie Fay tells him he's too old now that he takes communion. If you get confirmed then you get to have wine and bread at the altar but you have to share the same cup as everyone, even the really old ladies who have lipstick on their teeth, so it's gross. When I was little I thought the white circles they gave you were Milkybar Buttons but Ryan says that they are more like sugar paper that isn't sweet and that when you eat it it just sticks to the roof of your mouth and makes you gag. Getting confirmed sounds awful but I know Auntie Fay will make me when I'm old enough.

At home Auntie Fay checks on the chicken and puts the potatoes in for Sunday lunch. I don't want to be alone so I watch her in the kitchen and she tells me to get out from under her feet. Uncle Paul is watching football on TV and he smiles and pats the sofa next to him so I can sit down.

"Why have they stopped?" I ask him. "What color are we? How long is left? How come he is throwing the ball?"

"All right, love," he says after a while. "Why don't you go and help your auntie Fay in the kitchen?"

Back in the kitchen, Auntie Fay has the radio on and it is playing more church! I think Auntie Fay would live in church if she could. The cabbage goes on and I hold my nose because it smells like fluffs. Outside Ryan is kicking his ball like always.

"How long will it be?" I ask again.

"For heaven's sake, girl! Do you ever stop? It'll be a while yet. Why don't you go out and play with your friend? Is Sean about today?"

I shrug.

"What's wrong?" she asks, turning away from the stove. "Have you had a falling out?"

"Kind of," I say.

"Never mind," she says. "It'll all be forgotten soon. Why don't you go and make up?"

"I don't want to," I say, and Auntie Fay tuts and shakes her head.

"You'll forgive and forget soon," she says. "I used to fall out with my friends all the time! You learn to turn the other cheek as you get older."

"Does Jesus forgive sins?" I ask.

"Yes. If people are sorry."

"Even if they break the Ten Commandments?"

"Yes," Auntie Fay says.

"How does He know if you've broken them?"

"Because He knows everything."

"What other superpowers does He have?"

"They aren't superpowers, darling, they're miracles."

"What's the difference?"

"Superpowers are imaginary. Miracles are real."

"How does He know if you're sorry?"

"Well, that's why we pray," she says. She chops carrots and drops them into the boiling water. "We pray to tell God our sins and that we are sorry. And to say thank you or to ask Him to look after the people we love."

"What if—"

"Listen, lovely, I'm very busy here. Why don't you watch TV with Uncle Paul?"

I go to my room and draw the curtains. I close the door and I kneel by the bed and pray properly for the first time ever. I open my eyes and wait to see if I feel any different but I don't. Instead I take out the book we're reading in school and try to concentrate as hard as I can so I don't feel so bad anymore.

After lunch I help Auntie Fay wash up and Ryan goes to the fields with his friends. On Sundays they watch boring things like *Antiques Roadshow* and *Last of the Sum-*

mer Wine but I don't want to be on my own so I go into the living room with them.

The bongs at the beginning of the news make me feel like something bad is about to happen. I close my eyes and hope they change the channel but they don't.

A picture of Luke comes up on the screen. Auntie Fay starts talking about how awful it is like she always does, so I can't hear what the man is saying. Then they show a policeman talking outside the station and the cameras flash, clicking like chattering teeth, while some people shout out questions.

"It's heartbreaking," Auntie Fay says again, and it sounds like she might cry, so Uncle Paul pulls her in. "So close to home."

A different story comes on and they start talking about politics. I feel dizzy and sick. Mum told me once that the worst bit about doing something wrong was the guilt and that the only way to feel better was to tell the truth.

"Auntie Fay," I say. They both look at me.

"Yes, love?" she says.

"Can we light a candle in church for Luke?"

"Of course we can, my love. That's very kind, what a lovely thought."

"It's so sad," I tell her. "He was in my school."

ELEVEN

Him: Now

The front door won't catch when I close it. Instead it bounces back open like it always fucking does and I have to put my fingers in the letter box and pull it closed like that until I hear it click. Sometimes when it's doing my head in I just slam it over and over again and watch it bounce back open even though it doesn't work. The woman in the flat next door who's always peeking out of her fucking window gives me evils and I smile at her in the way that makes my cheeks hurt just to wind her up.

The lift stinks of piss so I take the stairs, running, and as they wind down I brace myself on the metal railing and jump the last steps of each flight and when I reach the bottom I have to catch my breath before I light the rollie I made before leaving.

In my pocket my phone buzzes but I ignore it. I haven't

got anything on me anyway. I can see the bus at the lights at the end of the road and I drop my fag and sprint to the stop, managing to get there just before he closes the doors. When I show him my ticket he takes it out of my hand and inspects it like it contains the meaning of fucking life. I feel my neck turn red while all the nosy old bitches crane their necks to see what's going on. The bus driver nods and hands it back. I feel like asking him how many counterfeit tickets he gets in a day to warrant that level of fucking scrutiny. Or just, *Nice work, Columbo*. But I can tell he's looking for any reason to kick me off this bus and so I climb up the stairs away from the judgy old fuckers and sit at the front.

I roll another cigarette and tuck it behind my ear. I put my feet up in front of me and I feel like I did when I was a kid. Dizzy and exhilarated with the novelty of being on the top deck of the bus. I always thought it was what being on a roller coaster would feel like, until we went to a shitty theme park on a school trip and I realized it wasn't even close. On the school coach they made me sit at the front next to Mrs. Crockett and every time I turned around on the seat to see what was going on behind us she made a noise like *Tsk! Tsk! Sit back down!* Like I was a fucking dog. Nearly three hours there and three hours back. It rained the whole day and Mrs. Crockett told my dad I took up all of her time and that they'd have to think carefully about taking me next time if I didn't improve my behavior. All bollocks but he didn't give a shit. I still have the key ring I nicked from the shop at the end but the paint chipped off and you can't read what it says anymore.

I press the bell and make my way down. As I get off I say, "Cheers," but the driver blanks me and closes the doors. I flip him off as he pulls away. I light my cigarette and pull up my hood and walk. It's ten minutes to Slimy's flat and I don't want to run into anyone on the way so I keep my head down and walk quickly.

A woman rounds the corner in front of me and when she sees me she tucks her handbag under her arm and quickens her pace. I flick my cigarette into the gutter and slow down so she knows I don't want her handbag but every turn I need to take she takes and I can feel the heat climbing my neck and my face, that sense of shame I always seem to have just for fucking existing around people like this.

She turns down the lane behind the precinct and I turn, as well. I try to keep my eyes on the ground but I can see she flicks her head over her shoulder every few seconds to check on me. Then she starts to walk so fast she's taking a small skip every few seconds and it's so fucking embarrassing I have to swing round and look at my phone until I can hear the click of her heels disappear into the distance. I kick an empty fag packet into a puddle and wait and when I'm sure she's gone I start walking again.

When I finally get to Slimy's flat, the streetlamps are starting to come on and the smell of cooking from other people's kitchens makes me realize how hungry I am. When Jiffo answers the door, the smell of skunk hits me hard, and there's a cheer from the boys in the flat: something happening on FIFA.

"What's happening, bro?" Jiffo says, slapping my back as he closes the door behind me. It's as cold inside as out. The curtains are drawn and the air is thick with smoke. I sit in the chair nearest the radiator and hold my hand to the metal: cold.

"It's fucking arctic in here, Slimes," I say, tucking my hands into my hoodie.

"Radiator's broken," he says without taking his eyes off

the screen. "Landlord…" He trails off. As he plays he tilts the controller back and forth, like a kid, his elbows up and out while he screws up his face in concentration. Slimy is so useless I almost want to kick his head in just to beat some sense into him, but he's a good guy and he'll sort you out if you need it, no questions.

"Have you tried bleeding it?" I ask. The clicking from the controllers increases and Wez cheers while Slimy groans. My question hangs in the cold air. Slimy puts down the controller and picks up a joint.

"Have you tried bleeding it, bro?" I ask him.

"Have I what?" he says. The smoke hangs above him.

"The radiator," I say, but he's already stopped paying attention. He takes another puff and holds it out to me, but I shake my head. Slimy, who licks his lips before every inhalation, always leaves the roach soggy and soft. I feel a wave of revulsion even thinking about it. Instead the spliff finds its way to Wez, whose nose wrinkles as he places it between his lips.

"Can I use your laptop for a second, Slimes?" I ask.

"Go for it," he says, selecting a team for the next match. I lean forward and take off the empty mug that's resting on top of it. The laptop is one of those big shiny red gaming laptops. Mad expensive. No one asks where he gets these things, but we know he's too fucking useless to steal anything. His parents kicked him out when he was fifteen but they give him cash whenever he needs it; they'll buy him an Xbox, big TV, nice laptop, trainers.

But for all the nice shit he owns, his flat is filthy: every surface is littered with empty cans dusted with ash, roaches and fag ends rattling in the bottom. There's black mold creeping along the walls and the sink is full of crusty dishes. My best guess is Slimy's parents kicked him out for living like a pig. I know I wouldn't want him stinking up *my* flat.

My heart starts to beat faster when I open the laptop and begin to type. This is why I've come. This is all I've been able to think about since I saw it on the news. Finally, she's back out.

When I was released again nine months ago I managed to slip back into society without much of a fuss. I've never interested them like she has. Why would I? I was exactly the way they imagined I'd be. No surprises there. It's always been about her: they look at her and they ask, *Why? What went wrong?* Those big wet eyes and the plaited blond hair. Either I was the one who led her down the wrong path or she's the devil himself, hiding behind the face of a fucking angel. But now that she's back out, suddenly I see them talking about me again, too.

Back in the unit, they made us watch a video for a science lesson. We watched all the experiments on tapes that flickered and rolled from years and years of use. Everyone in them had that mad seventies hair and we laughed at the shitty music. This one video they showed us was a reaction when you mix bicarbonate of soda and vinegar. Two things from the kitchen that you wouldn't think twice about. But when you mix them together they react so strongly you can launch a rocket. I watched it and I thought of her, thought of how the two of us together became something else, something unpredictable.

Even now, just the sight of her on the screen makes my heart thump harder. I read the article on BBC News. The screen is dirty and I wipe it with my sleeve but it doesn't help much. I look at that picture of her in the police van, that smile which only used to come out for me. What had made her smile then? I'd already been sentenced by the time she went to court. Maybe they'd told her she didn't have to worry, that everyone knew it was all my fucking fault. That was what Dr. Isherwood testified and it was the story they'd gone with. My own defense had relied on the classics: broken home, lack of supervision, behavioral problems. When they spoke about her they asked whether she could find redemption, if she could go on to lead a good life and do good things. When they spoke about me they asked, *Well, what did you expect?* They said I'd been dealt a bad hand, that it was just a sad ending to a sad childhood.

A hand on my shoulder. I jump and try to close the laptop.

"Bro, why are you looking at this shit?" Slimy says. "Sick. Pair of fucking pedos."

"What's that?" Jiffo asks. All the boys are suddenly looking over and I burn with hate as I wait for Slimy to pass back the laptop.

Slimy reads the article out loud. "They're back out now."

"Fucking council houses, never have to work again, plastic surgery," someone says. I grip my hands to stop myself grasping for the laptop.

"Made for life," Jiffo says. Everyone groans but they nod their fucking heads.

"The boy lived on my cousin's estate, two roads down from my cousin," Slimy says.

Everyone has an opinion and everyone has a fucking story. They all have a cousin, a friend, a cell mate who knew one of us, who lived near us or went to school with us or beat us up in prison. I try not to rise to it. When Jiffo passes me the joint I take it even though I can see the soggy roach and feel a curl in my stomach as I put it to my lips.

"If I knew where he lived I'd fuck him up," Slimy says

proudly. The smoke hits my chest like a punch and I have to suppress a cough. I take another toke.

"Well, my cousin said people kept vandalizing his house and shit. And they found kiddie porn on his computer, or something. That's why he went back inside last time. Shouldn't have let him out again."

"I would kick the shit out of him," Slimy says again, handing me the laptop and reaching for the joint. "Sick perverts."

"Wipe your fucking mouth before you take the spliff, you dirty fucking bastard," I say suddenly. Slimy takes a step backwards in shock. Everyone else is laughing, trying not to look at the hurt on Slimy's face.

"All right, chill the fuck out," he says. I see him look at the roach and it's like he's realizing for the first time that it isn't supposed to be wet.

"Mouthing off about kicking the shit out of people. Why don't you learn to mind your own fucking business before you start poking your nose into other people's?"

I can hear the squeak of barely contained laughter but someone pipes up, "All right, take it easy on him, Tanker."

"Fine," I say. Slimy squirms away with his joint and I stare hard into the laptop, looking at her face and feeling something between love and hate, blaming her for all of it, all of this.

Where is she now? Is she happy? Does she have to live like this? Surrounded by people who would kill her if they knew who she was?

I open Google and I type in Dr. Evelyn Isherwood, psychiatrist. It's there instantly, her new business address and the opening hours. Closed for the day but back open at 9 a.m. tomorrow. I take my phone out of my pocket and dismiss all the notifications. I write down the address and the phone number and save them. I click on the Google Maps link and switch to Street View. It's a nice clinic. Not as nice as the old one but, still. I zoom out and out again, looking at the town and its streets, knowing she is there, somewhere.

Right now it's a mess but I'll find her.

TWELVE

Her: Now

The security guard puts a hand on my lower back as we walk back to the staff room together. I look at his name tag, lined up perfectly straight against the top of his pocket. Jack, it says. I wonder if he already knows what I have done, if he has watched me on CCTV.

In the staff room Jack asks for my bag, looking me up and down. I hesitate, hoping that something will happen that will make all this go away.

"Come on then," he says after a while.

I hand over the bag, too ashamed to look at him, but I can hear him pause as his hand reaches around inside. When I look up Jack is holding the bra, moving the lace between his finger and thumb.

"I…" I say.

Then Jack pinches the price tag and smiles.

Suddenly he drops it, zips up the bag, and passes it back to me. He winks. "I'll walk you back out," he says, holding the door for me.

"Thanks," I say. I wonder if it's a trick, if he needs me to walk out of the store with it before he can say I've stolen it.

We walk in silence until we reach the automatic doors and then I hesitate, waiting for him to set off an alarm or something.

"So," he says. He's smiling and his eyes are shining with something. "You're not gonna mug me off, are you?"

"What?" I say.

"I've done you a favor," he says. "I know you didn't buy that. I don't care. Why don't you let me take you out?"

"Where?" I say. I don't know what he means and I'm sure it isn't what I'm thinking because why would he want to take me out on a date?

"I don't know. Cinema, Nando's, drinks. Come on then, let me have your number and you can choose where we go."

A date. I look at him; he's much thinner than the other security guards. He has thick eyebrows and dark brown eyes.

"I don't know my number off by heart," I say.

"Get your phone out then!"

"I don't have it with me," I say.

"You're mugging me off," he says, but he's still smiling. "Who doesn't have their phone with them all the time?"

I shrug. "I forgot it. Why don't you give me your number?"

Jack goes to the Customer Services desk and rips off a bit of the till roll and writes his number down for me. I fold it and put it in my bag.

"You'd better phone me," he says. He points at me and narrows his eyes, and as he walks away, he laughs.

* * *

On the bus I look at the number and try to work things out. Jack is okay-looking but I don't think he is really my type. Actually, maybe I don't really have a type. But there is something missing and I know from the past that men like Jack don't fill the gap inside me.

Instead of getting off at the home I stay on until the bus loops back around town and then I get off near the library. Inside I sign up for a library card and wait for a computer to become available. I have an email address that they set up for me when I left the unit but I have to get my address book out of my bag to remind myself of the password. Then I send Dr. Isherwood an email telling her that after thinking things over I've decided it would be best to have a phone after all.

There's still a lot of time left for me to use the computer so I search again for news about Sean and me and then I scroll down to the comments sections to read about how much people hate us. Back in the unit there were girls who cut their arms with razors unscrewed from pencil sharpeners, Stanley knives, broken glass. Anything they could open their skin with. Whenever I wanted to hurt myself I would read about the case. The words slice deep wounds and afterwards I feel invincible because I have hurt so much that now I am numb.

An email comes back from Dr. Isherwood.

Absolutely! Will sort this for you by next week. Leave it to me.

Sent from my iPhone.

Next week is too long to wait but I can't push her without making it seem suspicious. I will have to call Jack some other way.

I think of how suspicious Jack was because I didn't have a phone, the way that normal people can tell that there is something wrong with me because I don't have all the things that make a whole person.

They can give you an identity but they can't give you a life. There is so much missing: no family photos, no school friends, no restaurant reviews or old email addresses or ex-colleagues or love letters or clothes that need to be taken to the charity shop. You are brand-new and lack all the clutter that makes a person real. No past.

Then there's something else, something besides all the lack of physical evidence I exist. It's like if you painted a perfect copy of Van Gogh's *Starry Night*, even if it was completely identical to the real one, no one would want it. It isn't about how it looks, it's about how it got there. I think about the things people love, about the books and paintings and music, and how the artists tear off a piece of themselves and leave it in there—and that's what a soul is, that's how you can tell that something is real. And that's what people know is missing from me. There's a space inside me where a life should have been and it shows.

I turn off the computer and collect my bag while trying not to cry. The thing is, I can remember what it was like to be me and to have a person who saw into the tangled-up mess that I was, and still loved me back. But if all of that led to what happened, then what kind of person does that really make me?

THIRTEEN

Her: Then

Summer is nearly over already. Only one more week and then we have to go back to school. I will be in year four because I am eight now and that means I have a new teacher and a new classroom. I will miss my old classroom, where we could see the park from the window, and my old teacher. I wish things didn't have to change.

I want to ask Sean if he will still speak to me when school starts or if he is only my friend because it's summer but I don't. My cider ice lolly drips down my hand and I lick the juice off.

"Look," Sean says. He puts his whole mouth over the lolly and pushes it back and forth.

"What?" I say. I don't get it. I hate it when I don't get it.

"I'm doing a blow job," he says.

"Oh," I say. I still don't get it.

"Don't you know what a blow job is?" he says.

"Yeah," I say, hoping he won't ask again.

"What is it, then?" he says.

"It's rude," I say. I can tell it's rude and my face is hot and not just because of the sun.

Sean grins. "Do you know what a hand job is?" he says.

"Stop it!" I say. "I'll go home."

"You're such a baby sometimes," he says, throwing his ice lolly stick into the drain. I don't want the rest of mine anymore so I do the same.

"Let's go," he says.

"Where?"

"Surprise."

Sean is running before I can even stand up. I follow him through the streets, not sure where we're going, but that doesn't matter when I'm with Sean. At the next corner he stops and tries to climb a lamppost but keeps sliding down.

"Once," he says, "this boy in year six climbed all the way to the top."

"That's impossible," I say.

"No! He did. And he slid back down like on a fireman's pole."

"You're not supposed to climb them," I say. There was a special assembly and a policeman came. They played a video where a boy climbed up and got electrocuted and died and at the end we all got a sticker. "They're electric," I say to Sean. "You can die."

"That was pylons," he says. Then he starts running again.

Next time we stop I'm out of breath and my legs feel funny.

"Don't you know where we are?" he says.

I look around and it feels like being in a dream. Like I'm not really here.

"Is…" I start, and then walk, and Sean follows me, climbing up onto the garden wall and walking alongside me.

"You wanted to see where your old house was," he says. He spits into someone's garden.

My heart is beating faster as I walk and everything I'm seeing seems to get sharper edges and brighter colors. I recognize Mrs. Lyon's house and the one with the green front door and the garden with the wishing well and then…

"Where is it?" I ask Sean. "Where is my house?"

There's just a gap where my house should be, and when I look at it, it feels like being ripped in half.

"It burned down," Sean says, jumping down from the garden wall. "Duh."

"But…" I look at the space. It looks too small and I think maybe I'm remembering wrong because my house was big, it was enormous. I look up and down the street for where it really is.

"You know it burned down," Sean says. "Everyone knows."

I knew there was a fire. I knew the night I went to stay with Auntie Fay, when the doorbell went in the middle of the night and Uncle Paul turned on all the lights before he went downstairs. I kept hearing them say "fire." I heard them crying. I didn't want to know but I did. I knew my mum was gone, that she wasn't coming back to get me. Auntie Fay and Uncle Paul didn't go back to bed. I thought if I stayed in bed it wouldn't be real. In the morning, when the sun was really up and I heard Ryan go downstairs, Auntie Fay came into my room and shook my shoulder. I pretended to sleep. Auntie Fay shook me harder and I started crying before she could even start talking because it wasn't going away, the bad dream wouldn't stop.

But I thought there would be something left, something to show that Mum and I were here once, and that we were happy.

Now it seems impossible that I am looking at nothing because once it was everything. I step into the space and it's cooler because of the two houses on either side stopping the sun from getting in. Other than that it feels the same as anywhere else. I close my eyes and try to feel something but nothing comes. A tear creeps out and I squeeze my eyes tighter, make fists with my hands.

But then Sean pulls my hand open and holds it, his palm sticky from the cider lolly, and I can't stop the tears anymore.

FOURTEEN

Him: Now

Computers have always made sense to me. After Mum left, Dad got me an Atari as a distraction, and together we programmed our own games. He didn't do anything else for me, but he gave me that and maybe it was enough.

At the unit they liked to *encourage* us: all that happy-clappy shit to counteract the bars on the fucking windows. So when I told them I liked computers they made sure I got the lessons.

"Maybe you could get a job in IT," they'd say, smiling at me like I was a dog who'd learned to give his paw. As if any company hires an IT guy with a fucking record.

They stayed true to their word and they got me a diploma that's not worth the paper it's written on out in the real world.

Still, it wasn't completely wasted.

Most of this stuff even an idiot like Slimy could manage. He already has the Tor browser, so getting on the dark net is easy. It sounds so fucking mysterious and dangerous; like there should be reams of scrolling green code on a black background, some shadowy hacker in an unlit basement crossing over into some alternate cyberspace full of viruses and child pornography.

The reality is that almost anyone can get this far, can make a few clicks and order some weed and pills like you're browsing Amazon. Simple. Like I said, it must be, or Slimy wouldn't be able to do it.

It's not infallible, untraceable. You get ripped off; you get busted. That's why it's best to use someone else's laptop, someone who isn't on parole, or who doesn't have much to lose.

"Roll a joint," Slimy says, his bloodshot eyes staring lazily at the TV screen.

"Busy," I say.

"What are you doing?" he asks.

"Business," I say.

The problem last time I was out was that I used my own laptop, my own Wi-Fi. They weren't too impressed with what I did with my diploma but my options were limited. I was an entrepreneur, but not the right kind.

Slimy groans and heaves himself up to roll another joint. "Can't you do that somewhere else?" he asks.

"Chill," I say. "It's totally untraceable."

"I know, but…"

"I'll throw you a twenty bag," I say and he immediately pipes down.

Yesterday I sent an inquiry email to Dr. Isherwood's office saying I was looking for a new psychiatrist for my son and that his records were in the file attached. I didn't expect it to work. Most people are savvy enough to know not to open attachments from unknown senders but her PA must be the nosy type, hoping to rifle through someone's personal information. I made it juicy, dropped in a line about sexual misconduct. And now I'm looking through the contact details for most of her patients.

Most, but not all. I can't see anyone who might be her.

I open Isherwood's Outlook and poke around but, unsurprisingly, there's nothing there from my girl, either. Maybe Isherwood has finally moved on? That thought hits me in the chest and I feel sure that I've finally lost her for good, or that she's lost me. I'm angry, like she's planned this, but I know that she hasn't, and that if she's lost Isherwood then she's suffering more than I could ever make her.

I dig through Isherwood's messy email folders and accidentally stumble upon a new one, a subfolder named Iris. My heart speeds up because I think it's her, it must be, but the folder is full of adoption shit and emails from her solicitor. Congratulations, one subject reads. Inside, We are pleased to inform you that your application has been approved. Another from her solicitor explains how she goes about obtaining a birth certificate, another about changing the baby's name. Further back, flights to India and arrangements for visiting the orphanage.

I stare at the screen, unable to move.

"Tanker," Slimy says, leaning over the arm of the sofa, extending his hand, a joint pinched between two fingers. I take it and inhale deeply. The tip is dry and Slimy watches me while I take a drag.

"What are you staring at me like that for, bruv?" I snap. "Waiting for a fucking review?"

"Jesus, mate. Calm down. You looked proper pasty, like

you were spinning out," he says. He sighs and turns back to the TV.

He's right, though, I feel like shit. Heart pounding, dizzy. I can't figure out what to do with this new information, what it might mean.

I stare at the screen. A new notification pops up on Isherwood's Outlook, and it *feels* like one of those magical moments even before I look at it. Do you know what I mean? It feels weighted. I feel pulled towards the moment like it has its own orbit and my hands feel heavy on the trackpad as I slide the cursor to the inbox and click. Straightaway I know it's her, even though the name reads *Charlotte*. She's saying that she's thought about it and she's decided she does want a mobile phone and I know that whatever it is that's always brought us back together is still there and that it's still as powerful as it always was.

And now I know something that she doesn't. I know about Iris and I know that she won't like that at all.

FIFTEEN

Her: Now

I wait until the next evening and then I take the till receipt with Jack's number on it and hang around outside the telephone room until it's free. He doesn't answer so I leave a message but as soon as I put the phone down it's ringing and when I pick it up I recognize his voice.

"Who's this? I missed your call," he says.

"It's me. Charlotte," I say. "From work."

"What's up?" he asks.

"You asked me to call you," I say.

"You wouldn't have called if you didn't want to," he says. I can hear him smiling; I can hear his friends in the background: "Is she hot, Jacky-boy?"

I feel even more like I don't want to go out but we both know that I have no choice.

"I'll take you out on Saturday," he says. He's laughing and telling his friends to fuck off. "Shall I pick you up?"

"No. I can meet you there."

"Where are we going, then?"

It's been so long since I went out in the evening and had to choose what to do that I can't think of anything.

"Bowling?" he says. "Cinema?"

"Yes. Cinema."

"I'll text you," he says. "Give me your number."

"I lost my phone," I say quickly. "I need to wait until payday for another one. Shall I just meet you there at six?"

"Six? You're keen," he says. I don't know what he means so I just stay quiet. "Hello?" he asks.

"Yeah, six," I say again.

We agree to meet in the foyer on the day and as Jack hangs up one of his friends is shouting, "Is she moist?" I shudder and wipe the earpiece of the telephone before putting it back onto its base. Over the following days at work I hope that I'll see him so I can make an excuse and cancel. Maybe if he sees me again he won't want to go out, either, but we don't seem to have any of the same shifts and before I know it it's Saturday afternoon and it's too late to do anything except go.

When I arrive at ten to six and see Jack isn't there I feel relieved, like he may not come at all, but I wait until six just to be sure. I stand near the ticket machines and read the showings. If he doesn't come I can still watch something on my own. Then it's six, then two minutes past six, then five minutes past. I make my way to the counter and buy a ticket for a half-past-six screening. I'm handing over my money when someone grabs my shoulders.

"You're keen!" Jack says. He grins, all teeth, and I am assaulted by the various smells that come from his body:

hair gel, powerful cologne, strong mint on his breath. I take a step back and he replaces me at the counter. "What are we seeing, then? One for me, too, mate," he says, pulling out a twenty-pound note.

When he receives his change, I watch as he forces his wallet into his back pocket. His black jeans are skintight and give him a bowlegged appearance. He wears black patent-leather shoes with no socks and the toes come to sharp points at the tips. His white shirt is also tightly fitted and slightly see-through so that I can't help but see the impression of his nipples beneath. There's not a crease in sight and his hair is molded into crispy peaks.

I look down at my boot-cut jeans and loose gray T-shirt, the wrinkled navy hoodie I pulled from the washing hamper last-minute, and realize that perhaps this date actually means something to him. This makes me feel guilty and embarrassed on his behalf.

"Popcorn?" he asks me. I am conscious of his hand resting on my lower back as he guides me onto the escalator.

"No, thanks," I say.

"I need food. I'm fucking starving! I thought we were eating first." Jack rubs his stomach the way a child might and then adds, "Nando's after?"

"I've already eaten," I lie.

He looks hurt and I look away.

Jack orders himself some nachos and a slushed-ice drink.

"How long is the film?" I ask the person behind the counter, holding out my ticket.

"About two hours," he says, bored.

Jack seems quiet and I wonder if I hurt his feelings, but then I remember that it doesn't matter because I don't want to see him again.

We're so early that not even the adverts have started

and we are practically the only people in here. Even so, I can't help but feel embarrassed by how loud Jack is talking.

"So I do mixed martial arts three nights a week and we do sparring and stuff but the coach reckons I could compete so I'm just moving back in with my mum so I can focus more on that and drop my hours..."

He talks and talks and I can hear a woman giggling behind us and I'm sure it's about him. If even I know that people are laughing at us then it's obvious but Jack doesn't seem to notice.

"I got my black belt three years ago," he's saying. "But I wanted a new challenge, you know? And I always loved watching MMA, before it was popular..."

The lights dim and an advert starts but even then Jack doesn't stop talking until I shush him.

During the trailers he puts his feet up on the back of the chair in front of us and even though there's no one there it's rude and embarrassing. Jack chews loudly and talks about the previews: "She is *banging*" or "Looks like shit." But as people start to come in I realize that all of them talk and use their phones, too.

Mum only took me to the cinema for special treats. Birthdays, because there were never any parties, never any children my own age. Just me and her, a bag of sweets from the corner shop and a carton of juice, snuck in in her bag. And when the lights went down it was time to stop talking because you weren't supposed to ruin it for anyone else. If you really needed to talk because it was scary or confusing or you needed to pee then you whispered into her ear, the hair that had escaped her ponytail tickling your nose, cupping your hands around your mouth so the noise didn't escape.

Not now. The flash of a camera; someone is taking a

picture. Of what? It happens again and I turn. They are taking a picture of themselves. There is an advert telling people to put away their phones but even then they still talk and I have to poke Jack when he pulls his iPhone out of his pocket again.

It doesn't matter that the film isn't really good; every giggle and exclamation and buzzing phone feels like a finger jabbing me in the chest, and the person behind me keeps kicking the seat every time they move and there's a smell of lager-burps wafting from the person next to me.

Suddenly I am standing and I'm throwing my bag over my shoulder. Jack keeps his legs up, blocking my path.

"Where are you going?" he asks without lowering his voice.

"I have to get out," I say, my breath fast and my heartbeat thumping in my temples.

Jack brings his knees into his chest and looks absurd. It's like a birthing pose, his hands on his knees, his feet in the air. I squeeze past him and dash out and into the toilets. Someone has spilled a drink in one cubicle and another is clogged with toilet paper. I go from door to door, each toilet stinking and filthy, the panic rising with the anger, until I find one that isn't disgusting where I can close the door and cry.

This is why I didn't want to come back out here; why I wanted to stay in the unit, where it's clean and there are rules and everybody follows them. I think of the three meals they serve every day, how there are no decisions to make and I don't end up hungry and tired because I forgot to eat lunch again; how I never needed to worry about things like money and what to wear and whether people thought I was weird. I was never bored and I was never excited.

The nurses and the assistants made sure the time passed, always going forward, always accounted for.

The last time I was in the unit Dr. Isherwood told me she couldn't move again and so we'd have to see each other less. There were weeks and weeks without her, though she sent me letters and she called. The new doctor read all my notes but he didn't understand everything, so that when I said things like *there's a gap inside me* he would make me explain it even though I couldn't. Dr. Isherwood knew without me having to explain it, so the gap just felt even wider without her. I did what he told me to until I could be released again because Dr. Isherwood promised that she would come with me when I was, and she did.

And that's why I'm here.

I look around the cubicle and lean a shoulder against the wall. Dr. Isherwood made me leave the unit and now she isn't here for me.

I think about it more. I think about how this is the only appointment she has ever canceled. Something really bad must have happened to make her miss our session and I am only worried about myself and that makes me a selfish person.

I say inside my head, *I hope Dr. Isherwood is okay and that nothing happens to her and that her family is okay.* When I think it, I realize I really mean it: I am worried about her, for the first time.

I dab my eyes dry with toilet paper and wash my hands before leaving. I'm thinking of going to Tesco and getting something for tea but then I see Jack in the corridor, head down, his phone glowing in front of him, and I know I can't go past without him seeing me. Before I can go back into the toilets he spots me.

"Charlotte! Where are you—" he says.

"I don't want to watch the end of the film," I tell him. "I just want to go home. I'm really sorry."

"Don't go home. We can get some food?"

"I'm not hungry," I lie. I am starving. I have forgotten to eat again.

"Well, then I'll take you home," he says. His eyes are shiny and serious. "Where do you live?"

This isn't an option. I can't have Jack see where I live. All the mistakes I've made pass through my mind. Stealing from work, taking his phone number, actually calling him. They have led to this.

"Come on, Sharl," he says. "Don't mug me off, yeah?"

"It's Charlotte."

"Charlotte, then. Come on, babe. I did you a favor, didn't I?" Jack winks.

I think about it for a second.

"Just food?" I ask.

"One meal," he says. "If you want to go home and never see me again after that then that's fine."

"Okay," I say. There's a strange feeling just out of reach. Like when you've forgotten something but you can't remember what you've forgotten. Then it catches and it's almost a relief to realize what it is: Jack is a bad person.

SIXTEEN

Her: Then

After the funeral we all go to the pub and there are big plates of sandwiches and sausage rolls like they have in school at the end of term. I'm not hungry but Uncle Paul puts lots on a plate and rubs my hair and says, "Come on, love. You have to keep your strength up."

I eat the pineapple bit of the pineapple-and-cheese stick but then I feel sick again and when Uncle Paul isn't looking I put my plate under the table and walk off. Auntie Fay is crying again and the vicar has one arm around her and a hand full of tissues. The dress Auntie Fay bought me to wear is itching and too tight on my arms. A woman I don't know makes a weird face and then bends down and grabs me, holding me tight so my face is smushed into her dress. She smells of powder and perfume.

"You'll be okay, little lamb," she says. "It'll all be okay."

But she's crying and I can't believe her. When she lets go she kisses my cheek and I have to hold my hands behind my back to not wipe it off straightaway. After she's turned I rub my face with my shoulder and run to the food table and climb underneath where no one can see me.

I watch the legs and listen to the voices above them.

"It's so sad," one says.

"Terribly, horrifically sad," another says.

"That poor little girl. Can you imagine losing your mum when you're six years old?" someone else says. Her voice squeaks and then other legs appear to comfort her.

Then the vicar's legs appear and I know they are his because he is the only one wearing a dress *and* trousers. There is a napkin stuck to his shoe and it makes me laugh. Auntie Fay's legs aren't far behind.

"I can't, honestly, I can't," she's saying.

"Paul's worried about you, worried that you're not eating. And he thinks that because you're not eating it's affecting her, too."

"I'm trying to put on a brave face but—"

"No one expects you to put on a brave face, Fay. But you are brave, we all know you are, and we know you care about her entirely. To look after her the way you want to you need to eat, you need to look after yourself.

"In an emergency on an airplane, what do they say? They say you have to put your own oxygen mask on before you help others. If you're looking after someone in a crisis you need to be at your strongest, don't you? So come on, have a sausage roll."

Auntie Fay sniffs and laughs. "It's so hard, though, Father," she says.

"I know it is," he says.

"Every time I look at her…" She starts to sob. "I see him. She looks so much like him."

I cover my ears. I don't want to hear anything about him. He was a bad person and I don't look like him. I look like my mum and I don't know why she is telling the vicar lies.

When their legs go away I crawl out from under the table and into the room with all the games and gambling machines.

It's smoky inside and quieter, and because it's quieter the men talk in almost whispers as if you're not allowed to speak, like in a test or at church. I stand on my tiptoes and roll the white ball on the snooker table so that it bounces all over the place. The fruit machines flash colorful lights and I reach up and hit the buttons but nothing happens.

"All right, angel?" a man says. His face is dotted with little holes just like the dartboard. I nod. "How about you help me press the buttons?" He takes a coin from his pocket and lets me put it in the slot. The machine makes a noise like we've woken it up. "Up you come." He lifts me so I can see all the buttons. I push the red one and the spinners whiz round. "Press the middle one, love. Nice one. Press that one there. Now spin."

"Are we winning?" I ask but then the machine makes a sad noise and the man puts me down.

"Can't win them all, pet."

"Can we have another go?"

Before he can answer Auntie Fay comes in and starts talking really fast. When she does it at home Uncle Paul tells her to stop flapping.

"There you are!" she's saying. Then she's apologizing to the man. "We were looking for her everywhere!"

"She was no trouble at all," he's saying. "We were so

sorry to hear about…everything. Julia is in bits, she really is. If there's anything we can do to help…"

"Thanks," Auntie Fay says. "We know. Everyone's being so kind." She turns to me and reaches to grab my wrist. "Come on then, let's get some food inside you."

"NO!" I tell her. I snatch my arm back and hide behind the man.

"What's this about?" Auntie Fay asks. Her eyes go all shaky. "Just come with me and we'll put together a plate for later. You don't have to eat right now."

She reaches again and I scream and I run and dive under a table and keep screaming.

"I don't know what I've done!" Auntie Fay is shouting. She's shouting to no one and to everyone. She's crying but not with tears because they keep running out. I'm crying and there's more tears because I've been saving them up. "I can't do anything right! It doesn't matter what I do, I—I—I…"

"It's not your fault, Fay, love," the man is saying. "She's just upset; she doesn't know what she's saying."

"She hates me," Auntie Fay says.

"That's not true," the man says.

"Yes it is!" I shout. "I do hate her!"

Auntie Fay wails.

"You shouldn't say things like that, love," the man says. He comes over and he kneels down, leaning on the table. It creaks like it might collapse on me. "Even when you're upset you shouldn't say that. What's happened? You were all right a few minutes ago with me."

"It's her," I say. "I do hate her. She told the vicar that I look like my dad but she's lying."

Auntie Fay is suddenly on the floor with us and she's

crawling on all fours under the table and she has her hand on my ankle.

"That's not what I said, darling girl," she says.

"You're lying—I heard you! I'm not like him!"

"No, sweetheart, that's not what I meant. Oh, I'm sorry, I'm sorry." She crawls further under and crushes me in her arms. "You're not like him. You're nothing like him."

"You said—"

Auntie Fay lets me go and looks at me seriously. "Everyone looks like their parents a little bit, darling. I shouldn't have said it. I was being stupid and awful."

"It doesn't matter what you look like," the man says.

"No, it doesn't," Auntie Fay says. "You're not like your father. You're entirely your mother, right to the bones of you."

"I'll give you a minute," the man says, standing up to leave. The table creaks and Auntie Fay pulls me to her and curls around me.

"I'm sorry," she says again.

"I don't want to be like him."

"And you never will be. Never."

"Am I like my mum?" I ask. Auntie Fay stares at me and wipes my cheeks dry.

"You're so much like her it scares me," she says. "Because she had such a good heart and bad people knew it. That was how she got herself into so much trouble."

SEVENTEEN

Her: Now

We have to queue outside Nando's and Jack can't believe that I've never been to one before. He asks me several times, "Are you *serious*? You've never been to a *Nando's* before?"

They seat us in a booth and Jack immediately slides close to me and puts a hand high up on my thigh while I look at the menu. I push it off but it finds its way back. His other arm drapes around my shoulders.

"When are they coming to take our order?" I ask.

He laughs too loud. "You have to order at the counter!"

I start to slide out but he stops me.

"I'll go, chick. What are you having?"

"I'll go myself," I say.

"No, I'll go. What are you having?"

I tell him and I don't feel confident that he'll even re-member by the time he gets to the counter. I take out my purse and count out the money. It's too expensive but I don't feel like I have a choice.

"Put your money away!" he says.

I argue because the thing I learned before is that when men pay for something they can make you feel like you owe them something later and I don't want to owe Jack anything, so I insist.

"You're a bloody challenge, aren't you?" he says. "I like a challenge. Fine, we'll split it this time. Next time it's on me."

There won't be a next time but for some reason this doesn't help me relax. I sense the same thing about Jack that I've felt around men so many times, the ones that don't stop trying until you give in just to shut them up, just so they'll leave your house or give you the pills or go to sleep. The thing is that I was drunk back then and so it made it easier. Now it's hard to even be touched by Jack without shivering in disgust. It's not that he's ugly. I am not attracted to him but I can still tell he's good-looking. It's that I can sense there's something cruel inside him, waiting to come out.

I watch him at the counter. The outline of a black tattoo on his shoulder. The girl at the till smiles uncomfortably, a smile that every woman must practice, one that men like Jack can't decipher.

He returns with glasses and cutlery clutched in his palms and sauce bottles tucked under his arm. I wipe the knife and fork with my napkin and he laughs and asks if I'm a germophobe. I insist on getting my own drink and when I'm up I ask the girl at the till for a spare glass and I want to tell her I'm sorry about Jack but I don't know why.

Back at the table he puts his arm back around me and tries to force my face towards his for a kiss. I turn and his lips hit my jawline, and it hurts as he tries to twist my head back.

"Stop!" I say, suddenly, and it's so loud that some people turn and smirk.

"Fine," he says, flopping backwards. The girl at the till catches my eye and I'm too ashamed to look at her. "Why did you even come anyway?" Jack asks. "If you don't like me?"

"You made me," I say. I'm confused because this is obvious, isn't it? "You said that you'd tell the manager about that thing I took?"

"I've never said that!"

I think back and I realize this is true.

"Well, no, but you hinted that..."

"All I did was ask you out," he says.

"You said you did me a favor, though?" Everything looks different when I remember now and I feel stupid.

"I did!" he says. "I looked back at the security footage and it was really fucking obvious you were stealing. But you're cute and I thought you liked me so I kept it to myself."

It sounds again like the thing he's saying, but not actually saying, is that if I don't like him then he will tell the manager.

We eat and Jack stops trying to grab me and I think that maybe it will all be fine but when it's time to leave he insists on walking me home.

"I'm okay," I tell him. "Really."

"Where do you live, chick? Come on, I'll take you."

"No, really, it's okay. I have my bus ticket."

"I'll get on the bus with you. It's dark."

"I wanted to get some shopping first," I say.

"I'll come with you there, then."

I don't want you to know where I live! I want to shout. *Please! Leave me alone!*

But Jack isn't going anywhere, and rather than get on the bus with him, I suggest that maybe I could stay for one drink, just one, before I go home. I think about Jack on the bus with me, Jack moaning that now he's come so far out of his way it's only fair that he stays at my place. Jack smiles at the offer of a drink and I hope that he honors the deal and lets me go home after.

The bar is loud and dark and packed. People are already drunk and it makes me even more certain that I do not want to drink. Jack protests when I ask only for a Coke but I tell him that I don't drink anymore and he raises an eyebrow and says fine.

It seems easier to just let him hold my leg and play with my hair and speak into my ear, his breath thick with lager. I'm rigid and unresponsive but this doesn't stop him from trying, again, to kiss me.

When I finish my drink I pat his hand and tell him I really need to go now.

"I have to be home by ten thirty," I shout over the pounding music.

"Or what? You turn back into a pumpkin?"

"I'm going now," I say. "Thanks."

Because he still has a lot of drink left I assume he will stay and I can sneak away but he leaves it and follows.

Out on the street he offers to get a taxi.

"No," I say. I say it clearly so he can't get confused. "I don't want to go home with you."

"Who said anything about going home with me?" he asks.

There's a cab waiting at the taxi rank, so I slide in the

back and close the door but Jack climbs in the other side. In response I open my door again and try to get out but he holds my wrist and tells me he's just sharing a cab.

"But you don't know where I'm going," I say.

The taxi driver looks ahead impassively.

"Doesn't matter," Jack says.

I'm so tired of fighting that I tell the taxi driver the address for the home.

"See?" Jack says. "It's on my way."

Then he tells the taxi driver his address and I start to calm down. He leaves me alone and looks out his window until we reach the home. I cringe as he watches me get out and the way his expression changes as he sees where I live. The sign on the outside reads only Millbrook House but everyone surely knows what it really is, and how women in their dressing gowns smoke outside the gates.

I pay for the taxi and walk quickly towards the gate. Jack calls and I turn to see him leaning out of the open window.

"Next time you'll have to tell me how you ended up here," he says, grinning.

EIGHTEEN

Her: Then

The school dinner bell rings and I get in the line with everyone else in my class. I look around for Sean in the hall but I can't see him even though all the other year fives and sixes are there already, because the oldest classes get to eat first. I am eight now but when I am nine like Sean I will be able to go for lunch earlier and there will always be chocolate pudding left for dessert on Wednesdays.

I can smell the chips and my stomach feels empty. We move forward, too slowly, and I'm stretching to see what the dessert is when someone pushes into me from behind. It's like dominoes then, I push the person in front and they push the person in front of them. We all look back and see some older boys fighting towards the back.

"Gyppo!" Liam is saying.

It is Sean he's calling a gyppo and I'm so happy to see

him that I smile before I realize everything that's happening. Sean pushes the boy again, and again we all smush together.

I break out of the line even though it means I'll have to go to the back (because those are the rules) and I hold Sean's hand and say, "He's not a gyppo."

Sean pulls his hand away and wipes it even though my hands aren't sticky at all. His hands are covered in blue ink where he's been drawing on them.

"Is she your girlfriend?" Liam says.

Sean punches him in the mouth, a big wet slap sound, and it makes me cover my eyes.

Mr. Pocklington grabs Sean and Liam and takes them away. I follow and try to tell him: "Mr. Pocklington, sir, he called Sean a bad name, sir…" but he isn't listening at all. I follow all the way to the office and before he can slam the door I shout, "SIR! I saw it and it wasn't Sean's fault!"

Liam is holding his mouth and sniffling and Mr. Pocklington tells me and Sean to stand against the wall and wait for him to come back. Then he goes off to the nurse with Liam, who is crying.

"Why did you get involved?" Sean asks. His neck is all red and he's frowning at me like I did something wrong.

"Because he was calling you a bad name," I say. I put my hair in my mouth because I'm nervous and I'm hungry thinking about the chips.

"You made it worse," Sean says.

"Oh." I drop my hair. "I'm sorry."

"Shut up." Sean bangs the back of his head against the wall and his face is bright red like he might cry but he doesn't.

"Where have you been?" I ask him. "I haven't seen you all this week."

Sean shrugs. "Didn't want to come back to school."

"But you have to," I say. "Did your dad let you stay home?"

Sean laughs. "I mitched off, didn't I? But the school called and he came and found me and made me come in for the afternoon."

"Aren't you scared of getting in trouble?" I ask. My heart beats really fast even thinking about mitching off and the trouble I'd get into with Auntie Fay.

Sean shrugs again. "Don't care," he says. "It's fucking shit here anyway."

Mr. Pocklington comes back and Liam has some blue paper towel over his mouth but has stopped crying.

"Go back and have your lunch," the teacher tells me. "You," he says to Sean, "come with me."

"But—" I start.

Mr. Pocklington shakes his head. "I don't want to hear it. We've had this behavior before, haven't we, boys?" he says.

The boys both look away.

"But—" I say again.

"Enough. There's no excuse for this behavior. Go and finish your lunch. Now."

It's hard to concentrate after dinner because it's so unfair and it feels like no one ever listens and because the sun is coming in through the windows, warming me up and making me sleepy. When the afternoon break bell rings I rush to get out into the playground and see if Sean is still here. He isn't. I try not to cry and I do my walking that I like to do, following the walls all the way around the school, from the play area to the pond and past the school gates. I'm on my second time when I see Sean, crouched down at the side of the pond by himself, and I run until I'm right next to him but he doesn't look up.

"Did you get told off?" I ask him.

"What do you think?" he asks. He's scooping water up in his hands and letting it run off his fingers.

"It's not fair," I say, sitting down next to him. "Liam was calling you a gyppo."

Sean's neck turns red again and he snaps at me. "I know! Shut up."

"You're not a gyppo," I say.

"Shut up!" Sean punches the water and it splashes everywhere.

"I'm sorry," I say.

"Don't start crying again, please!"

"I can't help it." I sniff and wipe my eyes. "I thought we were friends but you don't want to be my friend anymore because we're back at school."

"I'm still your friend," he says but his voice is all groany.

"No, you're not. You don't want to be my friend because everyone thinks I'm weird."

Sean stands up and digs a hole in the mud with his shoe. "Look, you don't need to stick up for me," he says.

"Did Liam get into trouble? For calling you a—"

"No." Sean kicks a big bit of mud into the pond. "He gets away with everything just because his brother's a spastic."

"What's a spastic?" I ask.

"Come here," Sean says and I follow him back to the play area. "There." Sean points at a boy called Luke who's in the year above me. Luke has a bad leg and a bad arm because he has something wrong with his brain. When he walks he wobbles and he seems to go up and down and side to side and it reminds me of the way a butterfly moves, all clumsy and beautiful at the same time.

"Luke?" I ask.

"Luke's a spastic and he's Liam's little brother so that's why Liam can call me a gyppo and never get in trouble."

The bell sounds and we line up in our classes to go back inside. But behind me I can hear Liam and his friends saying it again, "Is that your girlfriend, gyppo?" Liam's eyes are still all red from where he was crying and his lip is bruised. Liam and his friends point and laugh and make kissing sounds and I get so mad that I forget that Sean told me I'm not supposed to stick up for him.

"Oy," I say. I try to say it like Auntie Fay does, where she looks in my eyes and points one finger at me. "Just because your brother's a spastic doesn't mean you can call everyone else names."

There is silence and Liam is staring at me with his mouth open the way I stare at Auntie Fay when she tells me off. I feel brave and right and I look at Sean to make sure he isn't mad at me but he looks really happy and like he's trying not to laugh at Liam.

I turn and walk back to my line, and everyone is looking at me like I'm important. We file in and sit back down. In the afternoons we do reading comprehension and it's my favorite part of the day but just as we get our books out Mr. Pocklington comes in. We all have to stand every time a teacher comes in but I don't know why. Everyone's chair scrapes across the floor and it hurts my ears. I used to cover my ears when it happened but everyone made fun of me so now I don't even though it kills.

Mr. Pocklington whispers to our teacher and they both look at me. Then I realize that Mr. Pocklington is calling my name and he's frowning. As I walk towards him, everyone starts to whisper and the teacher tells them to be quiet. Mr. Pocklington closes the door behind us and I follow him to his office.

Liam is in the waiting room where you get to sit if you're sick and your mum is coming to pick you up. He's crying and one of the ladies from the office is sitting next to him. When she sees us walking past she frowns, as well.

"Sit there," Mr. Pocklington tells me, and I sit on the chair on the other side of his desk while he leaves the room again. I feel like I'm going to get told off but I don't know why. When he gets back he sighs and shuts the door.

"Can you tell me what happened?" Mr. Pocklington says. He laces his fingers together and puts his elbows on the desk.

"When?" I ask.

"At the end of break. What happened between you and Liam."

"He was calling Sean names again so I—"

"Sean Jenkins?"

"Yes, sir."

"What was he calling Sean?"

"He was calling him a…"

"You can say it."

"A gyppo."

"Right. And he calls him this a lot, does he?"

"Yes. And it's a horrible word and he shouldn't say it. It makes Sean upset."

"You're right. So what did you say?"

"I said he shouldn't call people names."

"What else did you say?"

"I said… I said…just because his brother's a spastic it doesn't mean he can call people names."

Mr. Pocklington pinches his nose between his eyes. "Why did you say that?" he asks.

"Because it's what people say. That he's allowed to say anything because his brother's—"

"Do you know what that word means?"

"Gyppo?"

"No. The other word." I wait for him to say what because I don't know what he means. "Spastic," he says suddenly. He looks red and he blinks a lot.

"It means that you walk funny like Luke."

"It's a bad word for someone with a disability, like Luke. Did you know that?"

I shake my head.

"Who told you that word?" Mr. Pocklington asks.

I shrug.

"Was it Sean Jenkins?" he asks.

I don't move.

"Now that you know it's a bad word, will you use it again?"

I shake my head.

"Good. I know you wouldn't want to upset Liam, would you?"

"I didn't mean to make him cry," I say. My throat hurts.

"Can you tell me…why are you so concerned about Sean all of a sudden?"

"He's my friend," I say.

"Friends don't get friends into trouble, do they?"

I don't know what he means.

"Sean told you to say that word to Liam, didn't he?"

"No!" I say and it's true because he never told me to say anything to Liam. "He told me not to stick up for him but I did anyway because it isn't fair what Liam says to him, even if Liam's brother does have a bad leg."

"It isn't fair that Liam calls Sean names, you're right," Mr. Pocklington says. "But Sean is…" He sighs. "Sean is a troubled boy. He can be difficult and… I think that you would be wise to steer clear of him. Do you understand?"

"No," I say, because I don't; none of it makes sense.

"You should be friends with girls—and boys—your own age. Ones who are well behaved like you are."

"But I like Sean," I say.

Mr. Pocklington shakes his head and leans across the table. He talks really quietly and it makes the back of my neck tickle in a bad way.

"It may seem fun now but I guarantee that if you follow Sean down this path you will look around yourself one day and you will wonder how you got there. And then you will think back to this moment and you will wish you had listened to my advice."

NINETEEN

Her: Now

I arrive at Dr. Isherwood's office twenty-five minutes early but the secretary tells me she isn't in yet.

"What?" I ask. I'm sure I've heard her wrong.

"She's not in," she says again. "You're lucky there's anyone here at all. I'm only in early because there's tons of admin to catch up on. Our system went down last week."

"Do you know when she'll be in?" I ask.

"You're her first appointment and that's not for another twenty minutes," she says. It's actually twenty-three minutes but she looks like she's starting to get fed up with me so I don't say anything.

"Can I wait here?" I ask. There are new chairs at the far end of the room, a big green plant in the corner.

The secretary shrugs. "If you want." She says it in a sigh and has turned away from me, getting a file out of a locked cabinet in the back room and sliding the drawer shut with a bang.

I take a seat and breathe in the smell of fresh paint while I try to slow down my heart. I have looked forward to this appointment for days. Ever since the date with Jack, I've been practicing what I would say, whether I should mention him at all in the session. Dr. Isherwood would just tell me to stop seeing him, and then what could I say? I couldn't tell her that I'd been stealing again. I can't tell her what's really bothering me.

Not that it matters because she isn't here like she's supposed to be, like she always is. A little voice inside me says I'm not being fair and that makes my stomach twist, as if someone is wringing it out like a dirty rag.

Sometimes when we're mad at other people we're really mad at ourselves. That's what Dr. Isherwood told me once and I think that's how it feels right now. I shouldn't have stolen that bra set from work and I hate myself for it. If I could tell Dr. Isherwood the truth I know it would make me feel better, but I can't. I'm too ashamed.

The secretary tuts and sighs at things as she works. One time she catches me looking at her and her eyebrows pinch together and make her forehead wrinkle. I look away quickly but can't help glancing back, where I see her shaking her head like she's completely sick of me.

To pass the time I try to imagine what Dr. Isherwood would say to me if I did tell her about Jack, but if I knew what she would say then I wouldn't be stuck in this situation in the first place because she is always right. I can only do what I think I should do, which is nothing. Just wait for him to get bored of me and leave me alone.

Ten minutes before my appointment I walk over to the secretary's desk. She doesn't look up until I start talking.

"Do you think Dr. Isherwood is coming?" I ask. "Because it's my appointment soon and she still isn't here so..."

"It's still ten minutes until your appointment," she says. She stares at me like I'm an idiot. I blush.

"I know but...usually she's early and..."

"If you take a seat," the secretary says, "she will be here by your appointment."

"Would she call you?" I ask. "If she wasn't coming, would she call you?"

"Dr. Isherwood will be here when she arrives," the secretary says. I try to work out what this means.

I want to ask why she can't call her. Then I remember that I have Dr. Isherwood's telephone number.

"Please can I use the phone?" I ask.

"No," she says. She puts a hand on the receiver as if she needs to guard it from me. "The phone is for business use only."

"I only want to call—"

"If you don't take a seat I'll have to ask you to leave," the secretary says.

Back in my seat I browse the magazines and anxiously watch the clock hands move closer to my appointment time. When it is just one minute until my session it becomes so unbearable that I put my face in my hands and a little groan escapes, loud in the quiet room. In response the secretary sighs. Then it is my appointment time, then it is one minute past my time, and the secretary seems completely unconcerned. My mind races. Has Dr. Isherwood been hurt? Has someone she loves been hurt? Is it my fault for thinking bad things about her? Did I not care enough to stop it from happening?

At two minutes past the hour the door finally opens and

in comes Dr. Isherwood, her hair all blown about and car keys clutched in her hand, out of breath.

"I am *so* sorry," she says. "I'm having one of those mornings!"

I wait for her to explain but she doesn't.

"Kay, can you make us a cup of tea?" she says to the secretary. Dr. Isherwood shakes off her coat and pats at her hair.

I don't want a cup of tea but I don't say anything. Kay smiles as though nothing has happened at all this morning and I think about telling Dr. Isherwood how grumpy Kay is when she isn't around. I follow Dr. Isherwood upstairs; the old wallpaper has been taken off and the walls painted white. Everything looks and smells so new. In Dr. Isherwood's office there are the shelves full of her books and there are flowers on the desk. There are more picture frames than usual, their backs facing the room.

"I'm so sorry," Dr. Isherwood says again. She hangs her coat over the arm of the sofa and dumps her bag on the floor by the desk. She's not acting like herself. Normally she leaves her coat downstairs, her handbag out of sight. And when she sits down on the sofa she kind of slumps and makes a sound: *Ahhh.* Hangs her head back for a moment.

"So," she says, sitting up and crossing her legs. "How has your week been since we last spoke?"

"Two weeks," I say.

"Of course!" she says. "You'll have to bear with me, I'm still gathering myself."

"Are you okay?" I ask.

"Oh, bless you," she says, laughing. "Yes, I am okay, just a little rushed off my feet lately. I'm sure it'll settle once we've finally got everything finished here."

A whining noise interrupts the quiet, a sound like a mosquito hovering just by your ear.

"Ugh," Dr. Isherwood says. "There's a dentist above us." She points to the ceiling. "Every time he gets that drill out it goes right through me."

I don't like the new office and I don't know if I like the new Dr. Isherwood. She laughs all the time like she's drunk and she's not acting like a grown-up anymore.

"I don't like my job," I blurt out.

Kay the secretary knocks on the door and brings in a tray with two mugs on it.

"You're an angel," Dr. Isherwood says. "I swear I haven't had time to have a cup of tea in a week."

When Kay leaves Dr. Isherwood puts her tea down on the table and turns to me. "Sorry..." she says. "You were just saying..."

"It doesn't matter," I say. I know I am being petulant but Dr. Isherwood doesn't seem to notice.

"So how are you finding the job? Any better?" she asks. What is wrong with her?

"It's fine," I lie, waiting for her to realize her mistake.

"Well, good! I know it's not the most challenging job in the world but there's opportunity to progress once you have some experience and there are plenty of people there to potentially connect with."

"Hmm," I grunt.

"Now, I had something I needed to... Oh!" She jumps up from her chair. "I remember! I have something for you." She retrieves her bag and roots around in it. An empty tissue packet falls to the floor. "Here," she says, extending a box towards me.

It's an iPhone. It feels heavier than I remember them being.

"It's my old one," she says. "You need a *proper* phone, one for your emails and the internet. You just can't get on with anything less, so have this until you get your own."

"Thank you," I say, not knowing who—aside from Dr. Isherwood—I would email.

"I already gave this number to your parole supervisor, so they can call you if they need to speak with you regarding your appointments. I've also put in all your essential contacts," she says.

They fill only one page. There is Dr. Isherwood, my work number, my parole officer, and my social worker.

"Thanks," I say, trying not to show her how upset I feel when I look at how barren my life is.

"It'll fill up," she says, reading my mind. "Over time. You will meet people and they will get to know you and they will love you. I promise."

Hot fat tears roll down my face. Dr. Isherwood hands me a tissue.

"Oh dear." She crouches down and places a hand on my knee. "Is this why you were so reluctant to get a phone?" she says. "Does it make you feel lonely?"

I nod. But I think of the real reason, of the phone calls that came the last time, when Sean found me. Always an unavailable number; always Sean calling me. At first they were infrequent. We didn't say much; sometimes we said nothing at all. Sometimes we just listened to the open line, breathing very softly, until we fell asleep.

There were late-night calls where he would cry and ask me if it was all his fault. *No*, I would say, but he would ask again. There were angry calls, where he wished he'd never met me, where he wished I was dead. The worst were the calls where he was just like he used to be. Where he made fun of me and we laughed, our laughter catching in our throats and burning our eyes. Where I wasn't sure if I was laughing or crying anymore.

"Do you really not remember?" Sean would ask me again and again. He called me a liar; then he told me he was sorry. "How can you forget?" I told him about the underpass and how that's as far as my memory lets me go. I asked him to tell me what he remembered, but all he said was that he wished he could forget, too.

Then he was gone. The calls stopped suddenly and I wondered what I'd done wrong. I couldn't call him because I never knew his number. I thought he was punishing me. I felt the hole inside me yawn wide open until it felt like I might be sucked into the blackness. I could barely sleep but I could barely stay awake, either. When I did leave the house it was only to see Dr. Isherwood. I lied and told her I couldn't sleep because of the noise my neighbors made all night. She worried over me, and wrote out a prescription for sleeping tablets which I stuffed in my pocket and forgot about.

I put the television on to feel less alone but the sound clashed with the noise in my head and it felt like everyone talked too quickly, or that the music was too chaotic and loud and layered. So I muted it and lay in front of it for hours. Until one day I was watching the screen and I saw Sean's face. The picture of him they took at the police station when they arrested us both. His mouth a tight line, eyes hard. I knew that face: it was the one he used when he was trying not to cry. But that's not how the world saw it.

I scrambled to find the remote control to unmute but I couldn't. Instead I crawled to the TV and felt with my fingers until I found the volume buttons. The news reporter's voice grew and grew: "...computer was seized and the suspect was arrested. Police confirmed that Sean Jenkins would be held in custody but didn't specify the charges brought against him."

Dr. Isherwood pats my knee, which I know means she's about to stand up, and I want to hold her hand and ask her not to but I can't. She groans as she straightens up.

"My back is in bits," she says. "Now that you have that phone you *must* promise to call me if things get too much."

By "too much" she means what happened after Sean was arrested. We still have trouble talking about it. It is too painful, even for her.

"I promise," I say.

"You don't feel like that again now, do you?" she says.

"No," I say. I'm telling the truth but really it's impossible to know when you start feeling *like that*. It's almost as if you stop feeling anything.

"Do you think—" Dr. Isherwood starts but her phone starts to ring in her bag. "I'm sorry," she says. She roots around searching for it. When she looks at the screen her face changes. "I'm so sorry," she says. "I need to take this. I'm so sorry. Hello?"

Dr. Isherwood leaves the room and closes the door behind her. This has never happened before, either. Her phone has gone off but she's never answered it. All the things I was thinking about saying start to sink back inside me like swallowed vomit, burning all the way down. I feel like screaming: Dr. Isherwood is the only person I have and she doesn't care anymore. She was late and she wasn't listening properly, and now she's just gone.

I stare at the backs of the photographs on the desk and wonder which ones are new, and if they will show me what has changed the one person I had thought was permanent, consistent, mine. Outside Dr. Isherwood's voice grows quieter as she walks down the stairs.

I stand and walk towards the pictures. Is it bad? Would I be breaking her trust? I hesitate. If she didn't want anyone to look at them she wouldn't have put them on her desk. I reach and touch the frame of one. Dr. Isherwood knows almost everything about me; why can't I know anything about her?

TWENTY

Her: Then

After I had seen the news that Sean had been rearrested, I felt the hole inside me rip wider. Without him, I could suddenly see the rest of my life stretching out ahead of me. It would be a life without friends or laughter or crying. So I made a decision.

I packed everything I needed into a backpack and I got the prescription Dr. Isherwood had written me for sleeping tablets from my coat pocket. I left my keys on the kitchen table, knowing I wouldn't be coming back.

Outside, it was raining lightly, like the spray from a waterfall, misty and floating. I hadn't brought an umbrella.

On my way to the train station I went into a pharmacy and gave them my prescription for the sleeping tablets.

"Have you taken these before?" the pharmacist asked me. I nodded and the pharmacist handed me the box of pills inside a paper bag. I was relieved as I said goodbye. I wasn't sure if I could manage talking to anyone for any length of time.

Back in the rain I walked the ten minutes to the train station and bought a one-way ticket back home. I had to go back. I needed to remember what had happened, who I really was.

The journey took three hours. It seemed impossible that the past could have been so close this whole time. I looked out of the window and watched the world roll by, like a tape being rewound, as I was taken back to where I came from. As soon as I stepped off the train I knew I had broken the law. One of the conditions of my release was that I was never allowed back there ever again. As I left the station my phone rang. Dr. Isherwood left a voice-mail message, asking if everything was okay, and whether I had forgotten our appointment. I switched it to airplane mode and put it back into my pocket.

The town didn't look familiar at all and I had to look back at the sign above the train station to make sure I had got off at the right stop. Then, slowly, everything started to fall into place and I was walking the old streets without having to think about where I was going. The shop fronts were all different but when I tilted my head and looked up I saw that all the buildings were the same, the old architecture still as dirty and splattered with bird poo as it always was.

I knew I wouldn't find myself there. I knew I needed to get a bus to the suburbs, to the estates they kept at arm's length from everywhere else. The bus station was new, all glass and steel, a clock tower with a clock stuck at the wrong time. I closed my eyes and brought back the memories of Christmas shopping, my hand in Mum's, in the old bus station which was always damp and dark and smelled of stale urine and smoke. It had become the smell of going home, a bag full of Christmas presents and decorations. In the new bus station, the memory felt like someone else's life.

Everything that passed by the window as the bus took me home looked just as distorted as in town. It looked new, but only on the surface. There were still cracks where I could see through time. There was a new school building that gleamed even on the gloomy day but part of the old school still stood nearby. It was the comprehensive school that I would have gone to, that Sean would have gone to. That Luke… Then I felt something. Pain. I grabbed on to it and made myself feel it again and again.

I got off the bus at the edge of the estates and it felt like I was ten again. Here, nothing had changed. The pre-fab houses clustered around unkempt greens. The blocks of flats that had the bad reputations looked as though they still did. Even the little row of shops looked the same, though all the stores themselves had changed. The video shop where Sean's dad worked was now a vape shop instead. The flat above it had its curtains drawn and I wondered if Sean's dad still lived there now.

The streets were empty because of the weather. It was the afternoon and people were still at work, their children in school. It felt like I was the only person left alive or that I had frozen time and was walking around in a stopped world. Only the wind and the rain disturbed the stillness. Even the playing fields were empty. From a spike of the black railing that surrounded the park, someone had hung a child's coat by its hood. It was weighed down with rain and looked like it had been there for a long time, waiting to be collected.

I walked to the edges of the park, where everything had

started. Where I'd met Sean; where we had hidden in the undergrowth and listened to all the other children playing above us. This was where it had started and where it had all started to come apart. I walked down the bank and along the backs of the houses, remembering how it had felt to be small and invisible in the tangles of weeds and branches, and how they would scrape my arms and my cheeks like cat scratches, itchy and evidence that I'd been alive that day. We were agile, weaving through the brambles and squeezing through the gaps in the fences like urban foxes. Feral, fearless.

I left the park and decided to look at the houses from the front until I found the one I was looking for. Again, at first glance, it looked as though everything was different, but it was only superficial things like hanging baskets and front doors which had changed. Underneath, everything was still the same, and if I concentrated I could peel away the years and remember them as they were back then.

I stopped dead outside number 23. It still had the same low front wall, red bricks with smooth gray slabs running along the top. This is where all of Liam's friends would sit, lined up, swapping football stickers and cooling off with the bottomless supply of ice lollies his mum kept in the freezer, their bikes lying on their sides on the grass. But the grass was gone now, replaced with a patio surrounding a miniature tree with dark red leaves.

The porch had changed, too. Instead of the glassed-in area surrounding the front door—where muddy football boots and umbrellas and guests' shoes used to cluster in the corner—now there was just an overhanging roof and a small bench. Whoever lived here now didn't have the cluttered and chaotic life of the family who lived here before them and I wondered if they knew that this was *the* house, or if no one had told them that it was haunted with sadness and that it was my fault, me, staring into their windows and seeing only my reflection.

The rain had plastered my hair to my skin and my jumper was soaked through. I shivered but didn't feel the cold. I didn't feel anything, not like I should have. It was Liam who was always in the front garden, always surrounded by friends. Luke had always been in the back garden, alone, playing his strange games that only he understood. I took out my phone and googled our names, searching for the old pictures of the garden, the sports field and the disused swimming pool in the sports complex. Each image was like a pinch and I felt the bruises throb inside me. But I needed more.

I took a deep breath and opened the gate, which creaked so loudly I was sure that if there was someone in the house they would already have known I was there. The gate swung itself shut and I made my way down the path and stood frozen in front of the door. In one hand I clutched my phone, slick with rain, and with the other I reached to press the doorbell. It rang so clearly that I could hear it and I started to hope that no one was home because I realized it had been a terrible idea. I waited one second and then decided to leave but before I could step off the porch someone answered and called me back.

"Sorry," they say. "I was upstairs."

I turned and my heart stopped in my chest. It was Luke's mum. Her face changed when she realized I was not there to deliver or solicit anything.

"Can I help you?" she asked. Her voice was uncertain but she didn't know who I was, that much was obvious.

I shook my head. "Wrong house," I said. "Sorry to bother—" I lost my footing as I stepped down from the raised porch and fell with force. My phone skidded across the patio. Before I could get up Luke's mum was standing over me, reaching down and holding my arm.

"Are you okay? I'm so sorry. Here." She bent and helped me up, even though I protested. "That looked like a bad fall. Can you walk?"

"I'm fine," I insisted, but my legs weren't working as they should. My knees ached and my left arm was numb.

"You don't look fine," she said. She tucked some of her dark hair behind her ear.

"You're getting wet," I said, limping towards my phone. "I'm sorry for bothering you. Please, go back inside."

"Will you be okay?" she asked, tightening her beige cardigan around herself. "What house were you after?"

"I was looking for an old friend," I said. "I thought this was the right house but maybe not. Sorry." As I bent to get my phone I became light-headed and staggered forward. Luke's mum shrieked as I almost plowed headfirst into the garden wall. Then she was upon me again.

"You can't wander around like this," she says, taking my arm again. "Come in, get yourself together and go when you feel a bit better. Come on."

I hesitated but knew she was right; I didn't think I could go much further when I felt like that. I let her lead me inside the house, into the warmth. I had never been inside Liam and Luke's house before and if I could have forgotten everything that had happened I would have felt as though I was ten and had been invited to one of the parties I was always dying to go to. Parties with Super Soakers and every type of pop, those amazing cakes and games that everyone would talk about in school on Monday.

"I feel terrible," Luke's mum said, sitting me down on her sofa.

"Why?" I asked.

"Well, it's my porch you fell off! I've missed that step a few times myself," she said. "And you're soaked! I'll get you a towel and a cup of tea with some sugar. You need sugar for a shock."

Hot tears welled in my eyes.

"Don't you have an umbrella?" she asked.

"It blew inside out," I lied.

"I'm sure I've got a spare brolly. You sit there and I'll be back in a minute."

When she left, the silence in the house became oppressive. Beneath me I felt the sofa cushion dampen from my wet clothes. I stood and my knees throbbed in pain.

I looked around and realized everything inside the house was so clean and modern. This was good; it meant her life didn't stop completely after what had happened to Luke. But when I thought about it more I realized something. I understood the truth about what happens after someone is stolen from you. From the outside your world looks just like everyone else's: normal. But inside it leaves a hole that smolders at the edges, like a cigarette touched to paper, threatening to burn wider and wider until there's nothing left of you at all.

There was an alcove which led into a dining room and at the back of the house there were patio doors looking out onto the garden. The blinds were lowered and I couldn't see outside. I could hear Luke's mum in the kitchen, the clink of mugs and the boiling kettle. As I walked through the living room my shoes left gray footprints on the beige carpet and I hated the traces I was leaving of myself over her house. I shouldn't have come here; I knew it then. It was wrong.

The walls of the dining room were lined with photographs. Liam, growing older in each frame. From school uniform to graduation gown to wedding suit. He was still good-looking, still had that air of confidence all popular people have, people I knew I would never understand. They just seemed to exist without having to try. I looked at the pictures of Luke, which kept him frozen in time, always in his school uniform, or sitting in his mother's lap, their cheeks tinged from the holiday sun.

It hurt to look at him and so I forced myself to. I made myself remember his smile as we stretched out our hands to him and the way he looked back over his shoulder to check if his mum was watching as we helped him through the fence and into the playing fields. "I'll get in trouble," he said. We promised it would be okay.

"I've got you an old brolly. You can keep it," Luke's mum said as she came back in. She held out the umbrella like a baton. When she saw me standing in front of the photos she paused, confused.

"I got your sofa all wet," I said, pointing to the damp patch. "I'm sorry."

"Don't be daft!" she said. "Sit down for five minutes."

I sat, obediently, and rolled up my jeans to inspect the grazes on my knees. When Luke's mum returned again she had two mugs of tea and a bath towel over her arm.

"Thank you," I said, taking the drink and the towel.

"I'll just get us some biscuits," she said as she disappeared again.

The next time she came back she sat heavily in the chair opposite me and dipped a chocolate digestive into her tea.

"Thank you for all this," I said. Her kindness stuck in my throat like a pill, bitter and painful.

"It's no bother," she said. "I feel awful that you fell like that."

I squeezed my hair in the towel to dry it and forced myself to smile back at her.

"Sorry," she said. "Did you say you were local?" Her expression had changed.

"No," I said.

"But you were looking for a friend's house, weren't you?"

"Yeah. Just someone I used to know. They probably don't even live around here anymore, but I was passing through and…" I trailed off, shrugged.

"So you used to live locally? It's just that you seem familiar."

"No," I said. "I just knew someone a long time ago who lived here. I think I have one of those faces."

She laughed. "Who is it you used to know?" she asked. "I've lived here donkey's years so I'd know them if they're still around."

As I hung the towel over the arm of the chair I knocked my tea off the end table. Luke's mum jumped up and shushed me as I apologized.

"It's not your day, is it?" she asked, laughing kindly. "Sorry, what did you say your name was?"

"I didn't," I said. "It's Emma," I added, making up a name.

"Well, I'm Bernadette." She held out her hand to shake mine.

"I am so, so sorry," I said again. "I'll go. I've been enough trouble."

"You don't even know where you're going yet!" she said. As I stood the rain outside intensified, hitting the windows as hard as hail. I hesitated. I didn't want to leave the warmth of Bernadette's house, her company. "At least wait for this to ease off," she said, looking up at me from the floor as she patted at the spilled tea with the towel.

"Okay," I said, selfishly. "If it's not too much of a problem."

"I'd better make sure this doesn't set," she said, standing as I sat back down. "Here." She thrust the plate of biscuits towards me. "Get some of these down you."

I nibbled at the edges of a chocolate biscuit and took in my surroundings. I imagined what life would have been like if I'd lived here, with a mum as sweet and kind as Bernadette. To be allowed to spill things in the living room and have friends over—to have friends at all—and fill the house with noise and mess.

From the hallway I heard her phone ring and Bernadette shouted an apology to me before she answered it. "Oh, hi, love! No, no, it's no bother..." Her voice faded as she took the call somewhere else. I took a custard cream from the plate, split it in half, and licked out the middle. *Disgusting*, I could hear my auntie Fay say, as she always used to when I did this. *Eat it properly.*

I walked back into the dining room and looked again at the pictures. All of them seemed so happy. All the sadness and the anger had been skipped over, as though it had never happened. People only want to preserve and display the best of themselves. I thought maybe everyone was just creating a new identity, hiding what they really were.

At the patio doors I prized apart the metal slats of the blinds and peered into the garden. That, too, had changed. There was a water feature and a pond surrounded by stone frogs. They were the kinds of things that they probably couldn't have had with Luke around, all those things that would have got in his way.

"Right," Bernadette said as she came back in with the

bottle of carpet cleaner and a sponge. She stopped and looked at me. The blinds clattered as I let them go.

"Who was it you said you were here to see?" she said, putting everything down and folding her arms across her chest.

I couldn't say anything. My face burned and I looked down at my feet.

"Oh," she said. I could see she was trying not to cry. "You're just here to nose around, see where it happened."

"What?" I said. "Where what happened?" But my voice was wooden and unconvincing.

"Every time it gets in the news again we get people like you poking their noses in."

"No," I said. Then I started to cry. "I'm sorry, it isn't like that at all."

Bernadette was already going for the phone. "I'm calling the police. Get out," she said.

"No, please don't," I said. "I'm going. I'll go. I just—"

Suddenly she stopped looking angry and started to look afraid. The phone shook in her hand and she backed against the wall, my backpack behind her. As I approached, trying to get my bag, she screamed, thinking I was reaching for her.

"I just want my bag," I said. I was crying, too.

"You're not supposed to be here!" she said. Then, "How could you? Why would you do this?"

"Please," I said. "I am sorry, I'm so sorry—I'm trying to leave! Please just give me my bag."

"No!" she screamed. She lunged towards me and I blocked myself with my arm, pushing her to the side. She screamed again. I snatched my bag and ran to the door.

"Get out!" she shouted. "Get out get out get out get out get out—"

I slammed the door behind me and ran through the streets and out of the estate. Puddles ankle-deep soaked through my already sodden shoes and the rain whipped my face so hard it stung, cold against the warmth of the tears. I ran until I was at the flyover, at the mouth of the underpass, and though I knew I would have to go through it, exactly as it had happened, I couldn't. Instead I ran into the traffic and cars swerved and hit their brakes hard, their horns blaring, but I reached the pavement on the other side alive and unhurt. A man leaned out of his car window and shouted something at me that I couldn't understand.

Then I heard the sirens.

TWENTY-ONE

Her: Now

Dr. Isherwood sighs as she comes back into the room, and I take my hand off the photograph in front of me.

"I cannot apologize enough," she says.

I turn away from her desk, blushing, feeling caught red-handed. But she doesn't seem to notice as she talks and I am able to sit back down while she puts her phone back into her bag.

"That's okay," I say. I try to mean it.

"It really isn't okay and you're being very kind and understanding. It's just been absolute madness lately." She puts her fingers into her hair and shakes it loose. "But you have my full, undivided attention now, I promise."

She smiles at me but I see her eyes dart back to her phone in her bag.

"It's okay," I say again.

"I don't want you to think that I'm not completely here for you," she says, putting her bag behind her chair. "You must call me, now that you have your phone. If things get—"

"Too much," I interrupt, nodding. "I know."

When the police arrested me on that last day, after everything that happened with Luke's mum, Dr. Isherwood had driven the five hours to the station to see me. She was the only one who believed me when I said I wasn't going to hurt Bernadette. The police had laid out the contents of my bag: the sleeping pills, the rope, the Stanley knife, the pen, and the notebook. I tried to tell them I was only trying to remember what happened, so that I could tell the truth before I died.

"You should get a solicitor," the appropriate adult had told me.

"I want to see Dr. Isherwood," I said. "Please call Dr. Isherwood."

I could hear her from my cell as she came in, shouting my name and telling them I was vulnerable and shouldn't be on my own. I shouted back, I cried like a child; she was so close but so far away.

Dr. Isherwood knew straightaway that I would never hurt anybody, not on purpose. She knew I was going to hurt myself.

"I promise I won't do anything stupid again," I tell her now.

"It wasn't stupid," she says. "I just wish you'd felt you could talk to me—or to anyone!—about how you felt. You will, won't you? If you ever start to feel that way again."

"Yes, I promise." I say this to make her feel better but I don't know if it's true. When you start to feel like that the last thing you want to do is ask for help. You may as well ask me to climb Mount Everest. The idea that someone could help pull you out of that hole seems impossible and asking the most difficult thing in the world.

The rest of the session we talk about places I can go to find friends: taking an evening class, joining a gym, taking part in work events. I don't mention the dark cloud that hangs over work, or Jack, who now lingers nearby at all times, or else is watching me over the CCTV and, later, telling me what he saw.

I leave Dr. Isherwood's office with a few flyers for classes she found and a list we wrote up together of things I want to achieve and how to achieve them. When I am down the street I stuff the pieces of paper into my bag, knowing that I will probably throw them out once I'm back at the home. On the bus I take out my new phone and look through the sad list of contacts again. I set up my email address and the phone buzzes almost straightaway.

The sender's email is just a string of numbers and I would think it was spam except for the single word in the subject line: Petal.

TWENTY-TWO

Him: Now

I text: I'm outside. Lean my bike against the wall, take the cig out from behind my ear and light it. She texts back: Come up flat 37 I'll buzz you in.

I start to text her to get her fucking arse downstairs but delete it, crush the half-smoked fag under my foot and hide the bike in the bushes. I press the button for 37 and she buzzes me in before I've had time to take my finger off. The lift is broken so I take the stairs two at a time. There's light coming from behind her curtains and the door is left part open so that even as I knock it starts to swing wider. Inside, three dirty-looking kids wriggle on the sofa, looking away from the TV only for a second to check who's walking into their house. They are watching the menu screen for a DVD, playing on a loop.

"Where's your mum, then?" I ask. I put my hands in

my pockets. I'm always nervous around kids, never know what to say. One holding a sippy cup points to the television. "Shall I press Play for you?" I ask. I step carefully over the toys and bits that litter the floor and crouch down to the DVD player and start it to play all episodes again. One of them laughs and claps.

"Hang on a second!" comes a voice from the back room. The voice is followed by a skinny woman in black tracksuit bottoms and a white tank top. She holds out some crinkled notes to me with a shaking hand. I count them and pass her the Xanax. She pops two and dry-swallows them.

I take another look around the flat and at the kids, who stare unblinking at the TV.

"This isn't fucking Deliveroo, yeah?" I say. "Next time, meet me outside."

"Yeah," she says, not listening. "Thanks."

I leave but the flat seems to stay with me, reminding me why I never go inside. My head's been all over the place lately, thinking about *her*, thinking about what happened. Even now she has a power over me that no one else has ever had.

At Slimy's I tuck the bike behind the wheelie bins at the side of the flat and make my way up, looking forward to switching off for a while. I can smell the skunk as soon as I step off the lift. One of the boys lets me in; the air is thick with smoke.

"What's happening?" I say, slumping into my usual seat. No one replies. "Yeah, I'm all right, thank you, cheers," I say to myself. "Thanks for the warm fucking welcome."

"All right, Tanker," Slimy manages.

"What's got everyone so lively, then?" I ask. Some new guy I don't recognize passes me a bong. I take a hit that makes my chest feel like it'll explode and do my best not to cough like a pussy. "Fucking hell," I say, my eyes streaming.

"It's a bit poky," the new guy says, grinning.

I let go and cough and cough, my lungs assaulted. The new guy pats my back and I slap him away, unable to speak to tell him to fuck off.

I make my way to the kitchen, still hacking. Each time I try to take a breath a new fit starts up. I swill out a smudged glass and down some water, which I cough straight back up into the sink. Holding my breath, then taking a small sip, I start to get control back. My brain aches from the force of the coughing and my lungs burn behind my ribs.

When I get back into the room no one except the new guy even seems to notice what happened. The new guy grins at me with his smug face.

"Yeah, it's poky, man," he says, nodding. "Got to take it easy."

"Fucking poky," I say. "If you say 'poky' one more time I swear to fuck—"

"Poky," he says.

I lunge at him and grab his T-shirt in my fist. He turns his head away and screws his eyes shut.

"Yeah, I didn't fucking think so," I say.

Now people's heads start to turn and someone tells me to calm down.

"Who is this, anyway?" I ask.

"Cal," Slimy says. "He's all right, leave him alone."

I let the T-shirt go but only because I feel, suddenly, light-headed. Before I let myself sit down I grab the laptop off the floor and open it up. I stare at the screen but can't remember exactly what to do. I can feel my heart racing in my chest, beating so hard I start to think everyone can hear it. I look around to see if anyone is looking but they are all focused on the TV, except the new guy, what was his name?

"Oy," I say to him. "Fuck you staring at?"

The new guy smiles and shakes his head.

The panic creeps up me like ivy grows up walls. It rests on me; it shivers against my skin; I feel it all around me. A cigarette: I think the nicotine will help. I take my pack of baccy out of my pocket and the Rizlas are inside. The thin cigarette paper trembles in my hands. I look up and the new guy seems to look away quickly. Fuck him—just roll the cigarette, I think, pinching the tobacco between my fingers. I take a loose filter out of my pocket and put it in the end but my hands are shaking and I drop it twice. Beside me, I think I hear the new guy laugh gently.

When it comes to licking the paper my tongue is so dry it refuses to stick. I work up as much saliva in my mouth as I can and manage to get the paper to stick. I look at my work: loose tobacco hanging from the ends, paper not tight enough around the filter so that if I don't keep it pinched between my thumb and finger it will fall out. Generally a fucking mess, but it's all I have. I pat my pockets for my lighter but can't find it.

"Here," the new guy says, leaning forward with his own lighter. I try to take it but he flicks it and holds the flame out to me, like I'm his little bitch. I'm breathing so hard through my nose I almost blow it out but just manage to light the cigarette and sit back. The new guy smirks and I know he thinks he's got me there, he's made me look gay, but I can feel a cold sweat at my hairline and I'm too weak to do anything about it.

The cigarette helps; it is something to do while I stare at the laptop and try to remember what I was going to… The screen goes abruptly black and I stare at my own reflection.

There's a second where I think I've broken it and then I realize that it's gone to sleep, so I nudge it awake and start to type, slowly. Sometimes I have dreams where I'm coding, like I used to, but the keys keep moving around and I get it wrong over and over again. It feels like that now. I have to watch my fingers as they move over the letters, then check the screen to make sure it matches up. Am I typing too loudly? Am I hitting the keys too hard? No one seems to be staring this time, not even the new guy.

Get a grip. Sort yourself out.

I feel like I'm sinking into the chair.

"You all right?" the new guy asks, with that smirk again.

"Yeah, fine," I say.

"You Sean?" he asks.

"What did you call me?" I ask.

"Are you sure?" the new guy says, slowly. He laughs. "I told you it was a bit—"

I want to tell him to fuck off but I can feel myself start to retch. The laptop falls to the filthy carpet as I stand up and I feel everyone turn their heads in unison to stare at me as I run to the bathroom. I push the door closed behind me and bend over the toilet to release a stream of hot vomit that burns on the way up. It's noisy and I know they will all hear me and know that I'm spinning out but fuck it. The next heaves are dry. I flush to get rid of the smell of my own stomach contents; I shiver at the baseness of living, all that bile and blood and bone inside all of us. I blink away the tears in my eyes and look into the bowl: streaks of dried-on shit, flecks of some half-digested food. I heave again and again but there's nothing in me.

When I stand my legs feel like lead. I splash my face in the sink with cold water and look into the mirror: my pupils are wide as saucers, my skin pale as bone. I remember those old stories, of people off their tits on acid, staring into mirrors and seeing their faces melt off until they are staring at their own skulls. I've never messed with hallucinogens. There's too much hiding in the dark corners of my mind, too many monsters under the bed. But now I can imagine how it would feel and I wonder if the new guy has laced the pot with something stronger. Or is this paranoia? I look away from my hollow eyes and let myself sit again, give myself some time to right my brain.

I look at the corners of the room, all that black mold. It looks like it's breathing, swelling and receding. Out, in.

If I had the energy I'd go home; if facing the streets and the noise and the eyes of every passing person didn't seem like the scariest shit on the planet right now. Weak, I stand up and tell myself to have some sugar. That'll sort me out.

It takes all the bravery I can muster just to open the door and face the boys but I do it, trying to walk normally. Only the new guy turns around, like he's been waiting for me. I try to ignore him but something about him is just emanating bad vibes. *Vibes.* I really am fucking stoned.

The kitchen is a mess but Slimy can always be relied upon for munchies. I take an entire packet of shortbread back into the room, a can of Pepsi tucked under my arm.

"Pulled a whitey, did you, mate?" the new guy says.

Ignore him.

The laptop is exactly where I dropped it. Not one single lazy fucker bothered to pick it up. I get on to my email and there it is, finally, *her.*

Tanks? <3

That's all but it's everything.

Give me your digits, I write. I smile, already imagining the reply: What?

I delete and write out: Give me your telephone number.

TWENTY-THREE

Her: Now

When I get back to the home I rush up to my room and wait for Sean to call. The signal is bad and I wander from corner to corner trying to find a good place. I open the window, which sticks and screams in its frame, and crawl out onto the fire escape. My phone has three bars of signal and the sky is orange and purple as the sun sets. I sit back on the metal steps and look out over the roads and the rows of houses and my stomach dances with nerves. I shouldn't be doing this.

All kinds of things pass through my mind: that it's a trap and I've fallen for it and will be going back to the unit; that Sean won't call because he's realized I'm a bad person; that Sean *will* call but the phone is bugged and they'll arrest me.

The phone does buzz, eventually, and the screen reads Unavailable.

"Hello?" I answer. There's a long pause.

"All right, pet?" Sean says. It's his voice, changed by years and influenced by the accents of the places he's lived in, but it's him. I breathe a long sigh.

"How did you find me?" I ask.

"Now, if I told you that it would ruin it, wouldn't it?" he says. I know there's no point in pressing him. This time, I feel so much relief to hear his voice that I don't care.

"I missed you," I say, quietly. He doesn't speak for a long time. "You left me, last time."

He sighs.

"Wasn't my fault, pet," he says eventually.

"Are you still dealing drugs?" I ask.

"No," he says, but I know he's lying. "And what about you? What the fuck were you thinking, going back to Luke's house like that?"

"I was trying to remember," I say. "Like you told me to."

"I never told you to go to his fucking house, Petal. Jesus."

"I didn't know she was still living there! Everything just got too…too…" I close my eyes and try to block it out.

"How the fuck did you even stay out of prison on that one?"

"Dr. Isherwood helped me," I say. I hear him groan.

"And how is your doctor-slash-surrogate mum? Still sticking with you?"

"Yeah," I say, feeling shy. Sometimes I think he hates Dr. Isherwood or hates it that I love her. "Only…"

"Yeah?"

"She seems weird lately. Different. I don't know."

"How so?" I hear the interest in his voice.

"Like she's not really listening. And she's late or she isn't there at all. Or she *is* there but she's thinking about something else. You know?"

"As usual, pet, I have no idea what the fuck you're on about," he says. I laugh. It's been so long since I laughed that the muscles in my face feel stiff.

"I think she's sick of me," I say. "Except…"

"What?" he asks.

"Well, she still says I can call her anytime. She just seems…distracted."

"She gave you her personal number?" Sean asks.

"Yeah," I say. I blush because I only realize now how kind that is. "She even gave me her old phone when I said I needed one. Just until I get my own." Saying it out loud I suddenly feel stupid for worrying. Selfish, like always.

"What kind of phone?" Sean asks.

"An iPhone," I say. "Why?"

"Well," Sean says. Then he stops. "Nah, don't worry about it."

"What?" I say.

"Nah, it doesn't matter, honestly."

"What?" I say again, dying to know what he's thinking, even if it's dull, even if he doesn't want to tell me. Especially if he doesn't want to tell me.

"It's just that if you have her old iPhone and you have her personal number, she's obviously not that fussed about her privacy. That's all. It just shows that she must really care about you."

"Yeah," I say. It feels nice to hear him say it.

"Because you can find out pretty much anything about someone with those two things. You know?"

"You can?" I ask.

"Or maybe she's keeping tabs on you?" He laughs.

"What do you mean?" I get a knot in my stomach.

"I'm only joking, Petal. I bet someone like your Isherwood doesn't even think about things like location services and the Cloud. She probably doesn't even use Find My iPhone."

"So…do you think she's keeping tabs on me?" It's starting to get cold outside. The metal steps of the fire escape dig into my thighs.

"It's like I said, she probably doesn't even think about any of that shit. Go to Settings. What name does it say on the top?"

I take the phone away from my ear and swipe to look at the settings like he said.

"My name," I say. "Well, my new name."

"Charlotte Donaldson?" Sean says.

"How did you know?" I ask, feeling another chill, deeper than the one from the cold air.

"I have my ways," he says. "Do you like it?"

"Not really," I say.

"Yeah, you don't seem like a Charlotte."

"And what's your new name?" I ask.

"Neil," he says.

"No, it isn't," I say, laughing.

"Nigel," he says. "No, it's really Marvin. Marvin Parvin. I'm trying to keep a low profile with my normal-as-fuck name."

"Shut up!" I laugh again.

"Anyway," he says. I can still hear him smiling. "Is your email address showing?"

I look again. "No," I say. "It's Dr. Isherwood's."

"Scroll down," Sean says. "Is there a list of other devices?"

"Yeah," I say, trying not to sound excited. I read them aloud: "Evelyn's iPad, Evelyn's iPhone X, Evelyn's iMac…"

"Click one," he says. "Then press Show in Find My iPhone."

I press on the iPhone X and wait. A compass appears, then a map, then a little dot that throbs like a heart. I look at the street names and zoom in.

"She's shopping," I say. I smile. "How does this... Can she see me?"

"She probably doesn't know it's switched on," Sean says. "But if you wanted to be sure she's not tracking you, you could just turn off your location services."

"Why wouldn't I want her to know where I am?" I ask, confused. It doesn't seem like it would matter.

"You might want to go off-grid, I guess," Sean says. "Are you going to tell her you can see her?"

"I don't know," I say. "How come she doesn't know about it already?"

"Some people just don't realize the traces of themselves they leave behind on every fucking thing they use," Sean says. "She thinks she wiped it clean: no photos, no bank details, no passwords. But sometimes the things we touch stay inextricably linked to each other." He pauses. "You should know that by now, Petal."

I listen to him light a cigarette, the crunch of a lighter and the force of his breath as he exhales. Maybe I won't tell Dr. Isherwood about the phone. I like that we are linked; I like that she feels close to me.

"What if I did want to turn off my location?" I ask. Sean laughs.

"Easy," he says. He tells me how and I turn it off. "Now you're off-grid," he says.

"Well...not really," I say.

"Oh. Right. Like they'd let you back out without putting you on tag after the last time."

"Yeah."

"Well, that's easy to get around," Sean says. "If you know the right people."

"What kind of people?" I ask.

"Shady people." Sean laughs. "Know anyone who might be a little bit…bad?"

Jack, I think. I don't say anything. I listen to Sean as he talks about getting the tag fitted loosely on my next appointment, how easy they are to slide on and off, if you get the right parole officer. I tell him mine isn't done with my parole officer but with a man who comes to my house each week. I tell him the name of the company and Sean laughs again.

"Easy," he says. "Those companies don't give a fuck, seriously."

"It doesn't matter," I say. It feels like it always did with Sean, like I'm right on the edge of trouble. My stomach skips, like a bad caffeine rush. "I don't care about the tag. It doesn't matter if people know where I am."

"It might not matter right now, Petal. But what if you needed to be alone every now and again? Everybody should be allowed their secrets."

TWENTY-FOUR

Her: Then

Sean is so funny when he comes to dinner at Auntie Fay's house. She keeps telling him off for talking with his mouth full and waving his knife and fork around while he talks, but you can tell she finds it kind of funny, too. Uncle Paul keeps staring down at his plate trying not to smile when Sean tells them about school and all the reasons he gets into trouble. Ryan is over at his friend's house for a sleepover and I know it's because he hates Sean and didn't want to be around him. After dinner Sean asks to see my room and starts running up the stairs before anyone has even said yes.

"It's like having a bleeding tank in the house," Auntie Fay says, wincing at the banging he makes as he runs on the landing.

"Auntie Fay says you're like a tank," I tell him, upstairs.

"Why?" he asks but he isn't upset, he's laughing.

"Because you're so loud."

"You're a delicate petal and I'm a tank!" he shouts.

"Why don't you two go out to play?" Auntie Fay shouts from the bottom of the stairs. "It's still light."

My room is boring and there's no TV in there because Auntie Fay says eight-year-olds like me shouldn't have a TV in their room. So Sean runs back down the stairs and I follow him.

"Make sure you're back when the streetlights come on," Auntie Fay says. She's holding a hand to her head and being dramatic because Sean is jumping up and down for no reason.

"We will," I say, already being dragged out of the front door by Sean.

There are still plenty of other people outside, playing in their front gardens and walking dogs and watering the flowers.

"Your auntie Fay isn't that bad," Sean says.

"It's only because you're there," I say. "They are really bad sometimes."

"They seem all right," Sean says, and it annoys me because Auntie Fay is really strict and he would *hate* to live in their house because it's so quiet and they never, ever watch videos or have biscuits or buy cherry pop.

I follow behind him and he doesn't seem to realize I'm not speaking to him. Sean stops in front of the Messy House and points. I look at the windows, thick with dirt so you can barely see inside, but you can just make out that there are stacks of newspapers and books and clothes that are piled so high they block all the windows completely.

"What if you lived there, with Mr. Sampson?"

"Don't say that," I say. Thinking about living there makes me shiver.

The front garden is full of old furniture and washing machines and children's toys even though Mr. Sampson doesn't have any children or even a wife.

"I'll tell your auntie Fay you don't like living with her and you want to live with Mr. Sampson instead!" he says.

"Stop!" I say. Some of the windows are broken and smashed and I worry that Mr. Sampson is listening.

"I bet he'd love that," Sean says. "Fucking pedo." He spits into the rubbish in the front garden and it's rude even if he's really just spitting into a load of rubbish.

"Look at this," he says and runs down the side of the house.

"Sean! Stop!"

Down the side of Mr. Sampson's house is a lane that no one ever goes down; at school they call it Dead Man's Lane because, once, someone was murdered there. It's dark even in daytime and Mr. Sampson has put broken glass in the cement on the top of his wall so no one can climb over into his garden.

"Sean!" I say again.

"Don't be such a baby! Come on, little Petal, I want to show you something!"

I've never gone down Dead Man's Lane before and it's hard to take even a single step into the gloom, but I can see Sean disappear around the corner at the other end and so I run as fast as I can to catch up with him.

"Boo!" he says, jumping out at me when I get back into the sun at the other end.

"Not funny!" I say, getting my breath.

"Look!" Sean says. I look. The back wall around Mr. Sampson's house has crumbled and fallen down, leaving the big wooden gate standing in the middle, still padlocked shut even though anyone can get in now. The back garden is even worse than the front garden. There are two cars, orange-brown with rust and with all the windows broken.

Around the cars are loads and loads of old bikes, all rusty and twisted, and even more washing machines.

"Why does he keep all this rubbish?" I ask. Sean kicks at the broken wall, and bricks clank and scrape against each other as they shift.

"To hide all the bodies of the children he kills!" Sean says.

"Shut up," I say. "You're just trying to scare me." But I am scared.

"Where do you think he gets all the bikes from?" Sean says. "He snatches little girls who ride past on their bikes and then he strangles them and buries them under the rubbish."

"Shut up!"

Sean puts his sticky hands around my neck and I squirm.

"Look!" he says, pointing into the garden.

I cover my eyes. I imagine Mr. Sampson's face in the filthy window, his mouth wide and eyes white with anger, his long bony fingers tapping the glass.

"No, look!" Sean says, pulling my hands away from my face. "Look at that bike."

All the way at the back of the garden, right by the house, there's a bike, shiny and almost new. I cover my mouth to stop myself screaming.

"No!" Sean says. "I just made that up, about him snatching girls and their bikes. Don't be such a baby all the time!"

"You made it up?" I ask.

"It was a *joke*," he says. "But look at that bike!" Sean climbs the rubble and stares at the bike. "We should take it."

"We can't!"

"Why not? He takes everything he finds and then he

just leaves it out to rot. Why shouldn't we take it and actually look after it?"

"It's probably broken," I say. "Someone was probably throwing it away and he took it out of the skip or something."

"It doesn't look broken," Sean says. "We could fix it, anyway. It could be *our* bike."

"I don't know," I say, but Sean is already climbing into the garden.

"Just watch the back door and if Mr. Sampson comes out then yell and I'll run."

"Sean!" I whisper. He ignores me.

Sean has to climb and crawl along the mess, balancing on a bike seat, steadying himself on another bike's handlebars. Then he jumps onto the bonnet of a rusty car and it makes a huge noise that scares me and makes me cover my ears but he just laughs and carries on. He jumps onto a washing machine and slips and I can't look in case he falls and some rusty metal goes straight through him.

Finally he's at the bike, right by the back window, which is piled high with pots and pans and old tin cans. Sean tugs at the bike but it's stuck on something. I want him to leave it but I know he won't. He pulls again and it comes loose, causing a bunch of other rubbish to slide like a rusty avalanche into the side of the house. I watch the back windows and the back door but nothing happens. Sean awkwardly lifts the bike and manages to drag it over the top of a pile of microwaves. The front wheel is broken, bent.

"Just leave it," I whisper, too scared to shout. Sean can't even hear me.

I watch him heave the useless bike over all the rubbish. His face is bright red with the effort. He even picks it up and tries to throw it forward, over the tangle of bikes and scrap before the car.

Then I see the back door shudder.

"Sean!" I shout. "He's coming!"

Sean swears really loudly and jumps onto the car. Then he turns and tries to pull the bike after him but it's stuck again. The back door opens. It comes right out of the frame! Mr. Sampson comes out holding the whole thing up and placing it down back in front of the frame.

"Hurry up!" I shout. "He's there! He can see you!"

"Oy!" Mr. Sampson shouts. He's wearing his coat and his woolly hat, which he wears all year-round, even indoors during summer. He starts to climb the rubbish towards Sean and he knows the best ways to climb it and so he's faster.

"He's right behind you!" I scream.

Sean laughs and screams at the same time but he *still* won't let the bike go. He just gets it loose and lifts it onto the car when Mr. Sampson crawls his way to him and grabs the bike, too.

Mr. Sampson shouts again. When he opens his mouth wide I see he doesn't have any teeth, just a dark hole surrounded by bloodred gums.

"Sean!" I cry.

"Get off me!" Sean yanks at the bike, trying to get it free from Mr. Sampson. "Get off me, pedo!" Sean says, and he pushes the bike into Mr. Sampson really hard, so hard it sends Mr. Sampson flying back under the bike. He howls in pain.

"Oy!" someone shouts from behind me. "What are you doing? Get here!"

Before I have time to run, a man has grabbed my arm. I scream for Sean, who is still laughing and leaping among the junk until he reaches the back wall. He takes one look at me and the man holding my arm and starts to run.

"Sean!" I shout, trying to wriggle loose from the man's grip. Mr. Sampson howls again.

"What have you done?" the man asks, looking into the garden. "You've hurt him!"

"He was grabbing my friend," I say.

"What are you doing in his garden?"

"We wanted our bike back," I say, crying.

Mr. Sampson makes such a noise the man holding my arm says we need to call an ambulance. I pull away from him.

"You're staying with me," he says, trying to drag me into the garden so he can check on Mr. Sampson. When I look I can see there is blood on the new bike and Mr. Sampson's face is cut and bleeding. "It's all right," the man is saying to him. "I'll get you help now, don't worry."

The man looks at me and back to the garden, deciding what to do.

"Stay here," he says, letting go of my arm. I wait and rub the place where his fingers have dug in too tight. Slowly the man starts to climb into the garden and I run. "I know you!" he shouts after me. "You're Fay Patterson's girl!"

I run all the way home. The streetlights are coming on and I am so mad with Sean that I never want to speak to him ever again. At the front door I knock before opening it and kick off my shoes in the hall.

"Hiya, love," Auntie Fay says over her shoulder from the living room. "Did you have fun?"

"Yeah," I shout back. I am shaking. I want to go straight upstairs but Auntie Fay puts her crochet down and comes out.

"Sean's gone home, has he?" she asks.

"Yeah," I say. I'm still out of breath and my face is hot.

"Everything all right?" she asks. She frowns and inspects my face.

"Yeah," I say again.

"Have you had a falling out?" she asks. She pushes my hair off my sticky forehead.

"Yeah," I say.

"Oh dear. Well, you've spent a lot of time together, haven't you? It'll all blow over by the morning." She smiles and I try to smile back. "If you want you can stay up a little later and watch some TV with me and Uncle Paul. Fancy that?"

"Um," I say, looking at the stairs behind her. "I'm tired. I want to go to bed."

Auntie Fay frowns again. "Are you sure you're okay?" she asks. She puts her hand against my forehead. "You are a bit hot."

"I'm okay," I say.

"Hmm. Well, of course you can go to bed. Do you want me to make you a warm milk?"

"No, thank you," I say. "Good night."

I go up the stairs slowly so she thinks I'm really tired and I can feel on my back that she's watching me the whole way. I brush my teeth quickly and then go and lie in bed. It isn't completely dark yet and I can't sleep. I think of Mum sitting next to my bed when I was sick. I think of the green bucket with the sticker that wouldn't come off completely and how she called it the Sick Bucket and only brought it out when I was unwell. How she would lean and stroke my hair and we'd listen to the radio at night until I fell asleep, and how sometimes I would wake up and she would still be there, in the chair, holding the bucket between her feet.

I think of the place where she used to be, the space where we used to be together, empty.

Just as I am on the edge of sleep, the pillow a bit damp from my crying, there's a banging at the front door. For a second I am back there, in the house with Mum, hearing him bang to come in, waiting for the turn of the key in the lock of my door. But I am not there when I open my eyes. I'm in my room at Auntie Fay's house and there is a lot of shouting downstairs and it's not my mum, or him.

"Her and her friend have sent poor Mr. Sampson to A&E!" the man is shouting.

"Don't be so ridiculous," Auntie Fay says. "You've got the wrong girl. She wouldn't say boo to a goose, this one."

"I assure you," the man says, "it was her and her friend, *terrorizing* the poor man. They said they were getting their bike back."

"Well," Auntie Fay says, "she doesn't even have a bike, so you definitely have the wrong girl. Coming round here shouting at this time of night—"

"Get her down here!" the man says.

"Now listen," Uncle Paul says, and then his voice is too quiet to hear.

"It was her!" the man says. "And if you don't get her down then I'll call the police and let them sort it out."

I hold the covers over my head as I hear Auntie Fay coming up the stairs. She opens the door and light spills in. She sits on the edge of my bed.

"Sorry, love," she says, shaking my arm. "Did we wake you?"

"I'm scared," I say.

"Don't be scared, love," she says. "Mr. Lovell is downstairs. He thinks he saw you in Mr. Sampson's garden earlier with Sean, and that Mr. Sampson was quite upset and had an accident. I said it wouldn't be you but he's quite sure. Do you want to tell me anything? Did you go to Mr. Sampson's house?"

I hold the covers over my head and my own breath feels hot on my skin.

"It's better if you tell the truth," Auntie Fay says. She has taken her hand away from my arm. "Maybe you were there but Mr. Lovell doesn't know what happened?"

I stay still.

"Come on, love," Auntie Fay says. "Let's get this sorted. Just tell me what happened." Her voice is harder now and she tries to tug the covers away from my face.

"I can't believe it," she says to herself. "Oh God, I'm so embarrassed." She sounds like she will cry. Then she pulls the covers off entirely. "Paul!" she shouts downstairs. "Paul! Get up here!" She tries to pull my hands away from my face but I won't move. I hear Uncle Paul come up the stairs. "Either you get up on your own like a big girl and come downstairs to see Mr. Lovell, or your uncle and I carry you down to apologize. Come on! You're lucky the police aren't here."

"It wasn't my fault!" I cry. "It was Sean! He wanted the bike and he told me to tell him if Mr. Sampson was coming so I did and then—"

"What's the matter, love?" Uncle Paul says.

"It was her," Auntie Fay says.

"What happened?" Uncle Paul asks us but neither of us can talk.

"Up!" Auntie Fay says. "Now."

I get up and she makes me walk downstairs and I feel stupid in my nightie when Mr. Lovell looks at me. He has blood on his shirt and his eyes look angry and tired.

"That's the girl," he says. "She ran off when I told her to stay. She didn't care at all about Mr. Sampson."

"I'm sorry," I say. It comes out in a sob and I grab my nightie and hold it down on my legs.

"Mr. Sampson is in hospital. He's had stitches. They're checking to see if he has a concussion," the man says.

"Hey," Uncle Paul interrupts. "She's only a little girl. We don't know what happened."

"I saw it!" Mr. Lovell says. "The little boy was laughing and she was cheering him on."

"I wasn't!" I say. "I wasn't! I was telling him to get out!" I cry more and Auntie Fay holds me.

"That's enough," Auntie Fay says. "How dare you shout at her! Look at how upset she is."

"There're no tears there!" the man says. "Look at her, bloody crocodile tears."

"Get out," Uncle Paul says, pushing the man back. "She admits she's done something wrong and we will punish her as we see fit but I won't have you scaring the wits out of her, accusing her of all sorts. Get out."

"I will tell the police, then," the man says, stepping out of the door. "Seeing as you two aren't going to take this seriously. I'll call the police and we'll let them deal with it."

"You do that, then," Auntie Fay says.

"No!" I shout. It's too late; they've closed the door and the man is going to call the police.

Auntie Fay gets me a warm milk and calms me down, then she shouts at me until I'm crying again, then waits for me to feel better before sending me to bed and telling me I'm never allowed to see Sean again.

"We'll sort out your punishment in the morning," she says.

In bed I listen to Auntie Fay and Uncle Paul murmuring downstairs. When they turn the lights off and come upstairs I can still hear them talking quietly, about me and Mr. Sampson and Sean.

"But I don't think we should stop them seeing each other forever," Uncle Paul says. "He's a bit of a lad but still, when's the last time you saw her laugh like she did at dinner?"

"I know, I know," Auntie Fay says.

"She's a good girl. She knows right from wrong." Uncle Paul sighs. "Sean brings her out of her shell. Maybe they'll do each other some good."

TWENTY-FIVE

Her: Now

I sleep badly, keeping the phone next to my pillow, occasionally rolling over and checking the map to see Dr. Isherwood's dot on Hawkwood Avenue, which must be her home. When I do sleep I dream of dirt: shower curtains crawling with mildew, grouting clogged with brown filth that falls in thick lines into a graying bathtub. No matter how much I scrub I can't make it clean. Mr. Sampson's hollow mouth wails at me in the dark; blood trickles from a wound on his head; his neck is purple and his eyes bulge as if they will burst. I wake on a pillow drenched with sweat and check the phone again. Dr. Isherwood is still at home.

I lie in bed for a long time, poring over every detail I can remember about Mr. Sampson's house. It's so vivid it's like I'm there again, feeling that same terror and the hurt when Sean left me. I want to ask him if he remembers, too. Does he remember how the police made us write letters to say we were sorry? And how two police constables came to the school to talk about being kind to our elders and even though they never said our names, everyone knew it was about us. Does Sean remember all that rust, the color of dried blood, that throaty wail, and the mouth as black as night?

Eventually I force myself to get up, even though I don't have work until this afternoon. I shower, noticing the orange grime around each hole in the showerhead, the black that rings the taps in the sink, and the long hairs around the plug hole, on the tiles, stuck to the tiles. I look in all the cupboards for cleaning equipment but all the bottles are empty and the sponges and cloths so dirty and stiff with muck I can't bear to touch them.

I have no appetite but my stomach growls. I take a box of tea bags from my wardrobe and go to the kitchen, not expecting to see anyone else, but when I get downstairs there is a lot of chatter and noise, the clinking of spoons against bowls, laughter. The long table in the kitchen is almost full and a lot of the women are smiling. The chatter quells as I enter, people twisting to see who it is, then starts up again while I boil the kettle.

"Ooh, I'll have one if you're making," someone says.

"And me," they say in a chorus, laughing. They bring mugs and various requests: "Two tea bags, I like it strong" and "Leave plenty of room for milk."

I stress, no way to remember it all, no way I want to use all my tea bags. My eyes sting while I fill the kettle to the max.

"I'll give you a hand," a woman says, smiling. She has kind eyes, a piercing in the top of her lip, a tattoo of an angel on the back of her neck, dyed black hair.

"Thanks," I say.

The woman gets out a big box of tea bags from the cupboard.

"You don't have to squirrel your tea bags away upstairs like that," she says. "We share here." I think she's being cruel but then she nudges me with her elbow and winks. "And you can say hello, we don't bite!"

I smile.

"I'm Dani," she says.

"Hi," I say.

"And you are?"

"Oh, yeah. Um, Charlotte."

"This is Charlotte," Dani shouts and everyone shouts hello. I wave, they laugh, but it doesn't feel mean. Dani drops tea bags into mugs and sweeteners and sugars, somehow remembering everything with ease. I tentatively pour the water into each mug, watching Dani, waiting for her guidance. "Bit more in that one, love," she says. "Tide's out, is it?" She laughs, so I laugh, too.

"Right, you can put your own milk in, can't you?" she says, plonking mugs in front of people and a half-empty bottle of semi-skimmed in the middle of the table. I realize I haven't bought my own milk. Everyone helps themselves until only I'm left.

"Please may I borrow some milk?" I ask Dani, quietly.

"Give over," she says, elbowing me again. "Help yourself. It's like I said, we share here."

"Thanks," I say. I mean it.

Normally I would take my tea back to my room but I feel like I should stay, so I do. People chat, they talk over one another and it's hard to follow any conversation. Someone asks me about myself but by the time I start answering someone else has asked *them* something and they've turned away. As they talk their eyes flick between people and their phones.

I take my own phone out, relishing how normal all this feels. I smile as I switch it on.

"What are you smiling about?" Dani asks.

"Is it your new bloke?" someone asks.

"What?" I say.

"Whoever you were giggling to on the phone on the fire escape for hours yesterday," the blonde woman says, rolling her eyes.

"Ooh, is it the guy who dropped you off the other night?" someone else says. "He was *fit*!"

How do they know all this? I feel a rising panic.

"He looked like fucking trouble, he did," another says.

"How..." I ask. They all laugh.

"Can't hide anything around here!" Dani says. "Especially not from them lot."

"We were out having a sneaky fag and we saw you in the taxi," one says, laughing with a rasp. "Go on then, what's he like?"

"Um," I say.

"That doesn't sound good," Dani says.

"Where did you meet him?" the one who thinks Jack's fit asks.

"Watch out, she's after your man!" another says. They all laugh again.

"Work," I say. "He works on security."

There's an intake of breath.

"What?" I ask.

"Don't shit where you eat," someone says. More laughter.

"It was only one date," I say.

"Not into it?" Dani says.

"It sounds like she's into it," someone says. "Heard her flirting for hours yesterday evening."

"Then what's the problem?" someone else asks.

"I just…" I say.

"He looked keen," one of the smokers says.

"Maybe he's *too* keen," someone else says.

"Yeah," I say. "It's a bit like that."

They all laugh.

"I wish I had that problem!" Dani says. "Too keen! Fuck skinny girls!" Everyone laughs again and Dani elbows me to make sure I know she's joking.

"He looked like a player," one of the smokers says.

"How could you tell from there?" someone says.

"Too much gel in his hair. A pretty boy," she says.

"I like them rough," someone says. "I don't want my man to spend more time in front of the mirror than I do." Everyone murmurs in agreement.

"So, are you seeing him again?" Dani asks.

"I have to," I say. "At work."

More laughing.

"Sharl, you are *so* funny, babe," Dani says.

"Thanks," I tell her. I sip my tea. The smokers push back the long bench they've sat on together and grip their cigarettes and lighters in their hands. Others start to get up, too, saying things about viewing potential properties and meetings at the job center and the council. The life seems to drain from the room.

As they leave they put their dirty mugs in the sink and leave them there without washing up. Instead of complaining, Dani gets up and fills the sink, smiling. She brushes crumbs off the counter into her hand and puts them in the bin.

"Don't you mind?" I ask.

"Mind what?" Dani says, beginning to wash the mugs.

"Being left with all the washing up," I say. Already I feel embarrassed and wish I hadn't said it. But Dani shrugs.

"I like looking after people," she says. "They're not bad sorts," she adds after a pause. "They've just got a lot on their minds, that's all."

I help Dani wash up and then force myself to go out for a walk. I do a couple of laps of the lake and then go to Kelly's Café for beans and cheese on toast. It is midmorning and I realize that this means I'm having brunch. In the unit there was only breakfast, lunch, and dinner, all at the same time each day. I used to daydream about the meals between meals: brunches, afternoon teas, midnight snacks. Then once I got out I stopped being hungry almost at all.

Today, though, I feel almost normal.

The battery of the phone runs down quickly when I look at Dr. Isherwood on the map, so I try to stop looking at it as much. When I get to the supermarket, I can't resist one more peek before I put the phone in my locker. Dr. Isherwood has left home but she isn't at work, or shopping. I zoom in on the street and see the only thing there is a doctor's surgery. Worry starts to creep in. Maybe she is unwell and that's why she's so distracted and why she has to take phone calls even during our session and why she's been taking time off?

"Hello, stranger," says a voice behind me. I jump; I hold the phone against my chest so they can't see what I'm looking at. "You avoiding me or what?" Jack says when I turn around.

"No," I say, though I have been.

"And what have you got there? New phone?" He grins with all his white teeth.

"I only just got it," I say.

"Give it here and I'll put my number in so you can text me for that second date," he says, reaching for the phone. I give it to him reluctantly and without knowing how to say no again without being rude. But I tell myself that if I don't want to call him I don't have to. I hold my hand out waiting to get my phone back but instead of handing it over he puts it to his ear and pulls his own phone out of his pocket. His own phone lights up and he taps it and gives my phone back. "There," he says. "Now I have your number, just in case you forget to give me a call." He winks.

I wipe my phone on my trousers because his face has left a smear on the screen.

"I have to go now," I say. "My shift is starting."

"Text me," he says.

I realize I will have to. And I wonder, how far will I have to go to get rid of him?

TWENTY-SIX

Her: Then

There were three birthday cards on the windowsill in my room at the unit: one from Dr. Isherwood, one from Miss, and one big one signed by all the other girls in the unit. Each card had the number 18 in big bright print on the front.

Eighteen. My sentence of eight years was almost over and I was legally an adult, which meant I would finally be leaving the unit. More and more lately the social workers had been taking me out, trying to get me used to the everyday things that I had dreamed about: shopping, eating in cafés, walking and walking and walking. Sometimes it was overwhelming and we had to stop and come back in a taxi. Dr. Isherwood said it would pass and that I just had to focus on how exciting it would be. All that time stretching out in front of me. I read the cards again, one by one.

"This is it!" Dr. Isherwood's card read. "I will be here for you every step of the way."

Dr. Isherwood got me a book about positive thinking, a diary, and *Now That's What I Call Music!* I put the CD in my white ghetto blaster and looked at the diary: "To record all the wonderful new experiences you'll have xxx," it said.

I peeled off the plastic. There was a pen tucked into the side. I scribbled on the back of some of the wrapping paper to test it. Blue ink. I put it into a drawer and found a black pen instead. At the top of the first page I wrote the day's date, then paused, unable to think of anything else.

"Today I am 18," I wrote. Someone knocked on the door and I looked up. The doors were always open there during the day because that was the rule. Oliver was standing in the open doorway.

"Is my music too loud?" I asked, though I didn't think it was. Oliver was one of the youngest members of staff and all the girls fancied him like mad. His hair was brown and floppy and parted in the middle and he had lips that were red and pouty.

"Just saying hello," he said, inviting himself in. "How's it going?" He leaned against my dresser and looked at the back of the *Now* CD.

"Okay," I said, folding my diary shut and slipping it under the pillows. Oliver put the CD back and wandered over to the windowsill. "Birthday girl, are we?" he asked. One by one he picked up the cards and read them and I bristled.

"Yes," I said, wanting to take the cards away. As he read them he smiled and I wasn't sure whether he was laughing at me. It felt like he was opening *me* up and looking inside.

"No way are you eighteen," he said, looking from the

cards to me. I nodded. "No way. I thought you were, like, fifteen. *Fourteen*, even."

I shrugged. "People always say things like that," I say.

"Are you *seriously* eighteen?" he said again, laughing.

"Yes. Seriously."

"I like this one," he said, pointing to the CD player and nodding his head in time to the music.

"Me, too," I said. I looked at the open door, hoping he would walk out of it.

Oliver followed my gaze and seemed to understand. He made his way towards the door. But there he stopped and looked up and down the corridor. Then he pulled the door until it was almost closed.

"So you'll be leaving us, then?" he asked. He turned his mouth downwards and pretended to be sad. "But you're one of my favorites."

This confused me because until then Oliver and I had never spoken much before. And I was not like the girls who begged him to play pool or table tennis with them, who pulled him along by the arm, twisted their long hair around a finger and bit their bottom lips when he smiled at them.

Oliver sat next to me on the bed, close enough that our thighs were touching. He put a hand on my knee. His eyes over my body felt like a tongue.

"I think I'll miss you when you're gone. Are you going to miss me?" he asked. His hand slid further up my thigh; there was a burning in my stomach and lower, my face was hot, and I wanted to pull away.

I didn't know what to say. I wanted to say no but somehow I felt I couldn't.

Oliver's breathing got heavier. He closed his eyes and put his forehead against my temple. I hated the way his breath felt, hot inside my ear.

"You're so cute," he said.

"Thank you," I said, even though I wished he hadn't said it. *Go away, leave me alone.*

Someone knocked on my door and Oliver stood quickly. My mattress sprang back up like a pair of lungs filling with air. It was Miss, opening the door slowly in case I was changing my shirt or something.

"Are we decent?" she asked, her head tilted away.

"Yeah," I said. Miss turned back, smiling, but her eyes went dark when she saw Oliver leaning against my dresser.

"Everything all right?" she asked me, looking back and forth between us both.

I nodded.

"Just chatting birthday stuff," Oliver said. Miss narrowed her eyes.

"Why was the door closed?" she asked, pushing it all the way open and wedging the doorstop underneath with her foot.

"I didn't notice it was," Oliver said.

"Sorry," I said.

"Oliver, can you go and supervise the rec room, please?" Miss said. It wasn't really a question but an order.

"No problem," Oliver said. Then, to me, "Catch you later!" He held up his palm and I high-fived him even though touching his hot, moist hand meant I would have to wash mine again as soon as possible.

"Everything okay?" Miss said, standing over the bed.

"Fine," I said.

She studied my face to see if I was lying. "Are you sure?" she asked one last time.

"Yeah," I said. It was too embarrassing to tell her the truth.

After staring at me for what felt like five full minutes, Miss finally left, telling me she would see me later.

Whenever it was someone's birthday on the unit we all had a party where we were allowed to stay up an hour later and have music and a buffet and games for the younger girls. The older girls liked getting dressed up, swiping their lips with gooey, sugary lip gloss and spraying their hair with a fixant that gave me a headache between my eyes.

Lisa had lent me a tube of hair glitter for my party: like a mascara for your hair. But I didn't want to put glitter in my hair or dress up or go to the party at all anymore. Instead, I turned off my music and lay down on my bed, facing the wall. I felt the hard edge of my diary under the pillow and pulled it out.

I thought about writing in there about Oliver but it wasn't the kind of thing I wanted to remember, so I didn't. I put the diary into the drawer and closed my eyes, hoping I would forget it all when I was released.

Miss knocked on the door and woke me up from my half sleep in the evening. "Aren't you coming to your party?" she asked me.

"I have a headache," I lied.

Miss came over and put the back of her hand against my forehead. "Shall I get you some tablets?" she asked, pushing my fringe aside.

"Yes, please."

"What drink do you want?" she asked.

I said I wanted a cherry pop.

"Shall I get you a plate of food from the buffet?"

I shook my head.

"Not even for later? What about a slice of birthday cake?"

I shook my head again.

"I'll only ask one more time," she said. "Has anything happened that you want to talk to me about?"

There was nothing I wanted to talk to her about so I shook my head again. Miss sighed and told me she'd bring me a cherry pop and some tablets. I closed my eyes and listened to the music thumping from the rec room. Miss came back and left the drink and the tablets on the bedside table and closed the curtains.

"Am I allowed to have the door closed?" I asked her. "I want to go to sleep."

Miss agreed and closed it against the music but I still couldn't fully drift off. I was waiting for Oliver to open it, just enough to squeeze in, to slide into bed next to me. Because somehow I knew that Oliver wouldn't leave me alone until he got what he wanted, whatever it was, or until I left the unit. And I knew that out there it was going to be much, much harder to be left alone.

TWENTY-SEVEN

Her: Now

My shift goes slowly that afternoon. I am on the checkouts and the queue of people never seems to go down. My mood is low and I can't face smiling and making small talk with every person who comes to my till. It feels unfair that I can remember all the worst things with vivid clarity, while the memories of my mum become paler, more watered down day by day. Did I think of her too much, so that the image wore out like an old videotape played too often? Or, worse, did I not think of her enough?

Customers lose their patience with me when I'm not concentrating, and a woman taps her card against the reader again and again, sighing, tutting.

"Oh, it's not contactless," I say eventually. She rolls her eyes and stabs the card into the reader reluctantly, punching in the four numbers like it's a Herculean effort. I've noticed that customers will tap their cards indefinitely until you tell them the reader isn't contactless. Dr. Isherwood once told me about rats trained to press a button for a treat, how they would press it compulsively until they were obese and you had to take it away. Enough is never enough, I guess.

When the shift finally ends it is dark outside. I check my phone and see that Dr. Isherwood has gone home. I buy a bag of chips and a battered sausage from the chip shop, a can of cherry 7 Up and a Creme Egg. By the time I get back to the home it will be getting cold but it doesn't matter. Sean said he would call at nine and I need to get back and eat before then.

As I walk I swing the carrier bag with the chips in, sweating and steaming in the paper, wafting the amazing smell back and forth. It reminds me of the way the vicar used to swing the incense in church. But that smelled heavy and thick, like it was a smell designed to make you sad.

The women smoking at the gates of the unit all smile and say hello as I pass and I smile back. Even though I don't have time to chat I almost hope that Dani is in the kitchen but she's not. I eat my chips out of the bag, enjoying the sting of vinegar, the crunch of salt. The sausage I eat with my hands, knowing it isn't polite but not wanting to wash up a knife and fork. When I'm finished I screw up all the paper and put it in the bin. I take my can and my Creme Egg up to my room and wait for Sean to call.

I'll keep my phone plugged in until he calls so that we can talk as long as possible. I can't help checking on Dr. Isherwood (still at home) and wondering if she's okay. Now that I think of it I remember that she looked very tired at our last appointment. She wasn't as smart as she normally is, either.

I think of the worst thing it could be: cancer. I imagine

her getting thinner and thinner, her hair falling out. Maybe she would wear a paisley silk scarf tied around her head like I saw someone with before. It seemed more stylish and more dignified than a wig, I thought. Would she let me visit her in hospital, or would she disappear completely? Maybe she would insist I visit her but the courts would try to stop her because they would say it crosses the boundaries of the patient-doctor relationship. But she would fight because she cares about me and I would hold her hand sitting next to the hospital bed and read to her when she was too weak. I would tell her that I love her and it wouldn't matter if she didn't say it back because I know that it is true.

The phone buzzes in my hand. A notification appears at the top of the screen but disappears too quickly for me to see what it is. Worried that my signal disconnected the call, I unplug my phone and crawl out onto the fire escape again. It is cold enough to see my breath. When I check my phone I see there's a text message but I don't recognize the name. It says Bae. There's a picture that I click on but I don't recognize instantly what it is. It is dark but I can see the color of flesh, a finger and a thumb holding it at the base. I tilt my head trying to match the strange angle of the photograph. Suddenly I see it: a penis. I laugh, though it also feels like an intrusion of some kind, even if it's a ridiculous one. I wrinkle my nose and examine the picture further. There is no pubic hair, as if it belonged to a child, but it is obviously a man's erect penis. I text back: ?

The reply is a picture of a winking face sticking its tongue out and an aubergine.

Who is this? I write back.

Cold! How many men you texting? When we going on a second date then? Jx.

Jack? I ask.

You ducking with me babe? Yeah it's Jack, who else? While I try to work out what he means by *ducking* he texts again: *fucking. Xxx.

I go back inside, shivering, and plug my phone in.

I'm waiting for a call, I text him, can I talk to you tomorrow?

Have a think about where you want me to take you for our date!! he says. Then: Thinking bout you. Send a pic???

Good night, I text.

Harsh!!! he says. Thankfully he doesn't text again.

I wait and wait for Sean to call. I fight sleep, I play the radio and try hard to focus on the words. Worry and fear start to creep in, wondering if he's been arrested, if the police know we've been talking, if they are coming for me next. Eventually I tell myself I can rest my eyes. I turn the volume up high on my phone so it will wake me if he calls. *When* he calls. He will call. I pull the covers over me, staying in my clothes in case I need to go out onto the fire escape later. I start to fall asleep, thinking of Sean, missing him, wondering if he is thinking of me.

TWENTY-EIGHT

Him: Now

Lately I don't know what the fuck I'm doing. I watch the time I'm supposed to call her come and go. I light another joint, hoping this will be the one that chills me out like it used to, but ever since I hit that bong at Slimy's with the new guy's weed it just makes my heart race. Mad paranoia—it's like someone flipped a fucking switch. I had figured it was just the bad atmosphere over at Slimy's flat, the skeezy new guy and his staring and his thin-lipped fucking smile. But the dread has followed me home.

I spent all day inside with the curtains drawn, jumpy and agitated. Every time my phone buzzed it felt like a physical attack, so I turned it on to Silent, but even the light from the screen felt sinister.

And now I feel dirty, filthy. Hell has started to seem real and I feel like I belong there. What was I thinking, fucking with her life like that? Fucking with Isherwood? I try to tell myself that I hadn't expected it to be that easy. Who the fuck leaves Find My iPhone on when they lend it to a fucking *patient*? But deep down I knew Isherwood was a mess right now. Baby brain, she calls it in her emails. Baby Iris is up all night, not settling well. Isherwood worries that the baby isn't bonding. She's also constantly sick, back and forth to the doctor, rashes, coughs, temperatures, sickness, diarrhea. By the time I finish reading the emails I feel knackered enough myself. No wonder she's not thinking straight.

The thing that gets me about Isherwood is this fucking martyr act. Like she's the Patron Saint of Lost Children. Iris is a handful but she's worth it, she says in one of her long, whining emails where she eventually pats herself on the back for being so kind. Well, what about me? I was a lost child. The exact fucking same as her number one patient. Somehow it was okay to sacrifice me for the sake of the pretty little girl with the wet eyelashes and the plaits tied with pink bands. It was obviously the boy, too big for his age, the one with the angry stare and the bad attitude. It must have been all his fault. Look, he doesn't even cry, a monster.

Not that Isherwood's testimony would have made a difference to my sentence; the damage was already done. But the picture it painted in the fucking papers will outlive me. The painting stays vivid and present and I am the one left to twist and deform in the fucking attic.

The joint fails to calm me down. Instead I hear the headlines again, the chanting and the shouting outside the court. I feel eleven again; I remember how when they spoke to me I didn't understand half the shit they said.

I turn on the television but the voices coming from the

screen just make it worse. I'm hungry but the fridge is empty, I'm too paranoid to go out, and there's not enough in my bank account to order in. I remember something I read after my last sentencing: He's had his chance, someone said in the comments under the article about my arrest. Give them his real identity in prison and let them deal with it. Dead in a week, job done. Fucking sicko.

Most people don't know what it's like to be hated like that, by people you can't see, people you've never met. People who look fucking normal, like teachers and single mums and bricklayers and admin staff. They could be anyone and anywhere and they hate you so much they wish you were dead. It's like they stored up everything unfair that ever happened to them, everything that ever made them miserable and angry and scared, and they saw in you a target to take it out on. All of that shit pointed in laser-beam, red-hot hatred right at your chest and it makes it okay for them to be that full of bad energy, to feel all this murderous anger, because *you* are hated by *everyone*.

Almost no one knows what it's like to be the target, to feel like someone just looked at you a bit too long, like they've seen inside you and they know who you are, what you are. It's the way the new guy looked at me, at Slimy's. Only one other person would understand what I mean but I'm so fucked up I can't even call her. I want to tell her to ignore what I said, to forget about Find My iPhone and getting her tag removed. We have only each other and I shouldn't have ruined it. *I am not me*, I want to tell her. *Not right now.*

Soon the dread is so totally overwhelming that I find myself reaching for the pills that I sell. I hate the dead-eyed people I sell to but I need to restore some fucking equilibrium as soon as possible. I take two and swallow them

with lukewarm water, curl up on the sofa and watch the
muted television.

   Tomorrow, I think, drifting off. I will call her tomorrow,
and everything will be better then.

TWENTY-NINE

Her: Then

Sean takes off his royal-blue school jumper and drags it on the floor behind him.

"Won't you get in trouble for making it dirty?" I ask. Auntie Fay bought me a brand-new school uniform when I turned eight and said it had to last me until I was at least ten so I would have to be careful not to grow too much or to ruin it. It still has to last me another year and a half.

"Nah, he doesn't give a shit," Sean says.

"You shouldn't swear all the time," I tell him.

"So-rry," he says. He turns and walks backwards so I can see him make a face. "Didn't mean to upset you, princess."

"I'm not a princess," I say.

"You're a delicate little flower," he says in a silly voice. I laugh. "I won't swear, little Petal!"

"Can we watch anything we want?" I ask. I've already asked this but I can't believe it so I ask again.

"Yes!" he says. "Anything in the whole shop."

My heart is going faster because I haven't even been to the video shop since Mum died. Auntie Fay never rents anything and all my videos melted when the house burned down.

"Is it amazing living in a video shop?" I ask.

Sean shrugs. "We don't live *in* the video shop," he says, putting his tongue in his lower lip and making a noise. "We live upstairs, in the flat."

"Oh," I say.

"But my dad runs it, so we can just get any video from downstairs whenever we want."

We get to the shopping center and Sean pushes open the door of the video shop. The door makes a bleep-blop noise whenever it opens and the sound makes me remember Mum and the chips going soggy in the newspaper and I feel dizzy.

"I'll let you choose the video," he says, and he grabs my wrist and takes me into the video shop.

Bleep-blop. It makes my hair feel funny and my throat go dry.

"Seany," the man behind the counter says.

"Dad, can we watch a film?" Sean says.

Sean's dad looks at me like he's only just noticed me. Sean still has my wrist in his hand and I move behind him. His dad is big, with dark hair that looks like it needs a good brush and lines in his face that make him look angry.

"She's a bit young, isn't she, mate?" he says, looking back at Sean.

"No, because she's only in the year below me."

"Does your mum know you're here?" Sean's dad asks me.

"She doesn't have a mum," Sean says.

"Where do you live, then, sweetheart?" he says. I shrink a little bit more behind Sean. "Does she talk?"

"She lives down the nice end," Sean says. "With her aunt."

"And who's your aunt?" Sean's dad asks me. Sean starts to answer but his dad shushes him.

"Um. Fay," I say.

"Fay who?" his dad asks.

"Fay Patterson."

"Oh Christ. I hope you're allowed out here because I'm not getting on Fay Patterson's bad side. I've got enough bloody problems without any of that. Does she know you're here?"

Sean squeezes my wrist and I nod.

"She has to go back for tea but can she just stay until then?" Sean asks.

His dad rubs his face with his hands and sighs.

"If your aunt Fay is happy, I'm happy. Just don't get me into any trouble," his dad says. "Go on then, get something quick and bugger off upstairs."

Sean pulls me to the back of the shop and tells me to choose something. I look around but we're in the wrong bit and none of the good films are here. I try not to look at the horror shelves as I walk past but I peek because I can't help it and I see a face with no skin, the mouth open like it's screaming at me, and have to put my hand up to block it out.

On the good shelves all the videos are colorful and people don't scream from them, they smile. I choose the film and hold it out to Sean.

"That's for babies!" he says. I've already seen *An American Tail* but I love it. I didn't know it was for babies. I pick up *E.T.* instead but Sean puts it back. "Everything here is for babies!" he says. He runs off and comes back with a film called *First Blood*. "This," he says.

"You said I could choose this time," I say, and I feel my lip wobbling. "I don't want to watch a scary film."

"But it's not scary!"

"It says *blood* on it," I say. I have to wipe my eyes because I'm crying.

"But it isn't scary!" he says.

"Oy," his dad shouts from the front of the shop. "What are you whining about? Come here, the pair of you."

We go to the till and I cry more because I don't want to be told off.

"What have you done to her?" Sean's dad says.

"Nothing!" Sean says.

"Don't shout at me," his dad shouts.

"I wasn't!" Sean shouts back. I cry harder.

"You've brought her here and she's your guest so let her choose whatever she wants to watch, or she can go home and you won't have friends over again."

Sean screws up his face to stop the tears.

"Oh no," his dad says. "Is he going to start crying now?"

"No!" Sean says. He balls his fists.

"Did the precious little man not get his own way?" Sean's dad does a silly voice I've never heard a grown-up do before. "Princess Seany didn't get his own way and now he's going to start crying."

Sean's dad comes around the counter and Sean tries to run away but his dad catches him before he can and puts him in a headlock and rubs his head.

"Stop it!" Sean says, his face turning bright red.

"Fight back then, little man, fight back," his dad says. Sean wriggles free and slaps his dad on the arm. I cover my eyes. "Is that all you've got?" His dad laughs. "Let the girl watch her film," he says, returning to his seat behind the counter. "You shouldn't be watching that shit anyway."

"Well, I've already seen it a hundred times," Sean says. He swipes at his eyes, trying to get rid of the tears.

"There we are, then," his dad says. "No need to watch it again. Now bugger off upstairs and out the way."

Sean snatches the video box from my hands and goes into the back room behind the beaded curtain, which clicks and clacks behind him. I'm scared of Sean's dad but he doesn't even look at me when I go past him, as if he's forgotten I'm here at all.

The back room is full of videos without proper cases, shelves and shelves of them. Sean moves like he knows it all by heart. I go to each section and look at the titles.

"I found it!" I say, pulling out one of the copies of *An American Tail*.

"We're not watching it," Sean says.

"But your dad told you—"

"Shut up!" Sean hisses. "If you don't like it you can go home."

I look at the video in my hand and it goes blurry behind my tears.

"If you cry then you're definitely going home," Sean says.

I sniff and put the video back. I don't want to go home, I want to stay with Sean. So I follow him upstairs and into his house. It isn't a proper house because it doesn't have stairs to go to bed or the bathroom and most of it is all one big room. There is a kitchen inside the living room and the only way you can tell where the kitchen starts and the living room ends is because the carpet stops and turns into lino.

There is an ashtray on the table in front of the television and it smells bad. There's a plate with a fork and knife sticking out of leftover food, like the person eating it just vanished into thin air in the middle of their dinner. The sink is full of dishes and there are stains everywhere on the carpet.

"I'm hungry," I say. Suddenly I feel nervous, my tummy flutters, and I want to go back to Auntie Fay's. "I think I need to go home for tea now."

"You only just got here," Sean says. "Here." He pulls a chair to the kitchen counter and climbs up to reach the higher shelves. From the top he pulls down a big Tupperware box full of biscuits: Pink Wafers, chocolate Bourbons, Hobnobs, KitKats, Caramel Wafers, Trios, Gold bars. Sean holds the box out to me. My hand floats over the top while I try to choose. "Take it!" he snaps.

"All of them?" I ask.

"Have as many as you want," he says, climbing down. From a lower cupboard he brings out crisps. I take a packet of Quavers. Then he takes a whole bottle of cherry pop out of the fridge and two mugs. I peer into the bottom of my mug when he passes it to me and it is stained all brown but he is already poking the bottle of cherry pop into my face and pouring it, the bubbles dancing on my wrist like the tiniest drops of rain.

We take everything back into his bedroom, which is *really* messy, and when I see a pair of pants on the floor Sean goes bright red and kicks them under the bed.

"I can't believe you have a TV in your room!" I say.

Sean pushes the video into the bottom of the TV and the gray snow screen rolls into black. "I've always had it," he says.

There are stickers on everything and writing and drawings all over the walls where the paper is peeling off.

"Are you allowed to draw on the walls?" I ask. "Auntie Fay would *kill* me."

"My dad doesn't give a shit," Sean says.

I eat three biscuits and my crisps and drink all of my cherry pop in one go. I burp. Sean laughs. I laugh. Sean pours me more.

"You look like you're wearing lipstick," I say. Sean makes a kissy face at me. I shriek. When he smiles the pink at the corners of his mouth curves up like the Joker in *Batman*.

The film is boring; it's all talking.

"It gets good!" Sean says. He crawls across the bed to fast-forward it. When he presses Play it is too loud and I cover my ears. There is screaming and blood but it isn't scary, just noisy and boring. Sean fast-forwards again and then rewinds the same bit twice.

"You don't watch things properly," I say. My stomach hurts and I feel sick. I put the chocolate bar I'm eating down because I can't finish it.

It's even darker in the room now so I know the sun is going down and I will be in trouble if I'm not home before it's dark.

"I should go home now," I say.

"No," Sean says, sitting up. "If you stay we can watch whatever you want. Honest!" His face looks all twisted up with worry.

"I can't," I say. I feel bad, like I am being stretched like a tug-of-war.

"Fine," he says. He slumps back and hits his head hard against the wall. "Ow!" He curls up into a ball and holds his head.

"Are you okay?" I ask. I feel confused. "Are you crying?"

He springs up. "No, I'm not crying! Just fuck off if you want to go home so much! Go on!"

"I'll get in trouble," I say. "I have to go. I don't want to…"

I'm kind of lying because Sean's house is weird and I don't really want to stay but I don't want to be rude and hurt his feelings.

"I can come back tomorrow?" I say.

"Really?" he says. He won't look at me. Instead he picks at the edge of a football sticker on the side of his chest of drawers.

"I need to ask Auntie Fay," I say, "but maybe you could come to mine for tea?"

"Yeah," he mumbles. "Okay. Maybe."

"So will I see you in school?" I ask.

Sean nods.

"See you tomorrow," I say, leaving Sean leaning against the messy walls of his room, peeling the stickers and flicking the bits of paper into the clutter on the carpet. On my way out his dad doesn't look up from his newspaper at the counter. I used to think that living in the video shop would be the best thing ever but now I don't know anymore. Even though I know Auntie Fay will go mad with me when I get in I feel glad I'm not there anymore.

THIRTY

Her: Now

It's cold in my room because I slept with the window open, ready to climb out when Sean called. He didn't call. Still, I lie in bed with the covers pulled tightly around me, wondering if I will miss the call if I go to take a shower. Eventually I can wait no more and get up. I keep the phone resting on the edge of the sink in the bathroom and a few times I think I hear it ring and step out, cold and wet and naked, feeling embarrassed even though no one can see me. He doesn't call.

I dress and sneak out of the building, avoiding the other women because I don't have the energy to pretend I am okay. Dr. Isherwood's dot is at the office and I think about calling her and asking to talk but I don't know what I would say. Then I think I don't want to be a burden, not if she is sick.

Though I'm not hungry I go to Kelly's and order tea and toast. Every table is covered with spilled sugar, coffee rings, and sticky patches of tomato sauce. I wander from seat to seat before asking Kelly for a damp cloth to wipe the table nearest the window.

"I haven't had a single second yet today," she says, angry and out of the blue. "It's been nonstop."

I look at the empty café: the only other person is an old lady with candy floss—white hair, lipstick on her teeth, and a vague smile as she stares into the distance.

"Um," I say. "So, can I have a cloth, please?"

Kelly sighs; she shakes her head. "Where are you sitting?" she asks. I point to the window seat. "I'll be there right now, madam, if you'd like to take your seat."

"The cloth?" I ask.

"Yes! I will wipe your table down as soon as I can get a minute!" she half shouts. Confused, ashamed, I sit at the dirty table and hold my hands between my knees. What did I say wrong? Kelly appears and wipes the table down aggressively. Some of the sugar lands on my legs and I hold myself still because I somehow know that brushing it off will only make her angrier.

"There," she says as she leaves. "I'll bring your tea and toast now."

"Than—" I start to say but she has stormed off before I can finish. I look at the table and the waves of damp from the cloth, half circles and zigzags and some patches of dry where the cloth never touched at all.

I get a napkin and rub and rub at the edges of the pattern but it hardly makes a difference. Kelly catches me doing it when she returns and in frustration she puts my tea down too hard and it sloshes over the edge of the mug.

"Thank you," I say, looking at the white bread that I

didn't order and the tea dribbling down the porcelain, collecting on the red tabletop. I'm not hungry. My stomach cramps thinking of Dr. Isherwood and her illness, Sean and whatever has stopped him from calling me. But I remember what the vicar used to say: *You have to put on your own oxygen mask before you help others.* So I eat the toast, even though Kelly has only buttered the middle of the bread and not up to the crusts and even though it is white bread and I had ordered brown because I'm trying to be healthier.

Suddenly my phone rings so loudly that the old lady at the other side of the café makes a small scared noise. I apologize while I try to find it in my bag and turn to see her holding her hands over her heart and I worry I've given her a heart attack. The screen reads Unavailable.

"Hello?" I whisper into the phone.

"I'm sorry," Sean says.

"Why?"

"For not calling you. I was fucked yesterday, hungover. Couldn't face the chat."

"That's okay," I say. I am just glad he's all right.

"Nah, it isn't okay, though. You should be angry with me. Tell me to fuck off."

"I don't get it," I say.

"You're allowed to be mad with people if they let you down," Sean says.

"You didn't let me down," I lie.

"Come on! Fucking shout at me, tell me I'm a prick, do something!"

"I'm in a café," I say quietly.

"Well, anyway, I am sorry. All right?" Sean says this as if I have argued with him.

"Yeah. Okay," is all I can say.

Sean sighs and at the end he laughs a little. "You okay?" he asks.

"Yeah. You?"

"Not really," he says.

"Why?" I start to panic again. When I think of Sean not being okay, I don't feel okay, either.

"Just bullshit, just life. You know." We both sit quietly on the phone and that feels like enough. "Cheer me up, Petal," Sean says eventually. "Make me laugh."

The café is dead silent and both the old woman and Kelly seem to be staring at me, daring me to keep talking on the phone. So I grab my bag and hold my phone between my shoulder and face, and open the heavy front door.

"This guy," I say. "This guy from work sent me a picture of his penis."

Sean starts to laugh loud and hard. "How do you always say the last fucking thing I'm expecting?" he says. I laugh, too. "What did you do?" he says, so I tell him the whole conversation we had and he keeps telling me to stop because he can't breathe. I'm laughing but am not always sure what's so funny. I want to ask but I feel I can't.

"Did I say the wrong thing?" I manage, between giggles.

"Actually I think you were pretty fucking spot-on," he says. "You should show your boss, get him sacked. What a loser."

"Um," I say.

"Oh no. Don't tell me you like him?"

"No!" We both laugh again. A man passing by smiles like he's in on the joke.

"So? Ruin him! He sounds like a prick."

Hesitantly, I tell Sean about the underwear, about the date, about how I gave him my number so it's really my fault.

"It's not your fucking fault, pet. Jack's a fucking predator. What's he going to do now? Tell the boss he saw you pinching weeks ago and he's only just decided to say something? That he was just browsing the CCTV for the past few weeks and happened to notice you took something? He's bullshitting you, pet. Tell him to jog on, he's got fuck all on you."

It sounds good. I imagine myself saying these things, tough and cool, but I also know it will never happen. Sean just doesn't understand how hard it is to say no over and over again because when Sean says no, people listen.

"Anyway," I say. "Maybe I'll need him to help me one time, with my ankle tag."

"What do you mean?" Sean says, his voice all wary and thin.

"You said I needed to know someone bad, that they would know what to do. Especially because he works in security and he might know someone from the company who does my tag and—"

"Forget I said that; you don't want to go fucking around with that shit. I was talking bollocks. Leave it."

"But what if I need to go 'off-grid'?" I try to sound out the air quotes and feel silly doing it.

"What would you need to go *off-grid* for?" Sean mimics my silly voice and I blush.

"I'm worried about Dr. Isherwood," I say. "I think she's sick."

"Why?"

"Because she's tired all the time and she's not listening to me," I say. Then I feel like I am confessing something, admitting that I know it's wrong but: "She's visiting the doctor a lot."

"Look, don't worry about Isherwood, okay? She isn't sick."

"But she's not herself. What if they say I can't visit her when she's in hospital? What if I need to sneak in so that—"

"Stop, okay? I shouldn't have told you about the fucking phone-tracking thing. I was messing with you and it wasn't right. Forget it."

"What do you mean, messing with me?" It feels like a bone is stuck in my throat.

"I got jealous, yeah? Isherwood just *gave* you a phone so you could call her whenever. She probably fucking pays for it and all. I don't have anyone who would do that for me. It pissed me off, so I thought I'd mess with your head. It was shit, yeah? I'm sorry."

I hear Sean sniff, that noise he always made when he was trying not to cry.

"It isn't that bad," I say, trying to make him feel better. "At least now I know that she isn't well. I can look after her if she needs it."

"You're not listening to me!" Sean shouts. "Isherwood is fine! You don't need to look after her; you shouldn't be watching her on the phone. If she finds out you're tracking her she's going to be freaked out. It'll ruin everything."

"I think she left it on purpose," I say. It suddenly seems true, that this is her sign to me that she needs me as much as I need her. "I think she wants me to help her."

"You sound fucking insane," Sean says. "She's not sick! She's just…busy. She just didn't think about giving you her old phone because she's distracted."

"By what?" I wait for Sean to answer but he's silent. "Because she's not well!"

He sighs; it turns into a groan. "Look, Isherwood is fine. Trust me."

"How would you know?" I ask. "You don't even know her!"

"Because I hacked into her emails, okay? Fuck. Jesus fucking Christ. How do you think I always find you?"

I feel cold, suddenly. "Why?" It's all I can ask.

"Because you ruined my life! And I fucking care about you! You were my only friend."

"So…you want to ruin my life?"

"No. I don't know! I miss you. Sometimes I hate you. Sometimes I feel so bad about everything that I don't even know what I want anymore." Sean stops; he sniffs. "You're like a loose tooth I can't stop messing with. Stubborn, clinging at the root. You know?"

I close my eyes and try to remember loose teeth, dying for them to come out but fearing it, as well. That bitter taste of blood on the tongue. We are quiet for a moment.

I walk towards the lake, the phone against my ear.

"So what is distracting Dr. Isherwood?" I ask. "If she isn't sick?"

"She's fine, Petal, that's all you need to know."

"No, really," I say. "I promise I won't even look at the map thing again if you tell me."

Sean hisses air through his teeth.

"Please?" I say. "Come on, Tanks. Is she really okay?"

Sean waits a long time and then says gently, "It's good news, pet. She has a baby now."

"What?" I say. The cold hits me again; my breath is gone. "You're lying. You're still messing with me."

"I'm not, I promise!" Sean says.

"Then how come she hasn't even been pregnant?" I ask. After everything he's said I can't believe he's still lying to me.

"Isherwood adopted her, over the summer, while you were still inside."

"No but…wait. No." I have to sit down but there are no benches and so I walk backwards, towards the grassy verge at the side of the path. I sit on the damp grass.

"I knew I shouldn't have said anything," Sean says. "It's good news. Isn't it better than her being sick?"

No, I think. *No, it isn't. Dr. Isherwood won't need me anymore.* Then I remember how she left her phone tracker on for me and I realize he is lying. He is still trying to hurt me.

"Liar," I say. I feel eight again; I feel the same as I always did when he made fun of me. Except I have decided that I won't believe it this time, I won't let him ruin what Dr. Isherwood and I have. "You're jealous. You're messing with me because you wish someone loved you like Dr. Isherwood loves me."

"No," he says. "Not now. Petal, listen to me. The only person who's going to ruin it is you."

"Leave me alone," I shout, and I hang up.

I realize I have never hung up before. Sean calls back and I hang up again and again and again every time he calls. The world seems loud, the sounds of people and things competing with the noise inside my head. I put my phone on Silent and clutch my hands over my ears but it doesn't help. So I run. I run without knowing where I'm going; I ignore people who stare at my red face and the tears and my gasping breaths. I run until I reach a church, the railings painted green, a sign that reads St. Saviour's, trees as old as life, huge things that look tired and seem to sigh in the wind. It's quiet. So quiet I can hear the scuff of my trainers on the stone path.

The door is open and inside is dark, the light that gets

through the stained-glass windows tinged with reds and blues. It all smells like Sunday mornings: dusty books, incense, burned matches and candles blown out in the draft. A vicar fusses with something at the lectern but he is the only one here. He looks up and smiles. I force a smile and take a seat near the back. I bow my head, close my eyes as though I'm praying, and enjoy the silence.

THIRTY-ONE

Her: Then

After church on Sunday, Auntie Fay takes me to the front to light a candle for Luke. Lots of the candles are lit and we use a long stick to take the flame from one candle and light a new one. Auntie Fay holds my hands to help me and even though the stick is really long I still feel scared of getting burned and my hands shake. All the candles are in little red glasses and together they look beautiful and serious. Auntie Fay drops a coin into the wooden box next to them where you pay God to listen to your prayer. I look at all of the light and all of the red until Auntie Fay tells me it's time to go.

On the way out we shake the vicar's hand and he rubs my hair too hard. Auntie Fay knows everyone so it always takes ages to leave church. Ryan is running around the graveyard with some other boys. All the grown-ups are talking about Luke and how awful it is.

"It's a tragedy," Auntie Fay says, holding the golden cross around her neck. "But no one could have prevented it."

"They're saying it wasn't an accident," someone says. Auntie Fay holds the cross tighter.

"Didn't you know?" someone else asks. "On the news they're saying that Luke was seen with two other children. They're calling for witnesses."

"Children?" Auntie Fay says. "Well, then it was an accident, surely."

A woman with frizzy orange hair looks at me and then talks quietly, but I can still hear her.

"There were...marks, on his body," she says. Auntie Fay gasps.

"How awful. Oh, don't tell me any more, I can't—it's too terrible. That poor boy's mother," Auntie Fay says.

"Can we go now?" I ask, pulling at Auntie Fay's sleeve.

"Yes, in a minute, love, I'm just talking," she says. Then she starts on about Luke again even though she said she didn't want them to tell her any more about it.

"They think that maybe he was taken from the back garden," someone says. "When his mum wasn't watching him."

"That poor woman," Auntie Fay says again.

The woman with the frizzy orange hair looks at me again and it isn't a nice look.

"They said it was a boy and a girl that he was with," the frizzy hair woman says.

"Teenagers?" Auntie Fay says.

The frizzy hair bounces as she shakes her head.

"The boy has red hair and freckles," the woman says.

"They think he might be twelve, thirteen. But the girl...has blond hair. And she might be as young as eight."

The woman isn't looking at me now but it feels like everyone else is. I hold Auntie Fay's sleeve and kick at the loose paving stone. There is silence and Auntie Fay grips my hand too tightly.

"Well," Auntie Fay says. Her hand squeezes mine even tighter. "How awful. The truth will out, eventually."

Everyone agrees.

"I must get on now. I suppose this one is getting hungry, aren't you?" she says, turning to me. Her smile is fixed; her eyes are quivering and filling with water. I nod. "See you soon," she says. "Say goodbye now," she adds to me.

"Paul," Auntie Fay calls across the crowd. "I'm going to walk her home and get lunch started. Can you look after Ryan?"

Uncle Paul gives a thumbs-up and winks at me like he always does.

"Come on," Auntie Fay says, putting her head down and walking so fast that I have to run to keep up. She walks until we're around the corner and out of sight of the church. She bends down and she puts her hands either side of my head. "Listen, love," she says. She keeps stroking my cheeks with her thumbs, until my tears roll down and collect in the creases of her hands. "Listen..." She takes a deep breath. "Listen. You know you can tell me anything, don't you, love?" She tries to pull her taut lips into a smile. I nod but her hands hold my head too tightly. "If anything has happened... If you know *anything* about Luke..." The name makes me choke a little. "Tell me, sweetheart. Tell me and we can make it better."

I feel all the days of keeping it inside starting to leak out of me, the fluttering in my stomach turning into a quake, but I still can't talk.

Then Auntie Fay starts to turn angry, her face scrunching inwards. "What are you hiding? I know you're hiding something. Tell me! For God's sake, tell me what you've done!"

She's shaking me, hard, and I can't tell her to stop. I can't do anything. Suddenly she stops shaking me and puts a hand over her mouth and then grabs me with both arms and hugs me. "I'm sorry, I'm so sorry."

"I tried to help him," I say in a whisper.

"What do you mean, sweetheart?" Auntie Fay asks me. She looks afraid.

"It wasn't our fault. We were just trying to help him get home."

"Luke? You were helping Luke?"

"But a bad man took him away again," I say quickly, before the words can creep back inside.

"Tell me everything," Auntie Fay says. "From the beginning."

So I do.

THIRTY-TWO

Her: Now

I leave the church and instead of getting a bus back to the home, I walk. I claw at the scraps of memories and try to piece them together into something coherent, but I can't. I remember Auntie Fay's eyes as I told her about Luke, about the underpass. As I told her about the old man with his toothless mouth and his long bony fingers.

I am still deep in thought when I round the corner to the home but I look up at the giggles I hear as I approach. The group of smokers have their backs to me; the smell of cigarettes in the crisp air blows in my direction. One turns and says, "Here she is now, look!" The rest all make a sound like a cheer and I smile uncertainly, wondering what is going on.

Then the women part and I see, standing in front of them, Jack, a red rose in his hand.

"What are you doing here?" I ask.

The women all groan and tell me to be nicer to him.

"He's all right, he is!" one says.

"Give him a chance, love, he's made an effort!" says another.

"She keeps breaking my heart, see, girls!" Jack says. He pulls his mouth down like a sad clown, the rose almost drooping in his hand. The women all laugh and pretend to comfort him.

"I've come to take you out," Jack says. "Lunch, bowling, whatever. Lady's choice!"

"Can I talk to you a minute, please?" I ask him, smiling hard. All I want to do is crawl into bed and watch Dr. Isherwood's dot on my phone.

"See you girls later, yeah?" Jack says. He winks; they laugh.

Jack follows me around the corner out of sight of the women. When I stop and turn to look at him he offers me the rose and I make the mistake of taking it. He leans in and tries to kiss my cheek but I lean away and he misses.

I look at him and his hopeful face and suddenly I have an idea.

"I can't come out with you," I say, and I point my foot towards him and lift my jeans enough to expose my ankle tag. Jack finds this hilarious and doubles over laughing. I feel my face redden and pull the jeans back over the tag in case any of the other women come to see what's so funny.

"You naughty girl," Jack says. "I love it! What you get that for?"

"I didn't do anything," I say. "It wasn't my fault."

Jack laughs again. "You're fucking special, you are," he says. "It's always the quiet ones."

"Right. But anyway, I have a curfew here and the ankle

tag means I can't go certain places and they'll know if I'm not home on time. So—"

"If I take you out I'll have to get you back here in plenty of time, yeah?"

"Well, I was thinking that, um…" I try to think how Sean would say it. "That you might know someone who could help me out with it. You know?"

"How'd you mean?" Jack says. I can't tell if he's teasing me, if he already knows what I mean but wants to hear me say it.

"I guess I heard that sometimes, if you, like, pay someone…that they'll fit it looser so you can—you know—slide it off if you really need to."

"Why would you need to do that?" he asks. Now I know what he wants me to say, I know what he wants to hear and I know that if I say it then he will help me.

"If I ever wanted to stay over somewhere. I guess." I look away, feeling gross, but knowing that I have to do this if I want to know the truth about Dr. Isherwood.

"Maybe I know someone," Jack says. "Go get yourself dressed up for our date and I'll give my mate a call."

I run upstairs and I throw the rose into the bin in my room and look for my nicest clothes, which aren't really that nice but will have to do for now. I look at all my underwear, feeling an involuntary shudder when I think of how I will probably have to have sex with Jack later, and try to find a decent pair. All of the knickers seem grungy and dirty. Then I find the set I took, the emerald-green lace bra and pants. I rub the material between my thumb and finger, then shove it to the back of the drawer and choose a pair of baggy black pants that are only a little frayed and a flesh-colored bra. I don't want Jack to think this means anything to me.

I swing my bag back over my shoulder and go downstairs, every bit of my body telling me not to go, except for the tiny part of me that knows I must because I have to go to Dr. Isherwood's house. I have to find out if Sean is lying.

"That was quick," Jack says when he sees me. His phone is still in his hand. "Normally girls spend forever doing their makeup and hair."

"Yes, I've heard," I say.

"Low-maintenance," Jack says with a nod. "I like it."

I look at his phone, hoping he'll tell me it's sorted.

"So?" I ask when my patience runs out.

"You'll have to wait and see," Jack says. "First, I'm taking you bowling."

The date seems to last forever. The bowling alley is noisy and overwhelming and I have to wear shoes that have had hundreds of other feet in them before me and stick my fingers into holes in the balls that have had hundreds of other fingers in before. By the end of our three games I feel like I need a shower, not only because of the ghosts of all the other people who have been here before me but because of the way Jack insists on correcting my technique by standing behind me and guiding my arms, his crotch pressed into my lower back.

My phone keeps buzzing with calls from Sean. Whenever I get the chance I check on Dr. Isherwood. Still at home, even though it is a weekday and she should be at work. After bowling Jack takes me to a place that only sells desserts. Inside, all the furniture is black and purple; there are neon lights and glitter on the tables. If it wasn't for the ice cream behind the glass counter I would believe we were in a strip club.

I don't want anything but Jack forces me to order something, so I get three scoops of sorbet with some chopped fruit. Jack orders waffles that come topped with loads of different ice creams and wafers and chocolate. He takes a picture of it on his phone and then forces me to pose with him for a selfie.

The later it gets the more I lose hope that he can even get my tag loosened. I think that Jack has just been stringing me along when suddenly his phone rings and he answers.

"Half an hour?" he's saying. "No problem, mate, appreciate it. Cheers. See you then. Nice one. Cheers." Jack hangs up and turns to me. "Come on then, chick, time to get you off the naughty step."

Suddenly I feel my stomach lurch. Getting the tag loosened is the beginning of something. I realize this is just one more lie and that more will come because of it, until there are so many I won't know where it started.

THIRTY-THREE

Her: Then

Auntie Fay tries to turn over when the news comes on but I ask if we can watch it.

"I want to see," I say. Uncle Paul takes the remote out of her hand and they watch me as I watch the television. It is the top story; it is always the top story.

"Frederick Sampson was arrested today at his home following reports that he was seen with Luke Marchant…"

The news reporters are outside his house, the gate has yellow police tape across it, and policemen stand on the pavement making sure the people with cameras and the people with signs don't get too close to the house. They even have a helicopter that shows the house from above and you can see the cars and the bikes and the microwaves and the washing machines and all the bright plastic children's toys that haven't gone all funny and faded in the sun and the rain yet.

"I think it's disgusting," a woman on the TV says. She is holding a little girl's hand. "It could have been my little girl, that's what I keep thinking, my little girl. We only live a few streets away."

"Well, he's always been a little odd," says a man who has a bag of shopping in his hand. I know the shop is Lewis News because they have blue carrier bags and nowhere else round here does. "Quiet, you know. We thought he was just...you know. That he wasn't all there. Wouldn't have thought he was capable of this, no, not at all."

"They always say this," Uncle Paul says. "Always, 'Oh, he was so quiet,' or, 'We never thought he would do something like this.' We should have known." When Uncle Paul says this he sounds angry. I look at Auntie Fay and wonder if he's angry at me.

"Come here," Auntie Fay says to me. I try to sit next to her but she pulls me on her lap. "My big brave girl," she says. "Aren't you? They've got him now. Thanks to you being brave enough to tell the truth." She kisses my head.

I glance at Ryan, who is sulking in the armchair while we cuddle on the sofa. He's sitting sideways, his legs hanging over the arm of the chair. He scowls at me and I poke my tongue out at him.

"Is it over now?" I ask Auntie Fay.

"Well," she says. She rubs my arm like she's trying to warm me up. "We might have to go back to the police station again."

"Why?" I ask, pulling away. "You promised that if I told them everything then it would be over!"

"I just meant that you needed to get it over with, telling them. Then you would feel better."

But I don't feel better. I just feel the same fear coming back. I don't want to go back into the police station. We were in there almost all day before and the only pop they had was sugar-free and it didn't taste nice and they only had Rich Tea biscuits and I was starving but they still made me tell them the story over and over again. Then they said they needed to talk to Sean and I cried because I didn't know if Sean would be mad at me or not.

"Whyyyyyy?" I ask Auntie Fay, putting my face into her dress. She smells like cooking and washing detergent.

"There now, love, it wasn't that bad last time, was it? Everyone thought you were very brave, didn't they?"

"A proper little soldier," Uncle Paul says. He rubs my cheek with a rough knuckle.

"But…but…what if Mr. Sampson…?" I ask.

"They'll have him locked away now for good," Auntie Fay says. "You won't have to worry about him, I can tell you that."

The next morning I wake up late. I am too hot with how much sun is coming through the windows behind the curtains and it feels stuffy, like waking up inside the caravan Mum used to take us to for weekends away. So I stay in bed and try to remember as much as I can about the caravan and the fried breakfasts Mum made on the stove with all the pots and pans that were smaller than the ones at home.

"It's like being in a doll's house," she said once. I remember the button mushrooms from a tin and how she winked at me when she put in loads of butter. "We're on holiday, aren't we?" she said. "We can eat whatever we want."

There are voices downstairs, lots of them, and I wonder why Auntie Fay didn't wake me up like she normally does.

I get out of bed and peek down the stairs but I can't see the people from the landing. I can only hear them.

"...couldn't charge him with anything...just let him go..."

I hear words like "disgraceful" and "incompetent" and "useless."

"How can they let him go without searching the house?" someone almost shouts. "That's what I want to know. They haven't even searched the bloody house."

"How can they?" someone else says. "You've seen it. You couldn't find anything in there. Talk about finding a needle in a haystack."

"If Luke had been...there's no other way to say it; I'm going to say it...if Luke had been a normal child they'd be moving heaven and earth to find out what happened but because he was disabled..." Everyone murmurs like they agree with the loud woman who's talking.

I walk downstairs and when people see me in the hall they stop talking.

"What happened?" I ask, rubbing the sleep out of my eyes. "What's going on, Auntie Fay? Uncle Paul?" I almost don't see them in the crowd that has taken over the kitchen and dining room.

"Come here, sweetheart," Auntie Fay says, everyone parting so she can get to me. "We've just had a bit of a shock this morning, that's all. You should go and get yourself dressed and I'll talk to you about it when we've had some time to talk among ourselves. Is that okay?"

I stop and look at everyone. They are staring at me and I don't know why.

"Auntie Fay?" I say.

"Tell her, Fay," a man says. The man is really big, as big

as a doorway. "She should know after how brave she's been what the bloody police have done to thank her."

"Roy," Auntie Fay says in the same voice she uses when I eat chips with my fingers or pick my nose.

"He's right, Fay," the loud woman says. "She has a right to know."

"Know what?" I ask, more scared now, more than ever, looking at everyone's serious faces. "Am I in trouble?" I say eventually.

"Of course not, love!" Auntie Fay says, hugging me. I feel a tiny bit better.

Everyone else says the same; their voices go all high and strange and they say things like: "You're not in trouble," and, "You have nothing to feel bad about."

"What's happening?" I ask again. This time Uncle Paul steps forward and he kneels down so he is even smaller than me.

"Well, you know how the police arrested Mr. Sampson, because you were so brave and told them the truth?" he asks.

I nod.

"It turns out it isn't as simple as we all thought it was. You see, we thought that now that they knew the truth about Mr. Sampson they could lock him away and keep him there, didn't we?"

"They did lock him up," I say, confused. "They did. We saw it on the telly."

"Yes, but…to keep him locked up they have to say for sure that he did it. Do you understand? Right now, sweetheart, what the police say is that they need more time to prove that he did it, so that they can lock him up forever."

"But he did do it…" I say. "I told them. He grabbed

Luke's arm and he pulled him away from us and when we pulled Luke back, he…he…"

"I know," Auntie Fay says. "I know."

"You see?" the loud woman says. "You see this? *This* is all the evidence they should need."

Another woman starts crying.

"Is Mr. Sampson locked up?" I ask.

"No, sweetheart," Auntie Fay says. "Not right now. Once the police have enough evidence they'll arrest him again and—"

"If we're bloody lucky!" the big man says. "If they pull their fingers out and do their bloody jobs properly."

"Well, if the police aren't going to do their jobs properly, we'll have to," the loud woman says and everyone nods.

"What if Mr. Sampson comes back for me?" I ask Uncle Paul. "He said he'd come and get me if I told anyone…"

Everyone shakes their heads and tuts and sighs and mumbles.

"This is how the police look after witnesses," the big man says. "Look at her, she's terrified!"

"Wouldn't you be?" someone says.

"We should all be terrified! They've let this…this…pervert loose after what he's done."

"They don't care," another woman says. "They don't care about us or our kids. They don't care!"

Everyone agrees again. I start to cry and Uncle Paul hugs me this time. I can smell cigarettes but Uncle Paul isn't supposed to smoke anymore.

"We won't let him hurt you," the big man says. "We need to make sure he can't do anything else while the police are fannying about. Yes? We need to keep an eye on Sampson; we need to keep the press interested so that the police can't put off his arrest any longer. We need to let them know we are not going to let this go!"

Everyone is agreeing, loudly and angrily. I cover my ears and Uncle Paul hugs me closer.

"Don't you worry, love," the big man says, patting my shoulder. "We're all on your side. We'll protect you."

I don't want to go out because of Mr. Sampson and so we stay in all day instead. Auntie Fay makes Ryan stay in, too, and he's sulking so she tells him off. Uncle Paul has told work he can't come in and so he says we should all play *Monopoly*. Normally we only play board games at Christmas but it is the middle of summer and it feels weird. Ryan says he doesn't want to play *Monopoly*; he wants to go into the back garden and kick the ball around like he always does.

"The back garden is safe," Ryan whines. "I'm not even going anywhere!"

"Luke was in his back garden when he was taken," Auntie Fay says. "You know that. Don't be so insensitive, Ryan. I expect more of you."

"Mum!" Ryan says. "It's not *fair*. Just because *she*—"

"Don't you dare," Auntie Fay says, pointing a finger. "We're going to get through this as a family."

"She isn't family," Ryan mumbles but we all hear it. I start to cry.

"What did you just say?" Uncle Paul says.

"Nothing," Ryan lies.

"Yes, you did," Auntie Fay says. "What a spiteful thing to say. Apologize, right now. Come on."

"No," Ryan says.

"Then you can go to your room," Uncle Paul says.

"No, he can't," Auntie Fay interrupts. "No, he's going

to stay down here and play *Monopoly* and be a part of this family."

After everyone finishes arguing and I stop crying, Uncle Paul gets the board out and sorts out all the houses and the money and the cards because since Christmas they have all got mixed up together in a big mess inside the box.

"Right," Uncle Paul says when everything's in order. "Pick your pieces."

Ryan grabs the dog straightaway and I cry out.

"I want to be the dog!" I say.

"Give her the dog, Ryan," Auntie Fay says.

"No! It isn't fair!" Ryan says.

"Give it to her," Uncle Paul warns him. "You're too old for this. Now stop being so childish."

"Why does she *always* get what she wants?" Ryan says, holding the dog tight in his fist. "All of this is *her* fault! Everything goes wrong because of *her*!"

"It's not my fault! I didn't do anything wrong, did I? All I did was tell the truth."

Auntie Fay takes my side and tells Ryan to stop it or she'll give him a good hiding.

Ryan throws the dog back into the box and flops back against the armchair, curled into a ball. "She's a liar!" he says. "She's making everything up so she gets attention!"

"Ryan!" Uncle Paul snaps. "That's enough. Go to your room."

Ryan stomps off and Auntie Fay and Uncle Paul take care of me until I stop crying.

"Right," Uncle Paul says, clapping his hands. "Who wants to be banker?"

The phone rings all the time, and when Auntie Fay answers she stretches the cord as far as it goes so I can't hear what she's saying. When they watch the news they tell me I'm not allowed to watch with them because it isn't suitable and they close the living room door so I can't hear.

Later, the police come to the house and make me tell them the story again. Every time Auntie Fay tries to help by reminding me of something I've forgotten, the police tell her off and say she has to be quiet. Auntie Fay tells them it feels like *we* are the ones under suspicion, not Mr. Sampson, and that because they refuse to arrest Mr. Sampson, Uncle Paul might lose his job from staying home to look after us.

"It's like we're prisoners in our own home while that Sampson gets to roam free!" Auntie Fay says. The police try to calm her down but they can't. They tell us they'll be back another day.

Later that evening the doorbell rings and Auntie Fay tells me to go up to my room but I stop on the landing and wait to see who it is. When I see him, his dad standing behind him with his hands on his shoulders, I run down and hug him so hard I worry his eyeballs might pop out.

"Sean!" I say. He doesn't say anything and he doesn't even smile at me.

"Go on, lad," Sean's dad says, pushing him into the house. "You two go and catch up and I'll have a word with Mrs. Patterson a minute."

Sean won't look at me. Auntie Fay cups his face in her hands and tells him that she's missed him and all his noise round here.

"Do you want a drink?" she asks. "Anything to eat?"

Sean shakes his head and says no, thank you.

"My poor boy," Auntie Fay says and she does something she's never done before. She kisses him on the top of his forehead and when she moves out of the way, I can see a tear going down Sean's cheek.

"Come upstairs," I say, running up to my room. Sean kicks off his black trainers—the same ones he wears to school even though it's summer holidays—and he follows me slowly. In my room he leans against the wall and stares at the floor.

"I missed you," I say. Sean stays quiet. "Did you know they let Mr. Sampson out?" I ask.

"Durr," Sean says. "Everyone knows. It's on the telly all the time and there are people who stand outside his house all day shouting and waving signs."

"You're allowed to watch the news?" I say, surprised.

"I can do whatever I want," Sean says, rubbing his foot on the carpet so that all the bobbles are facing the wrong way, making a dark line in the beige carpet. I stop myself from rubbing it back.

"Are you allowed outside?" I ask.

"Yeah," Sean says. "Dad doesn't care. He says if the police can't sort it, the mob will."

"Mob?"

"The people with the signs. Dad says Mr. Sampson will get what's coming to him."

"What does that mean?"

Sean shrugs. "They'll probably kill him or something."

"Won't they get into trouble?" I ask. Sean shrugs again. I think about it. I wonder if it feels right, that they should kill Mr. Sampson or if it would be better if the police locked him back up. I think I would prefer it if the police locked him back up. "Auntie Fay says that all they need is evidence and then they'll lock him up forever."

"Dad says if they were going to find evidence they'd have found it by now," Sean says. "Dad says the police obviously don't care about spastics."

The word makes my face go red, remembering Mr. Pocklington and his office.

"What do they mean?" I ask. "What does *evidence* mean?"

Sean rolls his eyes. "It means, like, proof. Like if you stab someone with a knife and then they find the knife on you, they know you did it."

"Oh," I say. My heart races. "Um," I say. "If I show you something do you promise not to tell anyone?"

Sean nods but his cheeks go all white straightaway. I pull out the bottom drawer and feel around in the gap underneath it. When I feel the cold of the metal I close my fingers around it and hold it in my fist.

"What?" Sean says. "What is it?"

I hold out my hand and show Sean the little red racing car with the chipped paint that Luke had been holding when we pulled him away from Mr. Sampson.

"Shit," he says. "Why do you have that?" He backs away like I've shown him a knife.

"It dropped when Mr. Sampson grabbed him. I forgot I had it," I say. Sean shakes his head. "Honest! I didn't know I had it until the next day. I think I put it in my pocket and…"

"This is really bad," Sean says. "Really bad. We're going to get done if they find out you stole it."

"I didn't steal it!" I say, too loud.

"They'll think it's evidence," Sean says. "They'll say it's proof that you, that we—"

"But it wasn't us!" I start to cry again.

"Shut up," Sean says, his voice hissing like a snake. "You need to stop being such a baby. *Now.*"

"I don't want it anymore," I say, holding the car out to Sean. "It makes me feel bad."

"I don't want it, either! You need to get rid of it."

"How? I can't even go outside! You need to take it. Throw it in the river or something, please!"

"Hang on," Sean says. For a second I think he's going to take the car like I want him to, but instead he just stares at it in my hand. "We need to put it in Mr. Sampson's house."

THIRTY-FOUR

Her: Now

I expect Jack to take me somewhere shadowy and secret but instead we take a taxi to an industrial estate that is brightly lit by enormous lampposts and buildings where people are still working. The taxi stops outside Safe & Sound: Security Solutions and Jack hands over a ten-pound note, saying, "Cheers, mate."

I open my door and step out, looking up at the building.

"And you know someone who works here?" I ask Jack as the taxi pulls away.

"Most of my mates work in security," he says. "I know a couple of guys who work here. This one owes me a favor anyway."

As we approach the entrance, Jack puts a hand between my shoulder blades and rubs my back. It feels like a snake coiling around me, squeezing. I try not to jerk away.

Jack lets me go while he speaks to the man behind the desk in the foyer and waits while the man makes a call. Jack looks over his shoulder and winks. I stand behind him, not sure if I should take a seat. I pull the sleeves of my hoodie down over my hands and fold my arms across myself, suddenly cold.

The man at the desk gestures to the chairs behind us and Jack indicates we should sit down. My foot bounces as I wait in the chair, my trainer squeaking on the polished floor. To stop me, Jack places a hand on my knee, which only makes me squirm more.

"Chill," he says in a whisper. "It's no big deal. My mate says they do this all the time."

"Really?" I ask.

"Yeah. Don't worry about it. Just relax."

I keep myself still, looking at the walls around me, at the corporate colors and the glint of steel, cold and sharp as a knife-edge, that frames the doors and windows.

The lift doors open and a man appears, grinning the same grin as Jack, walking with the same Jack-swagger, arms outstretched.

"All right, mate, what's happening?" the man says.

Jack gets up and they hug, clapping each other loudly on the back.

"Same old, mate. Same old. How's it going?" Jack says.

"Not bad, like. Not bad." Jack's friend looks at me and his smile spreads. "Who's this, then?"

"This is *Charlotte*," Jack says, as if it's a joke I'm not a part of.

"All right, Sharl? I'm Andy. Nice to meet you." Andy holds out his palm and I pull back the cuff of my hoodie to let him shake my hand. His skin is warm and moist.

"Nice to meet you, too," I say. Instead of letting go of

my hand when I loosen my grip, Andy holds it for a second longer, and he frowns and looks as though he's about to say something before he changes his mind. He lets my hand go and I pull the hoodie back over my fingers.

"Right," Andy says, clapping his hands together. "Let's get you sorted."

We stand too close in the lift and the combined smell of their aftershave gives me a headache between my eyes. They talk. Jack asks Andy about "the missus" and Andy tells him about how being a dad changes everything.

"Don't go getting any ideas," Jack says to me, with a wink. My hand reaches instinctively for my upper arm, where they put the implant so that I didn't have to worry about getting pregnant. I suppose it stops them from worrying about me getting pregnant, too. Andy watches me as Jack talks, and his eyes narrow. I try not to look but I see him in the reflection of the mirror in the back of the lift, staring, and my skin tingles unpleasantly.

When the lift doors open we walk down a corridor, through an open-plan office and a minikitchen. All shades of gray and blue and white. There are coffee rings on messy desks and mugs abandoned with centimeters of cold tea left inside them, the milk turning chalky on the top. I look at the tidy desks, the ones where everything is lined up neatly and wiped clean, and wonder how the tidy people here can handle working in the same place as the messy ones.

"Here we are," Andy says. He holds open a door to a private office and lets us in first. On the plaque it says Andrew Grayling. Andy closes the door behind us and claps again. "So, would the patient like to take a seat?"

I look towards Jack.

"He means you, chick," Jack says. I sit in the chair and Andy spins me round to face him. He sits on one knee and

I lift up my foot with the tag on. He rests my heel on his leg and I remember Mum taking me for my first school shoes, the wooden measuring instrument that tickled as the man adjusted it and the shiny brown shoe that felt stiff and too tight with the buckle done up.

Andy turns the tag around to look at it and I remember the smell of the trapped water, cheesy and thick, and hope he doesn't notice.

"It's one of ours," Andy says. "This won't be a problem."

Andy stands and lets go of my foot. When he returns he has a small plastic key like the man who comes to my house has. He kneels, inserts the key and adjusts the tag. It loosens and I want to reach down and rub the smooth skin that was trapped underneath it but I resist.

"Job done," Andy says. He holds out the key for me to take and I put it into my purse with my loose change.

"Thank you," I say.

"No problem," Andy says. Again, he looks at me just a bit too long, and I blush.

"So, do I need to give you money?" I ask. They laugh.

"Keep your money, love. Jack's an old friend. Just don't forget to tighten it before your appointments. And don't mention you know me."

"Right," I say, sensing that instead of money, I now owe them both something else, something unnamed. The way Andy looks at me, a small smile that flickers every time Jack turns away, seems to say that now he is in control. Rather than giving me freedom, having the ankle tag removed only seems to have trapped me further.

"Cheers, mate, seriously," Jack says.

"What you got planned for the rest of the night, then?" Andy says. "Now that you're free to do anything?"

"Whatever Charlotte wants to do," Jack says. He pulls

me to him and squeezes me. The loose tag seems heavier on my ankle, dragging me down.

Outside, waiting for our taxi, Jack starts telling me about his house and how his mum will want to say hello but she won't bother us much.

"Um," I say, trying to pull away from his viselike grip. "I can't just stay over. I need to drop my tag back to the home. Remember?"

Jack looks like he's working it out.

"So we can drop your tag back at your place and then you can come back to mine," he says.

When the taxi arrives, Jack gives my address and we sit quietly, listening to the radio. But Jack squirms, unable to stand the lack of conversation.

"Are you having a good night?" Jack asks me. I nod but turn to gaze out of the window, unable to stop thinking about the way Andy had looked at me and what it had meant. Jack sighs loudly and leans forward, hugging the back of the leather headrest up front. "You don't want to take the flyover at this time of the evening, mate," he tells the driver. They argue for a while until the driver relents and takes a sharp turn, which makes me slide towards Jack. I put up a hand to steady myself and Jack puts his hand on top of mine.

At the home I expect Jack to wait in the taxi while I go in, but instead he pays the driver and gets out with me. What had I planned? To go in and text him to say I would not be coming back out? Even though it is what I want, I know I would have thought it was too cruel.

"I'll wait here," Jack says.

Just as I turn to walk through the gates, I realize something.

"My curfew," I say.

"What?" Jack says.

"I forgot, we have a curfew here. They check at the desk who comes in and who goes out. We all have to be in by 10 p.m. or we lose our residency."

Because I'm not lying, because I only just remembered, I hope that Jack can't accuse me of leading him on.

But Jack looks mad. "You said we only had to get the tag taken off," he says. "You mugging me off? After everything I've done?"

I feel embarrassed, guilty. "I forgot," I say again.

Jack rolls his eyes, like I am an idiot. "Fucking cock tease," he says.

"I'm sorry. I really wanted to go home with you but…"

Jack seems to soften. "You can sneak back out," he says. "You're good at sneaking, right?"

"No," I say. It comes out strong, certain. Jack takes a step back. "If I get caught sneaking out I'm going to lose my place here and then I'm going to be sent to prison. I can't risk it."

"But—" Jack says.

"No," I say again. "I'm sorry, I just can't. Not tonight."

I leave Jack at the gates. He doesn't threaten to tell the manager about the stealing. I realize Sean was right, about Jack at least. It was all talk. Inside, I sign in at the desk and walk as quietly as possible up the creaking steps. In the common area I can hear the television and the women chatting. I don't want them to see me, don't want to have to answer their questions about the date or see the way their eyes shine when they talk about Jack. In my room I take off my shoe and loosen the tag a little more. It slides right off and I hold it for a while, looking at it, wondering how many ankles it has been on before mine. I place it on the end of my bed. Then I lean forward and I scratch my ankle, the smooth flesh where the tag normally rests. I scratch and scratch and sniff my fingers, which do smell a little cheesy, then I pull my sock up over the skin.

I wait long enough for Jack to get a taxi or to walk away. I think about changing my mind, about staying in and watching TV with the women in the living room. Then I stare at Isherwood's dot on the map and I know I have to find out if Sean is telling me the truth, if she has a baby now.

I lock my door from the inside, slide up my window and crawl out onto the fire escape. My phone rings again: Sean. I almost answer, but know he will say anything to talk me out of finding Dr. Isherwood. I switch the phone off and put it back into my bag. I don't want it on. I know I need to be alone for what will happen next. Otherwise it's like people can see you, or they can sense what you are doing.

The metal clangs gently under my feet as I climb down the fire escape. I pass a lit window, but the curtains are thankfully drawn. Then past the kitchen window, which is dark: no one inside. Finally my feet are back on the ground and all I have to do is sneak over the front wall. Jack was right, I realize. I have always been good at sneaking.

THIRTY-FIVE

Her: Then

Even though Sean explains the plan to me twice I still
don't get it and it sounds scary and impossible. I thought
Auntie Fay would never let me stay over at Sean's house
in the first place but then she did because Sean's dad took
her into the dining room and spoke quietly until she said
yes. Auntie Fay packs me an overnight bag and gives us a
box full of the fairy cakes we made in the afternoon and
kisses me on the head, and Sean's dad walks us back to the
video shop where they live.

Sean lets me choose the video, so I pick *The Little Mermaid* because it has the best songs and then Sean's dad
turns the sign around so it says Closed and switches off all
the lights downstairs, even though the video shop doesn't
normally close until really, really late.

Usually at Sean's house we stay in Sean's room and Sean's dad stays downstairs in the shop, but tonight Sean's dad makes us stay in the living room with him. He puts on the video and asks us what we want from the Chinese. I don't like Chinese food except for chips and chicken balls, even though Chinese chips are more chewy than chip-shop chips. Sean orders loads of food and his dad says he has eyes bigger than his stomach and it makes me laugh.

It's weird sitting with Sean's dad and my Chinese chips are cold and there's no red sauce in Sean's house, but I am glad we are sitting like this because it means that the plan is canceled. The first part of the plan was to sneak out and we can't do that if Sean's dad is with us, so when Sean's dad says we should put on another video it makes me really happy.

Sean doesn't look happy. Even though he gets to choose the next video he is sulking and leaves most of his food on the plate, so his dad tells him off. In Sean's house they don't need to do the washing up straight after dinner; instead they leave the plates in and around the sink with all the other plates and glasses. When there are no glasses or plates left, that's when they do the washing up. But if they are in a hurry they only wash one plate or one glass and still leave the rest. I wonder if this is how Mr. Sampson started making a mess of his kitchen but then I think about his eyes and his black mouth and his howl and I get scared and have to try really hard to be okay again so Sean doesn't get mad at me.

When it is really late—when I am starting to get tired and we have watched two films and drunk all of the cherry pop—Sean's dad says it's time for bed. He tells me that I can sleep in the living room and that he will go and get a sleeping bag and Sean says I should stay in his room and they argue for a while about how there is no room on the floor in Sean's room and how if he wanted me to sleep in his room he should tidy up once in a bloody while.

"What about the TV?" Sean says.

"What about it?" his dad says.

"You can't watch TV if she's here, can you?"

Sean's dad thinks about it.

"All right, cheeky sod, if you can clear a space she can kip in there." Sean's dad looks at me. "But don't you dare tell your auntie Fay, okay? I'm in enough trouble with her as is."

That is how I end up sleeping on Sean's floor, looking at a sock with a picture of Taz on it and all the wires coming from Sean's computer thing he won't let me touch. I don't want to touch it in case I am electrocuted anyway.

"Don't fall asleep," Sean says again. He is talking quietly even though Sean's dad has the TV on *really* loud and keeps laughing along with it.

"I won't," I say.

Now my stomach feels sick because Sean says the plan will still work. We are just waiting a little while and we can go down the outside stairs from Sean's window that is called a fire escape.

"You promise you have the thing?" Sean asks.

"I promise," I say. The thing is the car, Luke's car, but it is hard to say it out loud. The thing is in the side pocket of my bag. I got it after Auntie Fay had already packed for me and I pretended I needed to go to the toilet before we left.

We keep waiting, Sean's dad still plays the TV loud and my stomach is nervous. I start to get sleepy but the floor is hard and there's a funny smell that helps me stay awake. Soon my shoulder is aching and I need to turn over again.

I don't even notice the quiet until the line of light goes dark under the door.

"OK," Sean says. He throws off the covers and his feet are on the floor next to my head.

"I don't want to," I say. I am afraid because I don't think I believed he would really make me go. Sean uses his foot to push me onto my back.

"You have to come," he says. His voice is sharp like smashed glass. "Get up now! Get the thing."

I get up, making sure I don't cry. We are both still in all our clothes because Sean's dad never made us get ready for bed the way Auntie Fay does. He didn't even make us brush our teeth but I brushed mine anyway. The toothbrushes in the cup on the sink were really old and all the bristles were pointing the wrong way and there were loads of bits of old bars of soap and razors all around the sink. It made me feel dirty even though I was trying to get clean.

I hold the thing out for Sean but he shakes his head.

"Put it in your pocket," he tells me.

"What if it falls out?" I ask.

"Don't drop it or I'm telling," Sean says. "I'll tell the police you stole it and it's your fault."

It hurts when he says it and I have to try really, really hard not to cry. I put it in my pocket and do up my shoes. Sean opens his window and it creaks really loudly. He leans out and looks around to check no one is there.

"Come on then," he says in a whisper; then he climbs out and is standing on the other side of his own window, looking in. There are butterflies in my stomach. Then I think that I'm afraid and it is night: there are moths in my stomach. Butterflies are for good times; moths must be for bad.

I climb out and my feet make loads of noise on the metal stairs and Sean tells me to be quiet. We leave the window open and climb down the stairs. This means anyone can climb in the window but Sean doesn't seem to care about this. The stairs go into the alley at the side of the video shop, where they keep the bins and all the cardboard boxes. Because it's dark I think it should be really cold but it's not that cold at all. I am shaking because I'm scared, not because I didn't bring my coat.

Sean goes to the end of the alley and checks there's no one on the street; then he says I should follow him and we walk quickly down the main street, past all the shops and into the streets with all the houses. When I don't walk fast enough Sean grabs my hand and drags me along. I don't want to go through the park because it's so dark but Sean tells me that this was the plan, because we can't go round the front of Mr. Sampson's house with all the people who are there with the signs. Sean says he doesn't know if they're there in the night but that we can't risk it anyway.

"Besides," Sean whispers, even though there's no one around, "we need to sneak in through the back door, remember?"

I try not to imagine that bit because it is too frightening so I just nod and hope he will stop talking. We go through the park and round the back of the council flats until we get to the right street. The moths in my stomach start to go crazy when I see how close we are. Sean just seems to be concentrating really hard and he keeps looking everywhere around us to make sure that no one sees where we are because this was the most important bit of the plan, he told me, that it is a complete secret.

We go down the street behind Mr. Sampson's house. All the houses have really high back fences and walls so you can't see into their gardens and on the other side are garages where people park their cars and keep their lawn mowers. You can see Mr. Sampson's house from ages away because his garden spills out onto the street behind it, as he never got his back wall fixed after it fell down.

Sean goes first and we stand by the bricks and rubble and look at the dark house. Mr. Sampson must be asleep, and this is the other important part of the plan.

"You need to be really brave now, okay?" Sean tells me. I nod but I don't feel brave, not at all. "Just follow me and be really quiet." Then Sean climbs into the garden and I have to follow him.

Every step Sean takes makes a noise. First the bricks move under his feet and then metal bends and clangs as he stands on top of the first washing machine. In the dark it's hard to see where we are going and the shapes look like tangled branches and piles of bones and spikes that will go right through us if we slip. I think of hands, hands like Mr. Sampson's, with long crooked fingers, reaching up through the rubbish and pulling us down. Then I squeeze my eyes shut and try to think about nice things, of the songs in *The Little Mermaid* and cherry pop and how Sean promised that after this we wouldn't have to be scared anymore because they would lock Mr. Sampson up forever and ever and ever.

I open them and carefully take the same steps that Sean did. I feel very good because I don't make anywhere near as much noise as Sean, even on the car, which is really rusty and noisy when Sean climbs on it.

Nearer the back of the house it gets harder to climb and a couple of times Sean takes a wrong step and all the bikes and junk lean and clank against everything. I cover my ears because in the quiet it sounds as loud as screaming.

Sean has to help me down at the end and then we crouch so that Mr. Sampson can't see us through the windows, if he is awake after all. The windows are all so piled with news-papers and plates and pots and pans and boxes that I don't think he could see out anyway, but Sean says we need to be extra careful tonight, so I don't tell him that.

"We need to take the door off together," Sean whispers. "Remember?"

I nod and crawl-walk to the back door to help Sean because it will be too heavy for him on his own. Sean puts his hand on the handle of the back door and takes a really long breath, and it makes me know he is afraid, as well, even if he seems like he's not scared of anything. I squeeze my pocket to check the thing is still there; then I put my hands out to make sure the door doesn't fall on us when it comes off. Sean pushes the handle down and the top of the door leans towards us. As the door comes loose it makes a terrible noise, like a ripping sound, really loud, and I think there is no way that Mr. Sampson can sleep through that.

I have to hold the door with Sean and it's really heavy and we both stagger backwards while carrying it.

"Push forward," Sean whispers, too loudly. We tilt it back towards the house and it falls against the wall with a bang but Sean doesn't stop to worry about it—he just goes straight inside and I follow him because it's even scarier to be left on my own than to go in.

It smells terrible inside. Worse than the toilets by the shopping center in town, about a million times worse. It's so bad I think I will be sick but when my stomach turns and I gag Sean turns quickly and holds his hand over my mouth.

He doesn't speak but I can see his mouth move: *Quiet.* He puts a finger against his lips and I try not to sniff the air. It is impossible to be silent now. The floor is covered in old plastic bottles and ready-meal containers.

After the kitchen is the hallway and that has old tins and newspapers everywhere. Above us there is a big hole in the ceiling that goes right through into the upstairs of the

house. The stairs don't have a bannister and at the top it is
so black we can't see anything else. But that is where Mr.
Sampson must be: upstairs and in bed, in the dark. I look
at the hole in the ceiling as we walk underneath it. That
big black hole, like Mr. Sampson's howling mouth. It feels
like he might be there, watching us through it.

I tug on Sean's sleeve. I want to leave. I want to ask why
we are still here. Can't we just drop the thing now and get
out? But Sean said we had to put it somewhere the police
could find it but Mr. Sampson couldn't, so that he couldn't
get rid of it before the police come to look. Besides, Sean
ignores me tugging on his sleeve and just keeps creeping
forward through the house.

Some light comes through the bumpy glass on the front
door. The light is orange, like fire, and lights up the piles of
rubbish closest to the door. But there is a space by the front
door that is clear, where the door has to swing open and
shut, and all the rubbish gets swept up to the side of the hall.

We go into the room that I think is supposed to be the
dining room. There are loads of clothes and cuddly toys and
books in here. This seems like it would be a good place to
put the thing but Sean shakes his head and points back out
of the door. I let him go first. Then we keep going to the
front of the house and the room that would probably be the
living room. We go inside slowly, both of us looking at the
window that faces onto the street, checking that no one can
see in. There is so much piled in front of the windows that
we know we are okay and that is when Sean turns around.

I turn, too, and I see Mr. Sampson, standing facing the
opposite wall, and before I can scream Sean holds his hand
over my mouth again. It is too late and even though he muf-
fles the sound, I have made a lot of noise and Sean starts to

pull me away, ready to run back through the hall and the kitchen and out, away, to home where it's safe.

Except Mr. Sampson doesn't turn to look at us like he should. Instead he stands very, very still. Sean goes back into the room and I shake my head, silently crying out for him to stop, but he keeps going anyway. That's when I notice the way Mr. Sampson is standing. The way his feet aren't quite touching the ground. Just the tip of his toe seems to brush the space on the floor that is clear around him. Everywhere else there are the papers and the bottles and the books and the clothes and the rubbish. But where his feet are there is just the floor.

I am too confused to scream. Then I am too frightened to scream. I watch Sean get closer and closer until he is right by the floating Mr. Sampson and then right in front of him and then Sean is stumbling back towards me and I almost scream again but Sean starts talking quickly.

"He's dead," Sean says. "He's hung himself. Don't be scared. He's just dead, that's all. That's good, that's good: it means he can't hurt us. He can't do anything now. Please don't cry, don't cry."

I am crying, though, and I feel like I'll never be able to stop.

"Just give me the thing," Sean says. "Give it to me."

When I give Sean the thing from my pocket, Sean pulls his jumper over his hand so he doesn't have to touch it. I don't want him to leave me, so I grab hold of his other hand and won't let go, even when he tries to shake me off.

"Please," I'm saying. "Please can we go now. Please."

"You just need to be brave for one more minute," Sean says. His voice sounds like he might cry, too. "Can you do that? One more minute?"

I nod but I still won't let go of his hand. So I let myself

be dragged closer and closer to floating Mr. Sampson, seeing the shape of his long bony fingers hanging down by his sides, all the time whispering to Sean to please, please hurry up. Sean starts to hold my hand tighter and I can hear him breathe, quick and loud, like he's been running fast. I close my eyes as we get in front of floating Mr. Sampson but peek to see what Sean is doing. That is when I see Mr. Sampson's face, all blown up like a balloon, dark purple like he's really, really mad.

"Sean," I whisper.

"Be brave," Sean says, squeezing my hand.

With his other hand Sean reaches up, standing on his tiptoes. I check that his feet are still on the ground; I see the way they touch the floor and look again at the way Mr. Sampson's don't, and a long squeak comes out of my mouth as I cry again. Sean ignores me and reaches as far as he can, pushing the thing towards the front pocket of Mr. Sampson's dirty shirt. One final stretch and Sean manages to get the thing into the pocket. He lets it go and his heels fall back to the ground.

"Okay," he says. "You were so brave."

Mr. Sampson jolts, like he's waking up from a bad dream, and then Sean and I both scream; we scream so loudly that half the street must hear us, and so we know that there is no point in trying to be quiet anymore, that we have to just run as fast as we can. And we do, we run, we knock over the piles in the hallway and all the bottles in the kitchen, we run out of the back garden jumping loudly from car to washing machine to back wall, and we run all the way through the park and the streets and up the fire escape and my lungs feel like they will explode.

We climb in through Sean's bedroom window, neither of us thinking about the fact that the light is turned on, even though it was off when we left. We are just happy to be out of the dark. Before we can sit down on the bed, Sean's dad comes through the open door.

"Where the bloody hell have you pair been?" he says. "I've been worried sick."

Please don't say you called my auntie Fay, I think. *Please.*

"We were playing," Sean says. "Sorry."

"Sorry's not good enough," Sean's dad says. "You'll need a better explanation than that."

"I—"

"Don't explain to me," Sean's dad says. "I've got the bloody police in my living room. You can explain it to them."

THIRTY-SIX

Her: Now

I follow the directions on my phone to Dr. Isherwood's house, where her dot blinks on the map. It is a one-and-a-half-hour walk and even though I'm tired, I'm sure I have to go now. It is like something is pulling me there, telling me I need to look out for her.

I walk in the dark and I am free to poke around in the memory of what happened that night long ago, like a tongue searching the cavity left from a lost tooth, impossible to leave alone. It is not that I had forgotten—you could never forget a night like that—but that it feels fresh, as if it had only just happened, as if I am seeing it clearly for the first time. It used to have the quality of a nightmare, not making sense in consciousness but leaving its mark, lurking in the dark. Now it seems as real as a nightmare is when you're asleep.

We told ourselves he hadn't moved, that we had scared ourselves, that we had knocked Mr. Sampson's body and set it swinging. Of course, now, we know differently. That nothing is so simple. You can find out anything online. Like how it can take hours to die by hanging, that Mr. Sampson might have still been alive when we found him. It is not so easy to take your own life, not as easy as taking the life of another.

How easy was it for your dad to strangle your mother? Easy enough to call it an accident? You once read that your father left her lying in bed while he went to buy the petrol, that before he left he turned the key in the lock of the little girl's room and put it in his pocket. When he came back he soaked the house in fuel, washed down pills with neat vodka, and lit the match. He died with his arms around your mother, like it was an act of love.

The map is hard to follow and sometimes I take a wrong direction and have to find my way back to the right street. At first I am cold but I warm up the quicker I move. When I am only thirty minutes away from Dr. Isherwood's house I see a twenty-four-hour Tesco Extra and go inside to think before I am at Dr. Isherwood's house and there's no going back.

The store is not completely empty, as I thought it would be. There are customers: a nurse, still in the light blue scrubs of the hospital, pushing a trolley; two twentysomething men, who are holding multipacks of crisps under one arm like a baby, a bottle of Pepsi swinging from one hand, a huge packet of Penguin bars draped over a forearm. They look pale and tired, and they smell strongly of weed, which makes me smile as they pass.

The employees are pulling huge pallets of food around. One is constructing a pyramid of tins of Roses and Quality Street near the front of the store. Boxes of fake Christmas trees are being priced up. Everyone says Christmas gets earlier every year but I can't remember it being much different. Auntie Fay never let us put the Christmas tree up until we'd finished the school term and she would keep the tins of sweets hidden until Christmas Eve, along with all the presents. But Ryan showed me where to look for them, in the top of the wardrobe in their bedroom, and we would peek and try to put everything back where it was supposed to be.

I always felt jealous of Luke's family, who put up all their Christmas lights and tree at the beginning of November. When other families did that, Auntie Fay used to say it was too bloody early and tsk under her breath. But everyone knew Luke and Liam's mum did it to make Luke happy, because he loved Christmas. Even the neighbors there started to put up all of their lights early because something about Luke being happy seemed to make everyone else happy.

There's so much to look at in the store: all the Christmas decorations and the aisles of chocolate and the scented candles and the magazines and books. I hardly think about what I'm supposed to be thinking about at all. It makes me forget I was ever worried about it in the first place. I start to wonder things like: Does Dr. Isherwood put her Christmas decorations up this early? Will she have a detached house or a semi? Will it have a front garden? I manage to make myself believe that these are the things I am really going there to find out about, quickly pushing away any thoughts about a baby or sickness. Instead I choose three chocolate bars and a Coke and go to the checkout to pay.

Outside, I follow the map on-screen and as I walk the traffic noises get quieter, the houses get further apart and some are protected behind big gates. My heart quickens when I reach the street where Dr. Isherwood lives. It is a quiet place, big Victorian houses all surrounding a small park in the middle, enclosed by spiked railings. Not a swings-and-slides park but a little shared garden: a square of grass with some benches, trees, and a stone fountain.

I walk around the outside of the park, looking at the houses. They are all three stories high, tall and narrow, with weathervanes and little chimneys and mosaic tiles around the doors and on the paths. It is impossible to know which house is Dr. Isherwood's, so I loop around and around, trying to choose one for her. Maybe it is the one with the magnolia tree blocking the front living room window. Or the one with the lion's head door knocker.

It's late and only one house has any lights on. The glow comes from an upstairs window, which is open even in the cold night, and I stand and look up, listening to the faint sound of a baby crying from inside. I am still looking up when a shape appears in the window and I have to step quickly behind the gate of the park, out of sight, my heart beating hard in case the person has seen me. I look again to check whether they have. The person still stands in the light, a baby held against their chest, reaching up to close the top window. And I recognize her straightaway: Dr. Isherwood, bouncing the baby gently and resting her lips against its head. I see her but she does not see me. I watch as she turns away from the window, disappearing back into the house, the light turning to dark.

THIRTY-SEVEN

Him: Now

I sit with my head in my hands, paralyzed. I can't call the police, I can't tell them who I am or why I think she is in danger. I can't tell them where she is. I can't say that I think she is somehow breaking the terms of her release. Why did I give her that stupid fucking idea about getting her tag removed? FUCK.

I punch the back of the sofa several times but my fist just sinks into the marshmallow-soft cushion, the stuffing degraded to nothing from years and years of wasters like me sitting against it, waiting for things to change.

There is only one thing I can do. I get up, put on a jacket and some shoes, and grab my bike at the door. I check the time: 4:53 a.m. Fuck it, I will just have to wake Slimy up. The bike doesn't have lights so I ride the empty pavements and take side streets lit by orange lampposts. It's so early not even the type A nutjobs who run in full fluorescent gear are out yet. Just me and the delivery vans, loaded with newspapers and milk and bread, miserable drivers sneering at me through the windows as I pass.

It is nearly 6 a.m. by the time I reach Slimy's block and by then the dog walkers are out and a man who runs past, breathing in tight little puffs which steam the air. I am sweating underneath my clothes. I roll my bike behind the wheelie bins and let it drop. Taking the stairs two at a time, I run until I'm at Slimy's door, pounding with the side of my fist. The noise sets off a dog in the next flat. I am banging for ages, nearby curtains starting to twitch, before Slimy finally comes to the door.

"Tanker?" he says, his hair sticking up in places, flat in others. "What the fuck, man?"

"I need to use your computer," I say. "It's an emergency—mine's fucked. Here." I hand him several strips of blue pills and a baggie of skunk. His face brightens.

"Come in, man. Must be an emergency if you're up this early," he says, laughing.

Only once I'm inside, I am not the only one who's up early. There is the new guy, sitting up and rolling a cigarette in the light from the TV, which is playing at a low volume.

"Calum," Slimy says to the new guy, "Tanker's just going to use my computer to sort out some business. I'm going back to bed."

"No worries," Calum says, eyeing me as I take a seat. He stares at me as he runs the tip of his tongue along the Rizla to seal it.

"Didn't you hear me knocking?" I ask him.

"Not my fucking flat, mate," he says with his shit-eating grin.

I brush the debris from the top of Slimy's laptop. Strands

of tobacco and stalks and seeds from shitty weed, balled-up cigarette papers from failed spliffs, dropped ash, a ring pull from a can—all scatter over the filthy carpet.

"Seems like you're here a lot, since it's not your fucking flat and all that," I say. I try to ignore the rising anger, to push it down so this prick doesn't know he's getting to me.

"Could say the same to you," he says. "Don't you have your own fucking laptop?"

I try to ignore him, instead concentrating on the screen. I get into Dr. Isherwood's email and calendar. On another tab I create an email address almost identical to the one created for Charlotte, one letter difference, and add this email to Isherwood's address book so that the contact looks no different. Then I send her an email.

Hi. I am not feeling good today, please can we talk? As soon as possible, please. Sorry. Things are getting too much for me.

Calum puts his rolled cigarette down on the coffee table and goes into the kitchen, where I hear the kettle boil.

I read the email again a few times. I don't want to scare the shit out of Isherwood but I want her worried enough to call and check everything's okay. I send the email and wait, smoking and refreshing the screen.

"Evelyn Isherwood?" says Calum, looking over my shoulder, a steaming mug of tea in his hand. I close the screen.

"What the fuck?" I stand and he backs away.

"Just wondering what's so important that you rushed over here at six in the morning," he says. That smirk spreads back over his face.

"Who the fuck do you think you are?"

"Chill," he says, laughing. "You're *seriously* paranoid."

I step closer and Calum resists taking the step back. I look at him there, his sad mug of tea in his hand, and I laugh.

"I don't know where Slimy finds fuckwits like you," I say. I turn back to take my seat; I sense him relax. Then I turn quickly and lunge towards him, watching his eyes bulge with fear. I stop before I touch him, only wanting to prove my point: that he wouldn't dare fight me. But Calum throws his mug at me. Scalding tea hits my chest and soaks my trousers. In the shock of it I almost lose him. He darts for the door, slipping through my grip like an eel, but he fumbles with the catch and doesn't make it out of the flat before I pull him back and throw him to the floor.

He is small, weedy, a little man who has never fought before. He puts his arms in front of his face but I pull them aside and punch and punch, feeling his cheekbone snap, feeling his blood on my knuckles. I let his arms drop, and keep hitting him even as my breath runs out and my punches become weak. Only when I am exhausted do I stop and only then do I see he is no longer moving, that his face is covered in blood.

THIRTY-EIGHT

Her: Then

The policemen in Sean's living room tell us that we need to come to the police station right away. Sean's dad tells them they are being a bit over the top and he only called because he was worried we were in danger and now we're home he can see there's no harm done. The police tell him that it's a little more complicated than that and he will need to come, too; they have to talk to him about something.

"Now, hang on," Sean's dad says. "I can't just take her to the police station in the middle of the night without her auntie's permission."

"We've got someone to bring Mrs. Patterson to the station, sir. No need to worry."

But Sean's dad does look worried. He looks really worried. He keeps rubbing at the back of his neck and looking around the room like he's waiting for someone to explain to him what's going on, except no one does.

"I don't want to go," I say. "I'm sorry we went outside. Can I go home?"

The policemen all look at each other but only one says anything.

"You should have thought about that before you went poking around where you shouldn't be," he says.

"Come off it, mate," Sean's dad says. "Can't you see she's bloody terrified? What's happened? I don't want to go anywhere until you tell us what's happened."

"We went to Mr. Sampson's house," Sean says. Sean is staring at his feet and everyone else is looking at him like they can't believe what he said.

"You did what?" his dad says.

"No, we didn't," I say,

"At least he's clever enough to tell the truth," the mean policeman says.

"Sean, mate, are you joking? Because it isn't funny."

Sean sniffs. "I'm not joking," he says.

"Don't say any more," Sean's dad says to him. "We'll come to the station," he says, turning to a policeman. "But you're not to ask him *anything* until we've got a solicitor. Do you hear me?"

The mean policeman smirks. The other nods.

"I appreciate that, sir," the nice policeman says. "If we could all go to the station now, we'll be able to call the solicitor when we're in custody."

"Wait a second," says Sean's dad. "Is this an arrest? Are you arresting them?"

The police look at one another like they aren't even sure.

"At the moment, sir," says the nice one, "we're just hoping to go to the station and ask some questions."

"No, no," Sean's dad says. "No, we're not coming. I know my rights. It's the middle of the bloody night and you're asking an eleven-year-old and a ten-year-old to come to the station? To answer some questions? No chance, mate. I'll call a solicitor and see how they think this should proceed but they aren't going anywhere tonight."

The nice policeman sighs. "In that case, sir, I'm afraid that I have to tell you that they are under arrest for breaking and entering, for perverting the course of justice, and for the kidnapping of Luke Marchant. As Sean's parent you are going to have to accompany him to the police station where he will be questioned. Mrs. Patterson has agreed to meet us there."

The mean policeman looks at me and says he's going to have to arrest us.

I cry and Sean reaches for my hand and holds it too tight like he will crush my bones, but I never want him to let go.

No one talks in the police car. Sean's dad sits between us in the back seat. It is still dark so no one is out and no one can see us in the back of the car and that is the only thing that is okay. I have cried so much that I have stopped making tears and now it's just my face that feels like it is crying.

The station is even more horrible at night. From somewhere in the back someone is shouting really loudly and banging on the door. I cover my ears. My auntie Fay and uncle Paul run in behind us and when they see me I think they'll be angry but they just look worried. They both come and hug me and ask if I'm okay. Then the police start asking them questions about me, like how old I am and my address and if I'm allergic to anything. Uncle Paul answers the questions but some things he doesn't know and then Auntie Fay gets annoyed at him for not knowing.

Then I have to have my photo taken and I'm not supposed to smile, they say, like when you have a picture taken for a passport.

Auntie Fay has brought me a change of clothes, and she and a woman policeman take me into a little room and I have to change out of my first clothes and into the new ones. They take all my old clothes and put them into a bag.

A different policeman takes me to another room with Auntie Fay. I ask what's going to happen.

"Have you ever done finger painting?" the policeman asks.

"Yeah…"

"Well, this is like finger painting. What we need you to do is to press your finger on this ink here and then press nice and firmly on this paper here. Okay? Do you understand? I'll help you to make sure you do it properly."

One by one the policeman makes me point with a finger and then presses it into a black ink pad that smells like permanent markers. Then he holds my finger and presses it onto a piece of paper, into the middle of a square, and rolls it back and forth. Last of all he takes my whole hand and pushes it onto the ink and then onto the paper, so that when we are finished my hands are covered in sticky black ink.

I whisper to Auntie Fay.

"What is it, darling?" she asks but doesn't look at me; she looks off into the distance.

"I want to wash my hands," I say, still holding them out in front of me.

"I'm sure they'll let us go and wash our hands soon, sweetheart. We need to wait and see what they want us to do next."

"But I want to wash them *now*. Please!"

"In a minute, love."

"Now!" I shout.

"Fine!" Auntie Fay says. "Excuse me, Officer, excuse me. She needs to wash her hands. Is it possible for her to wash her hands? She's terribly fussy about these things; she gets very upset."

"If you could just take a seat," the officer says. "We'll let you know what's going to happen next. Then she can wash her hands."

"This is ridiculous," Auntie Fay says. "It's three in the bloody morning, she's exhausted—we're all exhausted! You can't possibly want to question them *now*. When will we be allowed to go home so she can rest?"

There is a silence where the police officer looks very confused about why Auntie Fay is shouting at him.

"As my colleague explained," the policeman starts, in a really quiet voice, "she is currently under arrest for—"

"Yes! Yes, we know! I'm asking when we can go *home*!"

"You can't," the police officer says. His face looks very white. "You will have to stay here tonight, with her."

"Don't be so ridiculous," Auntie Fay says. "You can't put a ten-year-old in a custody cell!"

Everything is very quiet. The man shouting and banging in the back has stopped. I can feel him listening.

"These are very unusual circumstances for all of us," the policeman says.

"Do I have to sleep here?" I ask.

"No, darling, he's being silly. Uncle Paul is talking to the solicitor now and we'll get this sorted and take you home."

The policeman doesn't say anything even though Auntie Fay just called him silly.

"Where is Sean?" I ask. They made Sean go into a different room when we got in and I haven't seen him since.

"I don't know, love," Auntie Fay says.

"Why aren't I allowed to wash my hands?"

"I don't know, love! I don't know anything because they won't bloody tell me what's going on!"

The nice policeman comes back in and Auntie Fay starts talking to him and asking him all the same questions and eventually the policeman tells her to calm down and he says we can go to the cell and rest if we want to. I don't want to go back there, with the shouting and the banging, even if it is quiet right now. Auntie Fay says she'd rather wait to hear what Uncle Paul has to say after talking to the solicitor and the policeman sighs and says fine, come with me.

We go back to where all the policemen go to have a break. There are toilets there and they let me go and wash my hands. I wash them properly but even afterwards there is still black in the lines on my fingers and the soap in the toilets doesn't smell very nice. Then they take us into a room that has old sofas in with big flowery patterns all over them. You can tell they are old because some parts are really shiny from all the times people have touched them. There is another armchair and there are toys in the corner of the room but not good toys, they are the rubbish kind they put in the doctor's waiting room and in the bank. The ones that don't really do anything and you can't play proper games with.

They let us sit in the room and say they will bring blankets for us.

"That won't be necessary; we won't be staying long," Auntie Fay says, tucking her handbag next to the armchair. "Trust me."

The policeman sighs and says he'll bring them anyway.

"I'm tired," I say. "Are we going home soon?"

"Yes, love," Auntie Fay says. "We're just waiting for Uncle Paul now."

The door opens and we both hope it's Uncle Paul but instead it's just the policeman with the blankets and some bottles of water. He shows Auntie Fay a button she can press if she wants to talk to someone; then he leaves again.

Auntie Fay tells me to lie down on the big settee and then she puts the blanket over me like when I stay home from school because I'm ill.

I can't sleep even though I'm really tired. I open my eyes a tiny bit in case Auntie Fay is looking at me but she isn't, she is just sitting in the chair with her head lying back and her eyes closed but I can tell she isn't asleep because her lips are moving. I close my eyes again because it scares me.

I try to think of nice things instead of what's happening. I try not to think about floating Mr. Sampson or his bulgy eyes. I try not to breathe the sofa which smells like the old women in church.

Uncle Paul comes in quietly like he's trying not to wake me up, so I pretend to be asleep.

"Well?" Auntie Fay says, speaking really softly.

Uncle Paul does a long sigh. "It's not good, love," he says. "The solicitor says they can keep her here. Ten, apparently, that's the age of criminal responsibility—if you can believe it."

"Criminal?" Auntie Fay whispers back.

"Their words, not mine. I told them, whatever they think she's done, they're wrong. But they're adamant. Won't explain themselves now, of course. They say they've got evidence that she's...been involved with some very serious things. They need to keep her—us—here until morning when they can question her properly."

"What about Sean? Is he being made to stay here? I

need to talk to his dad…" Auntie Fay says. I can hear her starting to get up but Uncle Paul shushes her and tells her to sit back down.

"They're not here. They've been sent to a different police station."

"Why?" Auntie Fay says, louder than she meant to.

"I don't know, love. I don't know. Presumably they don't want any of us talking to one another."

"This is absolutely ridiculous. Let me speak to the bloody solicitor."

"You can't! I'm sorry, you can't. He's working on all this right now. Says we just have to sit tight. They have every right to keep us here for twenty-four hours."

Auntie Fay gasps.

"Then, if they can't charge her with anything, she can come home."

"They won't be charging her because she hasn't *done* anything. And will we be compensated for the humiliation of being taken from our home in the dead of night in a police car? How will they make up for the trauma they've caused a little girl and boy tonight?"

"I know, love, I know." Uncle Paul sounds really tired. If I wasn't pretending to sleep I would move so he could sit down and have a rest.

"And while we're going through all this, that predator is sleeping soundly in his house. How is that fair?"

There's a long pause while Uncle Paul is thinking of an answer, I think.

"Listen," he starts. "Listen," he says again.

"What?" Auntie Fay snaps after he doesn't say anything. Then he sighs.

"From what the solicitor has told me, it looks like Mr. Sampson is dead."

"What?"

"Apparently he's hung himself."

Auntie Fay gasps. "Well, if that isn't a sign of a guilty conscience... It's still terrible news. I don't mean to sound..."

"I know, love. It gets a bit more complicated."

"What now?"

"Well, what started all...*this*...is that people who were on night watch outside his house heard screaming."

"His screaming?"

"Children's screaming."

"Good God. There were children in there?"

Uncle Paul sighs again.

"They don't think it was them, do they?" Auntie Fay asks. I try to stay still.

"Sean's dad reported them missing around the same time as the call came to report the screaming from inside the house," Uncle Paul says. "They've put two and two together."

"And made five. What would they want to be going round his house for? You've seen her: she's been terrified of Mr. Sampson since the very beginning."

"I know, love."

"You can't think they're right. Surely you can't believe this?"

"I don't know what to believe anymore."

I hear Auntie Fay crying but Uncle Paul doesn't seem to go to her. I don't hear him saying it's okay or hear the swish of his hand on the fabric of her dress as he smooths her back. I can only hear Auntie Fay and her quiet sobs, like little hiccups. Then I feel my own tears leaking out so I turn over to face the back of the sofa. For a second Auntie Fay's crying stops and the room gets even quieter before she starts again.

"You go home, love," Uncle Paul whispers to her. "Ryan will be worrying. Go home, get as much rest as you can and come back fresh in the morning. I'm sure it'll be fine."

"I can't leave her. I can't do it. Ryan will be fine. Angela doesn't mind keeping him until morning. She's probably beside herself waiting for more gossip."

"That doesn't matter. Let her gossip. But Ryan will want to be home, with his mum. Why don't you just take a break?"

"No!" Auntie Fay shouts. It's so loud I jump and my skin goes all cold. "I'm bloody well staying here. Maybe you should go home, since you think your niece is stupid enough to go poking around that predator's house."

"One of us should be with Ryan," Uncle Paul says.

"What's that supposed to mean?"

"Oh love, I didn't mean anything. I just—"

"Am I not a good mother because I care about what's happening to her right now?"

"That's not what I was saying."

"It's what you're implying. Why don't you go? You're making everything worse. Just go. I will fix all of this."

Uncle Paul doesn't say anything before he leaves; I just hear the door click behind him and then Auntie Fay crying louder than before. I want to pretend to wake up and to ask her if she's okay and give her a cuddle like she would if it was me. But I don't think I can look at her because it will make me want to tell her the truth and then she will hate me. So I squeeze my eyes shut and try to remember a story my mum used to tell me before I went to sleep, about a monkey who needed to cross the whole jungle to get back to his family, and all the animals who helped him on the way. I can't remember it all, though, not properly. I can't remember how he got home.

THIRTY-NINE

Her: Now

I stare up into the dark windows of Dr. Isherwood's house, my tears drying cold on my cheeks, until I am so tired that I can barely stand anymore. I go back into the park, which is dimly lit by the streetlights which surround the square and by the full moon. When I find a bench I sit, then lie down, pulling my hood up over my head and tucking my arms tight around myself, using my bag as a pillow. Eventually I fall into something like sleep, cold to my bones and with the wood of the bench digging into my side.

I wake up because someone is shaking me. At first I can't remember where I am or why I am so cold. I find myself looking into a face that is creased with deep wrinkles, surrounded by a mane of thick and wild hair. Frightened, I jolt upright, twisting away from the man who is leaning too close to my face.

"It's all right, love, it's all right," the man says. "Just checking you're okay. What's a little thing like you doing sleeping out here by yourself?"

Confused, my teeth chattering in the cold morning air, I take in my surroundings and remember where I am. The man continues to talk but I have stopped listening. When I look at him closely I see that he is homeless. Behind him, in the back of the park, is a tent where he must sleep. I keep telling him I'm okay, that I was locked out, but he tries to give me money for a coffee. I open my bag and show him my Coke and my chocolate bars and eventually he seems satisfied that I am not in trouble and he leaves.

To try to warm myself up I start to walk around the park. It is one of those beautiful mornings, not cold enough for frost, but where everything is covered in a fine mist. It reminds me of getting up for school, the walk that Auntie Fay took me on, with Ryan walking far ahead of us, old enough to be embarrassed by our company. Eventually I was old enough to walk on my own, too, and Auntie Fay would wave me off at the front door. I would follow Ryan, but several feet behind him. Sometimes his friends would meet him and then I would have to walk even further behind.

I remember how the sky looked just like this in the months before Christmas, and how the atmosphere felt like it was building up to something. I remember going through the big school gates, the paintings on the windows of animals and flowers and things like umbrellas under a rainy cloud. I remember arriving alone and having no friends there to greet me. Sean was rarely there on time in the mornings, often not at all. So I would go into the cloakroom alone and hang up my coat on the hook with my name. I would wait in the classroom, sitting at the table in the seat I was assigned.

I would look out the window and watch the school gates and every day at the same time I would see Liam and Luke's mum, parking her car right in front of the entrance. She was allowed to do that because she had a special badge because of Luke. She would get out and open the doors and help Luke down from the car and she would hug him and hold his face in both her hands to kiss him on the forehead. Luke didn't get embarrassed about this the way that Liam and the other boys and girls did. Luke would smile and smile and still be smiling even when he was on his own and walking into the school. No one ever made fun of Luke because everyone liked it when Luke smiled. All the rules changed when it came to Luke. Sometimes it was hard to know what the rules were at all anymore.

My phone buzzes in my hand. I see Dr. Isherwood's name and I worry that somehow she has seen me, that she knows I am here. I breathe deep and answer.

"Are you okay?" Dr. Isherwood says. "I just got your email. What's happened?"

"Nothing," I reply, too quickly. So quickly I haven't had a chance to think about what she's saying. I don't remember sending her an email.

"I was worried about you," she says. "I'm sorry I didn't get it sooner but I just woke up and haven't had a chance to check my email until now. Typical. The one night I manage to sleep more than two consecutive hours and it's the one night you need me. I'm so sorry. Tell me now, tell me what happened."

"Nothing," I say again. "I was just...really down. I'm sorry that I worried you."

"Don't be sorry," she says. "I *always* want you to talk to me when you're feeling like this."

There's a noise from behind her and then I can hear the

cry of a baby. I can sense Dr. Isherwood being torn from me and my problems, back into her own world, her own problems.

"Listen," she says. I know that she wants to leave. "Shall we have a proper talk? Later on?"

"On the phone?"

"Or maybe you could come into the office? I have some patients this morning, but you could come in at around three o'clock?"

"Sure," I say, disappointed. "I can come in at three."

"Great, great." Dr. Isherwood's voice becomes higher as the baby's screams get louder in the background. "Well, I will see you then! Take care, bye!"

I don't have time to say goodbye before she has hung up. In the quiet she leaves behind I listen for the sounds of the baby's screams coming from inside the house, feeling so close yet so far away from Dr. Isherwood and her secret life. All I can hear are the birds and the whisper of leaves moving in the wind. I put the phone away, knowing now that Sean was right, and that since I have my answer there is nothing for me to do but go home.

But as I leave the park and take one last look back at the house I see her, Dr. Isherwood, in the doorway. I duck back inside the gates of the park. Dr. Isherwood is outside her house but so is a younger woman who has long black hair tied in a bun. And she is the one holding the baby. A big baby, with too much dark hair, sticking its fingers into its mouth while it screams and screams.

Dr. Isherwood is smoothing the baby's head and talking really quickly, and the girl is smiling and bouncing the baby as Dr. Isherwood kisses its head and presses the button on her car keys to unlock the doors of a dark silver BMW parked outside. I duck further back into the confines of the park and wait for the car to drive past and out of the cul-de-sac.

Then I am frozen. The girl has gone back into the house and closed the door but it feels impossible to leave. Who is she? Is she Dr. Isherwood's daughter and the baby her granddaughter? Maybe Dr. Isherwood had her before she met me. If this is true then it means that nothing—really—has changed. Perhaps the daughter has moved back home for a while and so Dr. Isherwood is just being kept awake by her baby. Maybe Sean got it wrong.

The door opens again and there is the girl and the baby in a pram. She closes the door behind her and pushes the buggy with the crying child inside it, walking briskly down the road.

As the girl rounds the corner I leave the park, following a safe distance behind, always hearing the baby shriek. I listen to the girl talking to the baby, trying to soothe her. It sounds like she has an accent but it's impossible to be sure as she is only saying things like "There, there, baby" and "Shh now, little one."

We come to a small high street. It's nicer than normal high streets and instead of pound shops and Greggses they have a deli and an independent café, and the store fronts match so that it all looks really pretty. The girl pushes open the café door and walks in backwards, pulling the pram over the step. I wait a couple of minutes, pretending to look in the window of the estate agent's but really looking at the reflection of the café across the street to check the girl doesn't come back out.

Then I cross and go into the café. Inside is warm and it doesn't smell of grease and bacon but coffee and fresh bread. I look at the menu, which is full of weird things like toast with goat's cheese and avocado and bagels with smoked salmon and cream cheese. And all the cakes cost more than three pounds fifty, even for really small ones. I take a look around and see the girl sitting near the back, waving a brightly colored toy in front of the baby, who cries but grabs for it anyway.

"Just a pot of tea, please," I say. It is still really expensive: four pounds. I have to use almost all the loose change left in my purse and the guy behind the till seems annoyed as I count it out.

"Where will you be sitting?" he asks.

"Over there." I point to the table next to the girl, and the barista hands me a wooden spoon with the number 8 painted on it in blue.

I take a magazine from the rack, a free local magazine that just has adverts and reviews for nearby restaurants and articles about people who live in the area who set up their own companies. I take a seat at the table and the girl looks towards me and smiles, so I smile back.

"Sorry," she says. "She has a bad mood today." The girl nods to the baby and shakes her head like she's weary but she smiles all the time. Now it is impossible not to notice her accent. It is something European but I am not good with accents and so it could be anywhere. All I know is that she can't be Dr. Isherwood's daughter and the thought sinks in my stomach like an anchor.

"That's okay," I say. "I don't mind."

"This one, she always has a bad mood. Very difficult baby." Again she keeps smiling, her cheeks flushed. She is beautiful, more than most people. Her smile makes it really hard not to look at her too much. I look at the baby.

"Is she yours?" I ask. Then I wish I hadn't because it is so obviously a weird question to ask. I realize it too late.

"No!" she says, laughing. "No, no baby for me. I am an

au pair?" She says it like a question that I am supposed to answer. She doesn't seem to have noticed that I asked a strange question before.

"Okay," I say. I want to keep talking but I don't know what to say. I try to think of things people ask others about their babies on TV and when I hear them in the supermarket. "How old is she?"

"She is nine months," the girl says. "She is trouble. Aren't you, Iris?"

Iris the baby responds with another agonized howl. The girl laughs.

"Oh dear," she says. "So much sadness today."

"Is she always like this?" I ask.

The girl finds this funny. "All the time, yes. All the time." She throws her hands in the air and makes a sound like *hooo*, like she is exhausted, blowing the hair out of her face. The waiter brings my pot of tea and I ignore it, trying to figure out what to say next.

"It must be hard work," I say.

"Yes, yes. Is difficult baby. But the mother, she is so nice. So nice."

"The baby's mother?" I ask, my heart pounding.

"Yes. She work too hard. The phone—always ringing. But she is so nice. How long she keep working, I don't know. I hope she keep working so I can stay but I don't know how long."

"What do you mean?" I ask.

"At first she say she keep working part-time but now, difficult baby, she want to work less. Want to be home with baby, all the time." The girl laughs again. "Some mums, they find it hard, leaving baby. I like to stay and live with them but—" the girl shrugs "—if Mum not working, she won't keep me." She shakes her head and sighs.

The girl stops trying to placate Iris, who is sobbing quietly now, half-distracted by the colorful things that dangle in front of her in the pushchair. The girl starts to pick at her blueberry muffin.

I feel I should pour myself a cup of tea but my hands are shaking too violently so I squeeze them between my knees to hide it. So Sean wasn't lying. Dr. Isherwood has a baby now. And she might not keep being a psychiatrist and then I won't even see her anymore. I try to stop the stinging in my eyes.

"What will you do if the mum stops working?" I ask the girl.

"There are other families," she says, as if it's nothing. "I just like this one more."

I wish I could tell her that she is right, that Dr. Isherwood is the best family she could hope for, but I have to pretend I don't know this and so I just nod as though I understand.

"What about the dad?" I ask, nodding to baby Iris.

"Oh," the girl says, like she's just remembered something. "No, no dad. The mum, she adopt baby. Is why she's so difficult, I think. No bonding, you know?"

I nod.

"Is hard. Is hard work adopting baby. Iris, she never want Mum to leave. Always cry for Mum. Mum leaves; Iris, she think her mum never coming back."

Iris is slowly falling asleep, her breath still coming in uneven huffs, but the tiredness is too hard to fight. The baby's face glistens with snot and tears and dribble. The girl leans forward and wipes gently with a soft cloth.

"Iris sleeps," the girl says. She puts her hands together like she is praying and looks to the ceiling. "Thank you, God!" she says in a stage whisper. I force myself to laugh.

Suddenly the café seems so much quieter. The absence of Iris's cries seems as intrusive as the noise itself.

I want to ask the girl more, but I can't think straight enough to work out how to ask it. Does Dr. Isherwood love the baby? Doesn't she get sick of Iris crying all the time? Has Dr. Isherwood actually *said* she wants to quit her job? Does she think about me? Am I the reason she wants to quit? Am I too much work?

The girl starts to shift in her seat. I watch her as she looks from the table to the toilet door and back at Iris in the pram. Reluctantly, it seems, she gets up and starts to fuss with her bag, hanging it on the back of the pushchair.

The girl slides around the side of the pram and tries to take its brake off without shaking it too much. Iris stirs, and the girl moves very slowly, carefully trying to wriggle the pram out between the tables. But every movement brings Iris closer to consciousness and even while her eyes are still closed her face begins to twist and grimace and little grunts of unhappiness pierce the quiet.

"You can leave her with me, if you like," I say.

The girl looks uncertain.

"No need to wake her up," I say.

The pushchair's wheel catches on a chair leg and Iris throws her head to one side with a groan, wrinkling her whole face up.

"I be two minutes," the girl says. She rolls the pram forward and pushes down the brake. "Thank you. Two minutes."

She half runs to the toilet and looks back one more time before she closes the door. I stare at the sleeping Iris, her hands clenched into fists like she's ready to fight. Then I can't look at her. I have to look away or I will cry. And

when I look away I see two policemen, peering through
the window of the café, looking right at me, and then they
are coming through the door.

FORTY

Her: Then

The next morning the policeman asks us what we want to eat but they only have horrible food and I don't want any of it. So they just give Auntie Fay a tea in a squeaky paper cup and then leave us alone again. Auntie Fay isn't talking to me; instead she just stares at the wall and every time her fingers move on the outside of the cup it squeaks. Then the policeman comes back and he has a whole variety pack of cereal and says I can choose whatever one I want so I choose Coco Pops.

The policeman brings me some paper and some pens so I can draw while we wait for the interview to start. I draw a picture of the gap where my and Mum's house used to be and then I draw me and Sean in the middle, holding hands. I put smoke at the top of the picture and then some fire. Then the policeman comes in to get us.

Me and Auntie Fay sit on one side of the table with a man who is our solicitor and says he's there to help us and make sure we get home. He says I don't have to answer questions if I don't want to and to ask him if there's anything I don't understand. I nod even though I am already confused and want to know what kind of questions they will ask. Is it like a test? How will I know if I say the right answer? But the man is scary, like a head teacher, and his face looks grumpy and I don't want to make him angry.

Two policemen come in then and sit the other side except they don't look like policemen because they're not wearing uniforms. They ask us if we want anything to drink and I ask for cherry pop but they say they don't have that and bring me a lemonade that isn't fizzy anymore. It makes my mouth feel wrinkly. Then they explain that they are going to record everything we say and so I need to say yes and no instead of nodding or shaking my head. They ask if I understand and I nod and one policeman laughs.

"Say yes or no out loud, okay? If you just nod then the tape can't record your answer. Do you understand?"

I look at the solicitor man and he tells me to say yes so I say yes.

The policeman presses a button on the tape recorder and says the time and the date like we do at the top of our exercise books in school before we start work. They ask me silly questions like how old I am and if I understand why I am there and I say yes even though I don't know why I am here. I think it is because Sean and I snuck out last night and then Sean told them we had been to Mr. Sampson's house but I'm not sure so I don't say any of that in case they don't know we snuck out. The solicitor man doesn't even seem like he's listening, he's just writing in a notebook; the bit of black ribbon to mark the page is stuck to his gray trousers.

"Can you tell us again, from the beginning, what happened on the day Luke went missing?"

I look at Auntie Fay.

"She's told you this," Auntie Fay says. "Several times! Every time it gets more and more traumatic for her."

"We just want to make sure we have all the details right. You can be brave, can't you? Can you tell us one more time?"

I nod.

"Out loud, please," the policeman says.

"Yes."

There is a little bit of quiet and the tape recorder makes a whirring noise.

"So what happened that day?" the policeman says.

"When we were in the tunnel we saw Mr. Sampson and he was holding Luke's arm."

"Before that. Can you go back and say what happened right from when you woke up," the policeman says.

I look at Auntie Fay.

"She can't remember all that!" Auntie Fay says. "I bet you couldn't tell me what you had for breakfast a month ago. And after everything else that's happened—"

"Let her try," the policeman says. "Can you try to remember for us?"

"Um. I was at home. Auntie Fay wakes me up but it wasn't really early that day because of the summer holidays. I have cereal for breakfast almost every day. I'm not allowed to watch telly unless I'm dressed first so I got dressed and then I watched telly."

"Good. What happened then? Did you stay in all day?"

"No," I say. I don't know why they're asking because they know I didn't. "Then Sean called for me and asked if I wanted to go out to play."

"Where did you plan to go?" they ask.

"I don't know."

"Where do you normally play?"

"Nowhere. We just go around and then we find things to do."

"Like what? What kind of things do you normally do together?"

"I don't know," I say.

"Have you ever been to the park?"

I nod.

"Out loud, please," the policeman says.

"Yes," I say.

"Is there anything else you both do? How about dares? Do you ever dare each other to do things?"

I shrug. "Sometimes," I say.

"What sort of things?" the policeman says.

"Why are you asking this?" Auntie Fay says to the police. Then she asks our solicitor if this is normal and everyone argues a little bit and then the police ask me again about what dares we do.

"Like to take something, in a shop or something," I say and Auntie Fay is so angry that she's glowing and I can feel her glaring at the side of my head but I can't look at her.

"What about daring each other to go into people's gardens? Have you ever done that?"

"Um," I say.

"It's better to tell the truth," the policeman says.

"Yes," I say.

"Whose garden have you been in?" they ask.

"Um… Mr. Sampson's garden."

"This was bloody years ago!" Auntie Fay says. "What's that got to do with Luke Marchant?"

"We just want to get an idea of what happened the day Luke went missing."

"We weren't in Mr. Sampson's garden then," I say. "Honestly! Auntie Fay! We weren't!" I almost start to cry and Auntie Fay tells them off again.

"All right, fine. So you went out with Sean and what *did* you do when you went out to play?"

I tell them about the playing fields and about our den we were building by the back fences. I have already told them all of this but they are pretending they can't remember. Then we left the den because it was too hot and we wanted ice lollies and so we went back to Sean's house and had Sun Lollies. It was hot in Sean's flat, too, and we said we wished there was a swimming pool and Sean said he knew where there used to be one and that he would show me it. So we walked all the way past the big estate and to the tunnel but when we got into the tunnel we could hear crying and that's when we saw Luke at the end of it with Mr. Sampson and Luke was trying to get away from Mr. Sampson but Mr. Sampson kept pulling him back.

We went up and we asked Luke if he was okay and he said he wanted to go home so we tried pulling him away but Mr. Sampson shouted at us and pulled him back harder. Mr. Sampson had his shopping trolley with him that he always had and it was full of rubbish. It's really hard to understand what Mr. Sampson says because he doesn't have any teeth and he talks funny but he was really mad and he pointed at us and he said he'd get us if we told anyone we saw him. That's what we think he said. Sean asked if he was taking Luke home and Mr. Sampson nodded but when they walked away they walked in the opposite direction from home, towards the place where me and Sean were going to go and see the old swimming pool. We were too scared to go there anymore, and we went home. Sean went to his and I went to mine because we were scared.

"Is that the truth?" the policeman asks.

"Yeah," I say.

"Do you think you've missed anything out?"

"No."

The policemen sigh and look at each other. Then they carry on asking me loads of questions, like what happened when me and Sean went into Mr. Sampson's garden before and if we felt bad that we'd scared an old man or if we were mad at him because he caught us. Auntie Fay has a go at the police for asking the questions and they ask her to be quiet.

"Have you been to Mr. Sampson's house since the time you saw the bike?" the policeman asks.

I don't know what to say so I don't say anything.

"Like we said, it's better if you tell us the truth," one policeman says.

"Sean has already told the police the truth," the other one says. "He stayed up really late last night because he wanted to tell them everything because he felt very bad about what has happened."

"What did he say?" I ask.

"We can't tell you that, because we need you to tell us the truth first. Do you understand the difference between telling the truth and telling a lie?"

"Yes," I say.

"Is telling lies good or bad?" the policeman says.

"Bad," I say.

"So it's good that Sean told the truth, isn't it?"

"What did he say?" I ask again.

"He told us the truth," the policeman says again. "That's all you need to do: tell us the truth. Let's start with what happened last night, when you went to Sean's house."

I tell them about the Chinese and the hard chips and Sean's messy floor and waiting for Sean's dad to go to bed.

Everyone is looking at me. The solicitor man has stopped writing and Auntie Fay is ripping little pieces off the top of the cup and dropping them on the floor, which she would never do at home.

"And what did you do when Mr. Jenkins went to bed?" the policeman asks.

"We wanted to go out and play," I say. "So we did."

Auntie Fay sniffs.

"In the middle of the night?" the policeman says. "Where were you going to play in the night?"

"I don't know," I say.

"Whose idea was it to go out and play?"

"I don't know," I say again.

"You can tell us the truth," the policeman says. "Remember, Sean has already told us the truth. Whose idea was it to go out to play?"

"Sean's idea," I say. I don't want to tell them about the plan because then I'll have to tell them about Luke's thing, the thing I accidentally took.

"Did he tell you where you were going?" they ask.

"Yes," I said.

"Where did he say you were going to go?"

"To Mr. Sampson's house," I say. Then Auntie Fay does a big cry and the police say that we will give her time to calm down. We wait while Auntie Fay has some tissues and a cup of water.

"Did he say why you were going there?" they ask.

"We wanted him to be locked up," I say. "So we were going to search the house."

"Is that true?" one says, like he knows it's not.

"Yes," I say. It is mostly the truth.

"What were you searching for?" they ask.

"I didn't know," I say.

"Have you ever seen this before?" one policeman says and then he gets out a clear bag like the kind Auntie Fay puts my sandwiches in and inside is the little red car. I can hear myself swallow in the quiet of the room and the policeman smiles a little bit.

"I don't know," I say.

"It's okay," the policeman says. "No one will be cross with you for telling the truth. That's all we want. Okay?"

"Yes."

"Yes what? Have you seen this before?"

"Yes."

"Where have you seen it before?"

"It was Luke's."

"How do you know it was Luke's?"

"Because he used to carry it everywhere with him."

"And was he carrying it the day that…the day you saw him in the tunnel with Mr. Sampson?"

"I think so."

"Did you see him carrying it?"

"I saw it on the floor."

"Why was it on the floor?"

"Because he dropped it."

"And when he and Mr. Sampson walked away, did they leave the car on the floor?"

"No. Yes. I don't remember."

"Did Luke pick it up before he left?"

"No."

"Did Mr. Sampson pick it up before he left?"

"Yes."

"Did he really?"

"Yes. I think so."

"Do you remember yesterday, when you did the finger painting?"

I nod.

"Out loud, please."

"Yes."

"Well, when we do that we get what's called a fingerprint. Do you know what that is?"

I look at the solicitor but he isn't looking at me, he is looking at the policeman. The policeman tells us all about fingerprints. They make me look at my fingers and I can still see the black ink in the lines he is talking about. The lines are so small and it seems like they swirl all over the place and the policeman says no one has the same pattern on their fingers, not even identical twins.

"Why?" I ask.

The policeman goes quiet for a moment.

"They just don't. Like snowflakes, they are always different. It's random."

For a second I have to think about it. All those tiny lines. You would need a microscope to see them properly. How do you know no one has the same lines? Do you have to check everybody in the world? Snowflakes don't look like they do in pictures. In real life they just look like white dots, like the bubbles from washing-up liquid. Do the patterns on your fingertips stay the same forever or do they change?

"Do you understand about fingerprints?" the policeman says.

"Yes," I say. I don't though, not really. But it doesn't feel okay to ask.

"So whenever we touch anything, we leave our fingerprints on there."

"What?" I ask.

They explain to me how when we hold things or press a

button it leaves invisible fingerprints and that scientists can put special dust on there to make them visible. Like magic pens? I ask. They don't know what magic pens are so I tell them about the invisible pen and then the color pens you scribble over with and it shows up. Yes, they say, like that. They say they did that on Luke's car and did I know whose fingerprints were on the car?

"Luke's?" I say.

"Yes, and others. Who else could have their fingerprints on the car?"

"Luke's mum?" I say. They say yes. "Luke's dad? Liam?"

"What about you?" they say. "Have you ever touched the car?"

"No," I say. I don't know why I am lying. Or I do know: it's because I am scared and they won't understand what happened because it all happened by accident. I don't remember how I picked up the car. It was just in my pocket when I got home and I was scared and I didn't know what to do. They don't know about how a little lie turns into a big lie and then a bigger lie until you're lying so much you can't remember what really happened.

"Your fingerprints were on the car," the policeman says, leaning in. "Can you tell us how they got there?"

"Are you telling the truth?" Auntie Fay says to me. Her whole face is cracking and breaking apart. I don't think she knows that tears are rolling down her cheeks. There's almost none of the squeaky cup left now, it's just on the floor, like snowflakes, all the pieces different sizes and shapes. "For God's sake, say you're telling the truth!"

"We'll have to ask you not to raise your voice, Mrs. Patterson," the policeman says.

"You're not lying, are you, love? You wouldn't lie about

this, would you, sweetheart? You haven't done anything, have you? Tell us what happened!"

"Mrs. Patterson, please. If you don't calm down—"

"I did touch the car," I say. "I picked it up."

All of the air comes out of Auntie Fay at once.

"It was all an accident," I say. "I didn't mean it. I'm sorry. I didn't mean it."

"Tell us what happened," the policeman says.

I am doing my best, I am trying to be good, but I don't know what the truth is anymore. If I knew what Sean had told them then I could tell them the same but I don't know and what comes out isn't right and I get so muddled I have to keep starting again. The police ask trick questions and they say they don't believe me and I cry, and they tell me not to cry and that I need to be a big girl and tell the truth but I don't feel like a big girl, I feel so little, like they have shrunk me, and every time they stare at me I get smaller but they won't let me disappear.

"Whose idea was it?" they ask me. "Who started it?"

"Sean," I say. "It was Sean's idea!"

Auntie Fay hugs me and the policeman tells me I'm a good girl and that we can stop for now.

"You'll never have to see him again," Auntie Fay says. "Don't worry. You'll never see that boy again."

FORTY-ONE

Her: Now

The policemen come into the café and they look around but it's like they don't see me and instead they stare at the blackboard behind the counter. Baby Iris starts to wake up and makes little noises. I will her to be quiet and not to draw attention to us but she starts getting louder. I stand and grab my bag, desperate to be outside, away from them, where they can't see me. Iris sees me getting up and it seems to upset her more and then everyone turns to look at me: both the police and the man behind the counter and I turn my back and hold the pram by the handles. I can't leave her alone, so I pull her with me. The brake sticks and I panic; I look at the wheels and see the lever and kick it off and pull Iris towards the door.

As I pass the policemen they smile and the barista be-hind the counter is turned away from me and making a coffee and I look back at the toilets and wonder what I am doing but it is too late because now the baby and I are outside and Iris has stopped crying and I am thinking how I just need to get around the corner where the police can't see me when I realize that I am already in too much trouble. I have gone too far.

Without knowing where I'm going, I start to walk. It has turned into a bright and crisp morning. Baby Iris seems happy, content. I turn another corner and walk faster. A taxi stops at a red light and I find myself walking towards it, waving. The driver flashes his lights at me and when the light changes he pulls over and gets out of the car. Why is he getting out of the car?

"Here we go—I'll help with that," he's saying, gesturing to the pram. I am shaking and I have no idea how to take a baby out of a pram or how to fold it up but the taxi driver disconnects the top of the pushchair from the other, handing me the baby in the top part. I climb into the taxi and put Iris in the footwell; then I realize that isn't right and put her on the seat instead. The taxi driver leans in and hands me a handbag I don't recognize straightaway. A second later I realize it is the girl's bag, hung on the back of the pram.

"Where to, love?" the driver says as he climbs back in.

I hear myself giving him an address I haven't thought of in years.

"That's a fair way. I'll need to charge you for how long it'll take me to drive back. Will cost you about two hundred and fifty."

I open the girl's purse and it is stuffed with twenty-pound notes. Does Dr. Isherwood pay her in cash? Is this all for baby Iris? My hands shake as I count out fourteen of them and pass them to the driver.

"It's kind of an emergency," I say.

"Righto," the driver says. He doesn't sound particularly happy but he drives and for a while we pass through every light and I can almost relax. I try not to look at the baby but I can't help it. She is staring at me in the unselfconscious way that babies and animals stare and when I look at her she smiles like she is in on a secret. I reach towards her and she takes a spit-covered hand out of her mouth and grabs my finger in her fist. My heart skips.

My phone buzzes once for a text. I let Iris hold my finger and try to take my phone out of my bag with one hand. It is Jack.

I know who you are, the message says. There is a link to an article. I don't need to read it; I know he has found out what I did. For the first time, it doesn't feel like it matters. I turn off my phone and put it back into my bag. The radio plays happy music; the driver taps his thumbs on the wheel to the beat. We hit the motorway and Iris starts to nod off. She still holds my finger. I stare out of the window, watching things fly past. There is a fox in the median, its body limp, the bright red of its insides spilling out. I look back at Iris, asleep. I smile.

FORTY-TWO

Him: Now

I run my hands under the cold water in the kitchen. Blood runs off my skin and over the dirty plates piled up in the sink. My blood or Calum's, I don't know. The blocked plug means the sink starts to fill with water, bits of food floating on the surface. The pile of crockery shifts and clatters, a noise that pierces the silence in the flat. I hear a groan from the living room.

"I'm sorry," I whisper, standing over Calum. "I don't know what happened."

Calum groans louder.

"Shut up," I tell him. "Please."

Slimy appears behind us. He's groggy, drugged. I can tell from the looseness of his face that he has taken some of the pills I gave him.

"What the fuck," he says.

"He got in my face," I say.

"This is bad," Slimy says. Calum tries to move his head, moaning loudly; blood fills his mouth, and he spits. Then Slimy starts to wake up. I can see him appearing through the fog; the fear starts to clear his eyes. "You need to go," he says. "Fuck. Jesus. He's going to need an ambulance. What have you done?"

Slimy backs away from me like I'm radioactive.

"It was a fight; he started it. It got out of hand."

"It looks like you were trying to kill him," Slimy says.

"You can't call an ambulance. They'll tell the police."

"I don't have a choice," Slimy says, still backing away until he hits the armchair and stands pressed against it.

"He's fine," I say. Calum coughs—more blood. I bend and grab one of his arms to pull him onto his side. "It looks worse than it is." As I say this, my hands throb. One bone in a finger of my right hand is definitely broken.

"I'm calling them," Slimy says, voice shaking. He moves towards his bedroom and I step quickly after him. The way he looks back at me over his shoulder, those terrified eyes—they make me feel like a monster.

"Stop," I say. He does, just like that. "If you call the ambulance the police are going to be searching your flat. How much has Calum got on him? Enough for possession with intent to supply?"

"This is a fucking nightmare," Slimy says. "This isn't fucking real. I thought you were all right. I thought you were a fucking mate."

"I am, Slimes, I am!"

"Don't call me Slimy," he says. His voice breaks. He grabs at his own hair. "I hate it! All of you come around here, eating all my food, using my laptop, my Xbox. You all take the piss! And now…"

"Calm down, S— What's your real name, bruv?"

"Mike," he says, his skinny chest rising and falling fast.

"Mike, mate, we hang here because we like you. Yeah? It's just a fucking nickname; we all have them."

"But—"

"Don't we all sort you out when you need it, yeah? When have I ever come empty-handed?"

I can see him accept this but he still looks afraid, looks at the exit behind me.

"Mike, don't do anything stupid, bruv. Just hear me out, yeah? If I get arrested for this I'm not coming back out. I've got too much on my record. I've never fucked you over, have I? He was baiting me. I was minding my own business and he got in my face. This isn't me. This was an accident."

Behind us, Calum starts to rise, leaning on one elbow.

"Don't tell them I was here," I say. I grab my backpack, take out everything I've got and drop it on the coffee table. I see Slimy's eyes widen, hungry. "See? He's fine. He's okay. All he needs is a fucking sit-down, yeah?" I unzip the inside pocket of my coat and drop down a load of cash. "I won't bother you again," I tell Slimy. "I'm gone. But let me take your laptop so I can sort some shit out."

"I don't know," Slimy says. He looks at the cash, then at the pile of baggies and pill packets on the table. "Fine. Whatever."

"There's some oxys in there," I tell him as I stuff the laptop into my backpack. "Let him have one in a couple of hours. He'll need some ice for now."

"What if he goes to the police?" Slimy asks.

"He won't," I say. I know that he has too much to hide, like me.

Before I step over Calum to the front door, I crouch. He instinctively flinches but I rest a hand on his shoulder.

"For what it's worth, I'm really sorry," I say. "Sometimes I don't know my own fucking strength, you know?" And then I leave, closing the door quietly behind me.

I dump my bike outside Starbucks and go in to use the Wi-Fi. If you look like me you can't just sit down, you have to buy something and even then you can expect the bitchy-looking girl behind the counter to side-eye you every thirty seconds until you leave. I get a coffee and sit towards the back where no one can look over my shoulder.

First I check Isherwood's email. Nothing. I check her Sent folder but there's nothing new there, either. I refresh and refresh and refresh until my coffee is cold and the queue at the counter swells, then dissipates. I try calling Petal again and again but, as expected, I go straight to voice mail.

Frustrated but not ready to give up, I resort to pissing about aimlessly on the internet, killing time until I can hit refresh again. I get a notification. At first I think, irrationally, that it's her, that she's found a way to let me know she's okay. Instead I realize it's a Google alert I set up for news about our case. I set it up in a moment of paranoia, convinced that Calum was a spy, a fucking undercover journo trying to out me. I physically cringe at the memory and I almost don't click at all. What is there they can say that they haven't already said before?

But then I think of her and my blood runs fast to my head. My hands even shake as I click the link. Immediately, my panic turns to confusion. It's not some BBC, Sky News, fucking *Daily Mail* article. It's some weird alt-right bullshit. A tiny site, badly put together and looks cheap as fuck. There's a headline: "CHILD KILLER'S NEW IDENTITY EXPOSED."

Beneath it is a picture of a woman who looks sad but

whose mouth is tweaked into a kind-of smile. She's holding a spoon. In front of her are three scoops of ice cream.

It isn't her, though. It can't be. I lean in. Her eyes are huge and sad and afraid and in them I see her. An absurd part of me thinks: *This can't be her because she is only ten.* I feel years rush by me, the weight of all that lost time, of her loneliness and my part in it. I have to scroll past it and put it out of my mind before it destroys me. She is a woman now. She is as real as I am. How am I only just realizing this?

Security officers Andrew Grayling and Jack Collins sensed there was something up with "Charlotte" from the start. "I thought she was fit, like," Jack said. "But she was weird. Like she was hiding something."

I read on.

As Jack got to know her, "Charlotte's" behavior started to get more and more bizarre. Not only did "Charlotte" steal from Jack's place of work, she also lived in a halfway house and wore an electronic tag on one ankle. It was only when he introduced her to long-time friend Andrew Grayling that he started to realize how much she was hiding.

Andrew thought he recognized her, though he couldn't quite place how. Andrew, who works with a leading security company, used his professional links to find out more about the mysterious girl who seemed to be taking his friend for a ride. "I thought she might be some kind of con woman or something, you know?" Andrew said. Little did he know the girl he was researching was one of Britain's most notorious murderers.

As I read, notifications for Google alerts start to ping one after the other. I can feel sweat beading at my hairline. My skin starts to itch.

> The Luke Marchant story is one of the most infamous cases in living memory. A story that broke everyone's hearts and a shining example of how the criminal justice system is BROKEN as Luke's killers have received MILLIONS of pounds to date in legal aid, benefits, housing and the cost of creating not one but TWO separate, new identities for both of these twisted, vile human beings. It just goes to show that so long as you're a TERRORIST or a PSYCHOPATH this country will support you financially while hardworking BRITS are left to rot. Until now she has been protected by a veil of anonymity and allowed to carry on her life as if nothing ever happened. Not anymore. The mainstream media won't be reporting this because they are RESTRICTED by LAW against telling you the truth. But we are not afraid to tell you the truth. To protect yourselves and your families, you need to know who she is. Jack had a close call; don't let it happen to you. Now we just need to find where Sean is these days…

The news alerts ping faster and faster into my email. I sip my cold coffee but it only makes my stomach feel worse, acid rising in my throat. Fuck. Shit. I click the latest alert and it chills me to the bone. A link to a BBC news article: "BABY IRIS KIDNAPPED FROM COFFEE SHOP."

The BBC include another picture of her now, her hair cut into a severe bob; the edges razor sharp, not a hair out of place. Unsmiling, the fear in her eyes hardened to something like hate. They don't name her, but sites all over the internet have linked to the article that does.

This is my fault. All of it. I want to ask what the fuck she was thinking but I know that she is probably asking herself the same thing.

Uselessly, I try her phone again and again. I try to picture her, wherever she might be, what she's going to do next.

And then it's obvious. I know where she's going, and I need to get there before anyone else does.

FORTY-THREE

Her: Now

The taxi slows; I open my eyes: traffic. I see the driver shake his head and rest his elbow against the window. When I open the window and lean out, I can see cars bumper-to-bumper into the horizon.

"Accident," he says.

Some way up ahead there are people who have switched off their engines and stepped out to stretch their legs. The car is still. I look at Iris, still asleep, but for how long?

The driver switches radio stations, searching for a traffic report. As he does so I catch just part of a news report: "…baby was taken from a café while her child minder was in the bathroom…"

Then it is gone. We listen to a traffic report and the driver rubs a hand over his face. His skin is pink with the stress of it. I want to move forward so badly that I could scream but instead I sit back and look at Iris, her eyelids as delicate as butterfly wings. Thick black lashes fluttering in her sleep. The car is warm, too warm, but I don't want to annoy the driver any further.

The presenter starts to give a rundown of local headlines.

"Can we turn this off?" I ask. "Just for a while. I don't want the baby to wake up while we're stuck here."

The driver turns it off without saying anything and we sit in the suffocating silence of the stuffy car, winter sun pouring through the windows, waiting to move.

Finally, the traffic starts to move again and with it my heartbeat seems to come back, like I've been holding my breath for the past forty-five minutes. At first we only crawl forward slowly and I feel I could get out and run faster than we will ever drive, but eventually the space between us and the car in front starts to grow and we begin to pick up just a little speed. That is when Iris starts to wake up.

I notice her frowning and wrinkling her nose in her sleep. She looks angry, fierce. Then the smell fills the car and I have to lean over and open her window, which only brings her closer to being fully awake.

"Someone needs changing," the taxi driver says. He sounds weary, sick of me and Iris.

"What do I do?" I say out loud.

The taxi driver looks into the rearview mirror to catch my eye. I see him frown.

"Only ten miles to the next services," he says.

I ask him how long is left in total and he sighs.

"If there's no more traffic—touch wood—we're looking at another half-hour, forty minutes."

Iris starts to grimace; now she is making little angry baby noises.

"Maybe we should stop, then," I say, though I want to keep going, I never want to stop moving forward, away from everything.

"Righto," the driver says. Back into silence. Only Iris complains out loud, unembarrassed by the smell.

The taxi driver says we'll meet back at the entrance of the services in fifteen minutes. As soon as I walk away I see him take out his phone and make a call. Inside I check for televisions or radios playing the news but there is only gentle Muzak and the sounds of the gambling machines in the little arcade room.

Baby Iris is screaming now so I walk quickly towards the women's toilets. There is a room especially for changing babies and I go inside and lock the door. Then I panic again. I have never even seen someone change a baby's nappy before, not properly. I waste some time rifling through the bag that was hung on the back of the pram, pulling out nappies, baby wipes and a folded-up mat that I think I am supposed to put on the baby-changing station before I put Iris on it.

Once everything is ready I take a deep breath and start to unbuckle Iris from the car seat. She fights me, pushing my hands away and screaming.

"I'm sorry," I keep saying. "I'm really sorry. I'm sorry."

She is stronger than she looks. As I lift her she wriggles and squirms, like eighteen pounds of pure anger. I lay her down on the mat and try to figure out how her onesie works. The whole time she resists me and I wonder if it is personal or if this is what it is always like. Not long ago she seemed to like me and it hurts me now that she doesn't. The process is disgusting but manageable. We get through it and as I lift her up she already seems calmer, blinking tears from her eyes and staring at me with that serious expression she has. I smile; she smiles back.

"Friends again?" I ask.

I put her back into the carrier and I wash my hands under hot water, though I cannot shake the feeling that I am covered in germs. For a second I think about leaving her here, to be found by the next person who comes in. A mum; someone better than me. I could leave the taxi driver, walk out to the motorway, step in front of a lorry.

But, as stupid as I know it is, I can't leave Iris now. So I pack everything away, looking at the bottle of milk and wondering when she will need that, if it will be enough, if I will need to buy more. When everything is in the bag I head back to the entrance where the taxi driver is pacing.

"Fifteen minutes we said," he tells me, shaking his head. "I'm going to hit the rush hour on the way back if we aren't careful."

"I'm sorry," I say. I feel relieved because his anger means he clearly hasn't seen the news while I've been gone or worked out what's going on.

"Right," he says. "Let's get going."

FORTY-FOUR

Him: Now

I'm on the train within the hour, passing through cities and countryside, back to the past. Sometimes I envy her ability to forget what happened. We are not the same. She was younger and had already been through so much. This is something I couldn't understand when I was an angry eleven-year-old but now it seems obvious. Though we were both there and we did the same things we had two different experiences. Everything that happened that summer took place in that space between us, space which we hadn't even thought of before, would never have known was there until those huge events shattered that invisible barrier and abruptly ended our childhoods. I grew up, fast. But her, she seemed to freeze.

This is why she is drawn back there; she is trying to find out who she is by figuring out what she did. To her it's a knot she needs to unpick, a splinter just under the skin, a word right on the tip of her tongue. But half of what she remembers is already tainted by years of stories she's read about herself. When she tells me what she knows about Luke and Mr. Sampson there are only ever the barest details of truth. All the color she adds herself, like an old black-and-white film rereleased in lurid Technicolor. The flourishes she gained from tabloid magazines and internet discussion boards.

So much of it is still fresh in my memory. I don't want to go back. It's like taking the stitches out before the wound has even healed. The wound will never heal, though, so maybe it isn't the same. Maybe it's more like performing a vivisection on myself, pulling back the skin so I can stare at all the stuff I already know is inside me but now have to look at in all its bleeding, pulsing realness.

And it fucking hurts. I am so far away but it already fucking hurts.

FORTY-FIVE

Her: Now

The driver continues through the town center and past everything I once knew so well. Beneath the roads we are driving on is the underpass where Luke cried and I held his hand and we walked slowly because Luke could walk no other way. I think about how loud it seemed then. Like it was impossible that no one could hear us. But the roar of traffic drowned it all out.

When we turn off the main road, through a quiet residential area and onto the country roads, I tell the taxi driver he can stop wherever he likes.

"Here?" he says. "There's nothing around here. Let me take you to the address."

"This is fine," I say. "I want to stretch my legs."

Sick of me now, the taxi driver pulls over abruptly, yanking up the hand brake and letting his seat belt snap back as he steps out of the car to help me with Iris.

We are on a country road; there are no sidewalks. Brambles snag my jeans and my hoodie as I step out. The driver has assembled Iris's pram and is clicking Iris back into place.

"She's a good one, isn't she?" the driver says, not looking at me but at Iris, who smiles back at him with warmth. "You're lucky: she's a very calm baby."

"Do you think so?"

"Oh yeah. You should see my grandson. She's an angel, trust me."

"Thank you," I say. I think of all the girl told me, that Iris is so difficult, that she never stops crying, and I allow myself to imagine Iris must like me. Maybe Iris can sense I am like her: misplaced, misunderstood, miserable. Together, we make sense.

The taxi driver closes the boot. I hand him another twenty pounds, which he tries to refuse but eventually takes.

"You've been very helpful," I say.

"It's been a pleasure." He gets into his front seat and starts the car. As he drives away he waves out of his open window, before disappearing around a bend in the road. Everything is quiet then. No insects, not even any wind.

The pram bounces on the uneven road but Iris doesn't seem to mind. We are not far away now, anyway. The route is firmly fixed in my memory. In the distance I can see the smokestacks of the steelworks. I can see the towers and structures that loom over the countryside like a dystopian city. There are blackberries on the bushes next to me.

"Look, Iris," I say. "A robin."

It is nice to have someone to talk to as I walk. Iris listens as I tell her how we walked this way before. How we expected, at any moment, someone to see us, someone we could hand Luke over to, but no one came. We wanted to show him the swimming pool. I tell Iris I will show her the swimming pool, if it's still there. Does she like swimming? Iris doesn't answer. I liked swimming. Sometimes we would have to bring our bathers and a towel to school, I tell her, and we would all be buzzing with excitement.

After assembly they would line us up and tell us to choose a partner. No one ever chose me, but it didn't matter because we were going swimming. The teacher would take a girl who was sulking because her friends had partnered up and left her out and they would put her with me. She wouldn't like it but she didn't have a choice. We had to walk to the pool like that, in a line, paired in twos, holding our bags with our towels and bathers. We walked all the way to the leisure center and the smell there was amazing; as soon as you stepped inside you could take a deep breath and smell the pool.

I was a good swimmer, I tell Iris. Auntie Fay sewed the badges onto my swimming costume. The swimming instructor said I was part mermaid. I liked that. And after we'd done our lengths we were allowed to play; there were floats and a little slide and at the end they'd put on the wave machine.

Then we had to go back. That was always the worst part. You never got dry and so parts of your clothes would stick to your wet skin, and your hair would be soaking and it would dry a weird texture, and your teeth would chatter all the way back to school. But for the rest of the day you could smell the pool on your hair and remember the waves, remember when everyone forgot not to like you and let you play with them, splashing and racing and floating.

"Here we are," I tell Iris. We are in front of a pair of rusty gates, the brambles growing through the gaps. There is a sign that says Trespassing Is a Crime and another that says Danger. Then there is the faded sign that says Sports Village for Boys and Girls! On it there used to be a bright painting of a swimming pool full of children, but it is so faded now you can't even see it anymore. I push the gates and they open until the chain between them strains. There is enough room for me to get through but not enough for the pram.

I unstrap Iris, expecting her to cry out, but instead she seems very calm, content. I hold her tight against my chest and cover her head with my hand as I squeeze through the gap in the gates.

"Don't worry, Iris," I say. "It looks creepy but there's nothing bad here."

It does look creepy. Even though I am a grown-up now and I know not to believe in haunted places, my heart beats fast and I feel the hairs on the back of my neck stand up. The path leading up to the old sports complex is so overgrown it is like dusk even in the middle of the day. I hold Iris closer, her head on my shoulder.

Further in and there are the rotting wooden shells of the old towel rental and ice-cream stalls. It was like this all our lives: dead, forgotten, abandoned. Once, before I was born, it was a place alive with children and screaming and sunlight. There is a tennis court and a bowling green and what was once a café that would have sold chips and sausage in a paper cone and Crusha milkshakes and Slush Puppies. There were the changing rooms running along the back, a white wooden building filled with mothers wrapping children in soft beach towels.

For me it has always been dilapidated. An empty place,

forgotten. At its center, the pool. Empty save for the filthy water that collects at one end, the drain partially blocked with leaves and muck.

I expect to feel something, but I don't. Instead, I just look at the place and think of the years it has been left to crumble. How no one cared enough to take it away, to build something else, to return the land to nature. Nothing. Everywhere I have been I have left these holes behind me, little gaps in the world, like the gap inside of me.

There is a rustling and I spin around to see where it is coming from. I imagine police, armed, guns raised, a megaphone. The rustling gets closer and I hold Iris tighter.

"Where are you?" I shout. I feel absurd, silly. "Please. You're scaring me."

Iris weighs heavy in my arms. I know I won't be able to run, not fast enough. I move to the edge of the empty pool, twisting and turning to look for motion in the bushes.

"Don't be scared," a voice says back. "I'm coming out. Please, don't...do anything stupid."

The voice sounds like it is coming from another place, another time. Every noise in this place seems distorted, dulled.

"Who is it?" I ask.

"It's me," the voice says, clearer this time. Twigs snap underneath his feet. When he emerges from the tangle of leaves he was hiding behind and stands tall, I see he is huge, six-four, broad and muscular. His hair is shaved close to his head and he looks mean, angry. I take a step backwards. "It's me, Petal," he says. "It's only me."

The man stands at the opposite end of the long, empty pool. I squint to see his face better, notice the spray of freckles on his cheeks, that his shaved hair is rusty brown.

"Sean?" I say, uncertain.

"It's me," he says. "Don't be scared."

"How did you know that I would be here?" I ask.

Sean shrugs his big shoulders. "I just knew," he says. "When I saw you on the news—"

"I'm on the news?" My arms feel weak. For a split second they loosen their grip on Iris and she slips down my torso. I look down at her, at the toes of my shoes against the lip of the pool, and hike her back up.

Sean tells me that it was Jack and Andrew who named me, that the internet made the connection between what he said and the news about a kidnapped baby. Sean slowly starts to move closer to me.

"I didn't kidnap Iris," I say. "Or at least, I didn't mean to. It's all just happened."

"I know, Petal, I know," Sean says.

"Has Dr. Isherwood...has she said anything? Is she okay?"

Sean takes a step closer to his edge of the pool. "Not about you," he says. "She's scared, though, Petal. Of course she is."

"I would never do anything to hurt her," I say. "I wouldn't hurt Iris."

"We know that. Isherwood knows that. But it's her baby. She's obviously going to worry."

"She doesn't trust me," I say. "She's never trusted me."

"You know that isn't true. Isherwood loves you. I know she does."

"She won't now. She won't ever again." I start to cry and Iris starts to squirm and I am so tired it is hard to keep hold of her. Iris pushes away from my body and seems to slip from my grasp like soap. I catch her as she reaches my stomach, and I pull her up awkwardly, first grabbing one arm, then the other.

"Do you want me to help with her?" Sean says.

I am out of breath from the effort of lifting her back up but I shake my head.

"Maybe it would help if I held her for just a while, give your arms a rest."

"I'm fine," I lie.

"Okay." Sean moves back a little. He is acting like I am holding a bomb and I might set it off at any time. "Have you thought about how you're going to give her back?"

"I thought about putting her in the pram and, maybe, leaving her somewhere safe."

"Like where?"

"Maybe a church or a toilet. You know, a baby-changing place."

"And then where will you go?"

I swallow the lump in my throat and my eyes sting. "I don't know."

"You can still fix this," Sean says. He is lying. There is no way back.

"I've really messed up," I say. I put my wet cheek against Iris's soft head.

"It's bad," Sean says. "But you can make it a little better. You could call Dr. Isherwood, tell her where you are, hand Iris back to her, and say you're sorry."

"Do you think she'd ever forgive me?"

"I do. It just might not be the same as before."

Iris starts to slip again. I hold her under her armpits, and use a knee to push her back up.

"I don't think you're holding her right," Sean says. "Can I come closer? I can show you how to hold her properly."

"Yeah. You can come here."

Sean walks towards me along the edge of the pool. Brown leaves crunch under his feet. When he is close I can see him properly, see the old Sean underneath all the years. I look into his eyes and time seems to rupture and all the lies we told spill out like blood from a wound.

Without thinking, I take a step back and I feel the edge of the pool slip away under my foot and suddenly I remember, I remember everything.

FORTY-SIX

Her: Then

"Come on," I say, reaching my hand through the broken fence. "Come with us. We can show you something. Do you want to be our friend?"

Luke smiles. His lips are pink from an ice lolly we saw his mum bring him a while ago.

"Do you want to see our den?" I ask him. "We built it ourselves."

Luke nods and gets up, walking towards me with his clumsy walk. He needs to crawl to get through the gap I've made. I hold the fence open for him and he comes out.

Now I am supposed to keep him here, in our den, but Luke sees the park and wants to go there.

"No, Luke," I say. "Stay here. We need to wait for Sean."

Luke is already crawling up the hill and into the fields.

I laugh and follow him. I say, "Luke! Luke! Where are you going?"

Luke starts to walk to the swings but changes his mind when he sees a dog down the other end of the park. The dog sees him and runs to him, ears bouncing, tongue hanging out of the side of its mouth. Luke laughs. The owner calls the dog back and it gallops away and Luke sees someone blowing bubbles and starts towards them.

"Luke. Luke! Do you want to come and see something really good?" I ask, but Luke doesn't pay me any attention.

"Oy!" Sean runs from the bottom of the park, and when he stops by me his face is bright red and his forehead is shiny with sweat. "I told you to wait with him in the den."

"He wandered off!" I say. "Look, he's enjoying himself."

"His mum is going to notice he's missing now. We need to take him back."

The plan was that Sean was going to go round to Luke's front door and knock, asking if she had seen Sean's cat. I was going to get Luke to come into our den. Then when Luke's mum went back in and noticed that Luke was missing we were going to take him back round the front of the house and say we found him. Then maybe Luke's mum would invite us to parties in the future because she would know we were good and not bad like everyone says we are.

"We can go the long way," I say. "Luke's having fun. Aren't you, Luke?" Luke doesn't listen to me but he is smiling and laughing and so anyone can see that he is having more fun than staying in the back garden all the time.

"She's going to call the police," Sean says. "She'll be really scared."

Sean seems bigger, lately, and always worried about things he never used to worry about. It already feels like he's growing away from me. After the summer we won't even be in the same schools anymore and then I don't know if he will want to be friends with me or if he will have all new friends.

"But Luke's okay," I say. "She'll like us for looking after him."

I catch up to Luke and hold his hand. In his other hand he carries the little toy car he takes everywhere. Luke is small for his age, even small compared to me. Auntie Fay said that's because he was born really early and when he was a baby he was so small you could hold him in your two hands pretty much. Auntie Fay said it was a miracle he was okay. Uncle Paul said it wasn't a miracle; it was the doctors who made him okay.

I hold his hand and I pull him away from the bubbles, which makes him upset.

"Do you want to go and get some sweets?" I ask him. "We can go past the shops on our way back to your house and get some sweets."

"I don't know…" says Sean but Luke is already agreeing and starts his wobbly walk with me through the gates and out of the park.

"The longer he's missing, the happier his mum is going to be when we take him home," I say. "If Luke gets upset then we'll go home straightaway."

"We can't take him to the shops," Sean whispers. "Then people will see us and they'll know we didn't take him straight home."

Luke seems happy enough and doesn't seem to notice when we turn the opposite way from the shops and more towards the main roads. We have to walk way more slowly than usual because of Luke and it's annoying because it takes longer to get anywhere and it's so hot in the sun.

"Do you want to go in the tunnel?" I ask Luke. We are

standing at the end of the underpass that goes beneath the road. If we go under there it will be cooler and Luke won't get sunburn but Luke shakes his head.

"I don't want to," he says.

"I know it looks scary but it isn't," I say.

"Let's just take him home," Sean says.

"He's fine," I say. "Come on, Luke, let's go in the tunnel."

Luke starts to cry. He pulls his hand out of mine and it slips out easily because my hands are all sweaty.

"Come on," I say. "Don't be a baby."

"He doesn't want to," Sean says.

I grab Luke's arm and pull him along. Instead of walking he falls over and his knees scrape the pavement. Then he starts to cry harder.

"Get up," I say.

Luke gets up, and limps slowly behind me and I squeeze his hand in mine. I want to hug him, I want to slap him, I want to calm him down and make him happy again.

"I want to go home," Luke says. "Where's my mum?"

"Luke," Sean says. "Listen to this." Sean stamps his feet on the floor and the sound bounces off the walls. "Hello!" Sean says. The walls say, *Oh, oh, oh.* Luke laughs. I stamp my feet, too; I shout. Luke laughs and stamps his good leg; his laughter bounces off the walls. I hate Sean because he makes Luke smile and I don't. I stick my foot out and Luke trips over it and starts crying again.

"Shhh," I say. "You're okay! Aren't you, Lukey?"

"I want my mum," Luke says.

"We should go back. Now," Sean says. We turn around to go back the way we came when we hear rattling from behind us. We all turn to look at the other side of the tunnel and that's when we see Mr. Sampson pushing his trolley full of rubbish.

"Hurry up," I say to Luke, pulling him. He falls again and this time he won't get up.

"Let's run," I say to Sean.

"We can't just leave him!"

Mr. Sampson's trolley rattles closer and closer to us. I try to pull Luke up but he stays on the floor. I drag him but I'm not strong enough to drag him far.

Mr. Sampson rolls his trolley right to us and stops to look at Luke on the ground. Even in the middle of summer Mr. Sampson is wearing his long, thick brown coat. Mr. Sampson makes noises but I don't know what he's saying. Luke starts to look afraid of Mr. Sampson now that he's up close. I notice that one side of the old man's face droops lower than the other.

"We're taking him home," Sean says.

Mr. Sampson makes more noises. He points a long knobbly finger at Luke and then at me; then he waves it back and forth like he's telling me off. He smells of cigarettes and damp. As he talks, bits of spit come out of his mouth and I can see his horrible pink gums where his teeth should be.

Then Mr. Sampson bends down and says something to Luke. Luke turns his head away and starts to cry. Mr. Sampson curls his scary hand around Luke's arm and tries to lift him up. Luke cries out, and his little car clatters to the floor.

"Leave him alone!" I say. I grab Luke's other arm and pull him. Mr. Sampson spits and talks some more and Sean keeps telling him that we're looking after him and he's fine with us. Eventually Mr. Sampson lets go of Luke's arm and starts to roll his trolley away. He looks back over his shoulder. His wrinkly forehead wrinkles more; he sighs like he's sad and rattles away. I pick up the little red car and put it in my pocket.

"We need to take him home," Sean says again.

"We can't go now. Mr. Sampson might be waiting for us."

"No!" Luke says.

"Don't worry, we won't let him scare you again," I say. Luke stands up and this time he holds his hand out to me so I can take it. It's wet because he's been wiping his tears and his nose with it but he holds my hand tight and it feels as though he is starting to like me and that is suddenly very important.

"Show us that place you were talking about before," I say to Sean. "The place with the swimming pool."

"Not now. It's too far. Luke's mum is going to be crazy by now."

"I want to see the swimming pool," Luke says.

"Let's just take him there and then we'll come straight back, okay?"

"What are we going to say when he tells his mum we took him to the pool? It's stupid. We have to go back."

"Please!" Luke says.

"Luke, you can keep it a secret if we take you there, can't you? You can't ever tell anyone because if you do then we can't be friends anymore."

Luke nods.

"Do you promise?" I ask.

"Promise," Luke says.

Sean sighs and looks both ways down the tunnel.

"We need to be quick," he says. "We can't stay long and then we have to go back. And if we see anyone we have to go straight back, okay?"

So we follow Sean. We follow him through the tunnel

and down a lane and under the pigeon bridge where the floor is covered in bird poo and in the dark corners of the bridge, beneath the railway, the pigeons all coo softly like ghosts. I nearly tread on a dead bird, a baby fallen from the nest. The other birds have started to eat it, picking it apart. Its little beak is open like a silent scream.

Then we are out the other side of the bridge and into the light again. The roads are quiet. Little insects fly above our heads and I can hear crickets in the field. There is no one around except us, like we are the only people left on the earth.

Sean leads us to a big rusty pair of gates and pushes one back so that we can squeeze in. Luke needs help so I let him lean on my shoulder as he goes through.

Inside looks like a secret garden. Plants have grown through the buildings, in through cracks in the wood and out through the broken windows. I imagine vines slithering to my legs like snakes, wrapping themselves around my ankles and dragging me under the ground.

At the center of it all is the swimming pool. It's empty, like Sean said it would be. A big white basin in the ground. Sean and I stand on the edge of the pool and look down. It's high, even at the shallow end, and in the sticky summer air I can imagine diving into the cool water, the sun shining off the surface as though I'm swimming in diamonds. Not like the pool in the leisure center in summer, the way it seems even hotter than outside, like swimming in old bathwater.

"How come they closed this place?" I ask Sean, who knows everything.

"My dad said it cost too much to keep going. He says if rich people used it then it would still be open, but because it's just us the council don't care."

I think about this. I think about what he means by "just

us." Does he mean normal people? Or is the opposite of rich something else. Does it mean we are poor?

"Luke," I say. "Come here."

Luke will not come closer to the edge of the pool.

"I said: come here!" I grab his hand and pull him hard towards me. Luke starts crying again and I feel bad but also annoyed because I haven't done anything wrong this whole time and he still doesn't like me.

"Be gentle with him," Sean says. "We should be getting back now. This was a really stupid idea. Let's just get him home and forget about it."

"Can I come over to yours after?" I ask.

Sean looks at his feet; he puts his hands in the pockets of his shorts. "Nah, my dad's been in a bad mood lately, so I'd better not have anyone over."

"I want my mum," Luke says, his lip shaking and watery snot dripping from his nose.

"You can stay over at my auntie Fay's if you want," I say. "She won't mind."

Sean looks past my head, somewhere else. "Nah," he says. "That's okay. I think I'm going to play computer games. It's too hot at your auntie Fay's."

It's always too hot in Sean's flat but I don't say it.

"I want to stay longer," I say. "I don't want to go home yet."

"Fine," Sean says. "You're on your own, then."

As he walks away he looks back and I know he is expecting me to follow but I don't. I hold Luke's hand tight, maybe too tight, and pull him to me.

"Come and hug me, Luke. Let's be friends and not fight."

But Luke won't hug me. He pulls away, trying to follow Sean, so I pull him back harder. Luke turns and slaps me.

It's a weak slap and it doesn't hurt but it makes me sad and so I shout at him.

"No, Luke! Naughty! We don't slap!"

To show him we don't slap I slap him back. It is maybe a bit too hard. His cry makes me feel worse so I slap him again.

"We don't cry!" I say. "Babies cry."

Luke stops pulling and instead tries to push me. I almost fall off the edge of the pool.

"Naughty Luke!" I say. "We don't push!"

I push him back and he pushes me again.

"We don't fight!" I say. When my hand hits his arm it makes a loud slap and my palm stings. Luke cries harder and tries to slap me back but instead his nails catch my skin and leave scratches on my arm.

"Ow! Naughty! We don't scratch!" I scratch him back and the place where I slapped him turns red with white scratches down the middle. Luke lunges forward and grabs me, this time he tries to bite me but just leaves a wet patch of spit on my skin. I hold his hand and bring it to my mouth.

"We don't bite!" I say. His skin tastes like sunblock and salt.

Luke doesn't stop hurting me.

"We don't pinch," I say. *We don't slap. We don't kick. We don't hit. We don't spit. We don't scratch. We don't push. We don't stamp. We don't fight. We don't kick. We don't punch. We don't bite. We don't scream.*

"We don't push!"

This time Luke's foot slips off the edge of the pool. I watch him fall. His body, which seemed featherlight, falls like a brick. He doesn't have much time to scream before he hits the ground. I hear the back of his head crack against the bottom of the pool. His eyes are open; he blinks once, twice.

"Luke? I'm sorry, Luke. I didn't mean to push you. Luke, please say something."

Luke says nothing. His eyes move in his head but don't look at anything.

"What have you done?" Sean asks me. I jump. I hadn't even noticed he was there.

"We had an accident," I say.

"You pushed him," Sean says. "I saw you do it!"

"No, you didn't!" I say. "I didn't do anything! He fell over!"

I look at Luke. A halo of red is forming on the white basin beneath his head. His eyes stare terribly at something in the distance, like he is seeing something we can't.

"Please," I say to Sean. "It was an accident."

FORTY-SEVEN

Her: Now

I squeeze Iris against me as tight as I can without crushing her. My hand moves to her head. I must protect her head. I close my eyes, waiting for the crunch of my skull as it hits the concrete. Instead I feel a hand clutch the sleeve of my hoodie, feel the force of being pulled back onto solid ground. I fall sideways, my shoulder curling painfully underneath me. Iris cries out in shock but the sound is muffled by her face pressed into my T-shirt.

"Fucking hell," Sean is saying, over and over again. Then, "Are you okay? Is the baby okay?"

I loosen my grip and she cries louder and louder but it sounds beautiful because it isn't the silence of someone whose skull has cracked against the floor.

"I think so," I say.

Sean bends and scoops Iris from my arms. I let him.

Sean holds her like he's done it before, bounces her, soothes her.

"She's all right," he says. "Aren't you? Yeah, you're absolutely fine."

"Thank you," I say. It doesn't seem like enough. "It was my fault," I add.

"You just missed your step, that's all."

"No, I mean, Luke. I remember. I think I always remembered but I tried so hard to forget. It was me. I did it. You tried to lie for me."

"I shouldn't have. If I'd just told the truth then…"

We don't need to say it. All those lies, how they made everything worse. That's what they talk about in all the books, the articles, the BBC documentaries. The lies, the deception.

That day, when we left Luke, his eyes were still open. Every now and then a slow blink. What did we think? That someone would find him, help him? The horrible truth is I don't think we thought of Luke much at all. Those eyes scared me too much. So lifelike but without life, without understanding. Luke had gone, slipped out of the fault line in his fragile skull.

I tell Sean everything now. The things we never talked about. All the things we should have done differently, or that others might have done. The total darkness of those two days between Luke's disappearance and when the police found his body. The shock as my hand touched the cool metal of the red car in the pocket of my shorts and how it seemed to beat like a telltale heart from beneath my drawers.

How sure we had been that Mr. Sampson would report us to the police. We weren't to know that there was no electricity inside his house, that he lived in such solitude that until he himself was arrested he had no idea a boy had even been taken.

How the police hadn't believed it could really be us. Only after we'd been caught breaking into Mr. Sampson's house did they truly accept that we had lied and by then we had already ruined more lives. All those lies toppling like dominoes, taking down Mr. Sampson, the people who had defended us, our families or what was left of them, ourselves.

The only way to feel better is to tell the truth, my mum said. But she was the only person I could tell the truth to, who would have forgiven me, who would still have loved me.

Sean and I sit and talk, our legs hanging over the edge of the pool. Iris sleeps in his arms.

"You need to call her," Sean says. "The sooner you call, the better it will be for you."

"I'm scared," I tell him. "She will hate me."

"She won't hate you, Petal. She loves you. Why else would she move around the country for you?"

"What if I'm really a sociopath?" I ask. "How am I supposed to tell?"

"You're not a sociopath. The opposite. Why would you think that?"

"It's what people say."

"Don't you ever talk to Isherwood about this stuff?"

I try to think. "No," I say eventually. "I don't ask her things like that."

"Why not?"

"Because I'm scared she won't want to help me anymore if she finds out there's something wrong with me."

"Maybe it wouldn't be so bad if you saw someone else for a while. This is stuff you need to talk about."

"Did you talk about it?"

Sean is silent. We bang our heels against the side of the pool. I imagine a different life, a different time, where our bare feet rest in cold, clear water. Instead we stare into the space, nothing.

"You should call her," Sean says again. I nod.

"You can go. You don't want to get into trouble."

Sean doesn't go anywhere. He bounces Iris on his knee and pretends he hasn't heard me.

"I'm not going to do anything to her," I say. "Don't worry."

"I know. But what about after you've called? I don't want you to do anything stupid."

I try not to look at him. "I just don't think I can do it anymore," I say. "I'm so tired."

I imagine jumping. For a few seconds I would know what it was like to fly. The jagged rocks at the coastline, the foam of the waves as they crash.

"One thing at a time," Sean says. "That's all you have to do." Sean reaches with his free hand and I knit my fingers with his. "Call her."

I turn on the phone and notifications flood in. I take a deep breath and press Dr. Isherwood's name on the screen. She answers immediately.

"Hello?" Her voice is cracking, pained, terrified. It splits me open. "Where are you? Have you got Iris? Is she safe?"

"Iris is okay," I manage. "I'm sorry."

"Can you tell me where you are? Please stay on the phone!"

Dr. Isherwood is panicking and I don't have time to answer one question before she starts asking the next. I let go of Sean's hand so I can wipe the tears out of my eyes. I do my best to explain, though I can't, even I don't understand what has happened. I start talking about Luke and how I remembered what happened, how being here brought it all back to me.

"You're still there? Stay there! The police will help you. We understand! We all understand!"

Dr. Isherwood isn't listening. I try to tell her that I pushed Luke, that I lied, that all those lies have filled me up and weighed me down and now I want to tell the truth but she just won't stop interrupting, talking about Iris, talking about the police and how I need to stay calm.

"Listen to me!" I hear myself scream. "Why won't anybody listen to me?"

Sirens. It is impossible to tell which direction they come from. I drop the phone.

"Go!" I tell Sean. Iris twists and seems to be reaching for me. Sean hands her over. "Get out!"

"I'll stay," he says.

"No! Please! I don't want to ruin your life again. Just go!"

I scream against the sirens, to let them know where I am. Iris screams with me. Sean runs, looking back over his shoulder, hesitating, but he runs.

FORTY-EIGHT

Him: Now

I spent months wondering if running was the right thing to do. Leaving her felt like leaving a piece of myself there and at first I didn't know how I was going to go on. I had to read about all the untrue and fucked-up assumptions people made about her and why she did what she did. It was painful not to be able to tell her that they were wrong, that I knew she was a good person.

They were months where I stagnated, suddenly not sure what to live for. The guilt of leaving her to face the consequences by herself when I knew I'd had a part in it. She only did what she did because of me.

Then I realized that I had only made things worse. Maybe she pushed Luke but I made her lie. Everything that came after, that was my fault, too.

If I could speak to her I would tell her I was sorry. I

would tell her that she has all the stuff inside her that makes people good. I would tell her she deserves to be loved and that it will happen, one day, when she lets it.

She didn't want to ruin my life, she said, not again. So I get up and clean my flat because I owe it to her. I throw out my phone and stop dealing. I get a shitty job at a hardware store with shitty pay because it's honest and decent and actually, over time, I even start to like it. I like the smell of the wooden sheds in the garden section and the stupid names they give to shades of paint and the routine of getting up and wearing that fucking fleece in the winter.

I meet someone and instead of worrying about hiding who I was I show her who I can be. I take her for dinner and kiss her on her doorstep and meet her parents and even though she jokes that I'm her bit-of-rough I feel accepted and welcomed and warm in a way I haven't since I was a small kid. Since her auntie Fay let me stay over and I pretended to be asleep when she touched the top of my head and said good-night.

It is too late to go back and change what's happened. This is fucking obvious but for years it didn't seem so clear. All we can do is move forward and leave new marks on the way.

If I could speak to her now, I would tell her that all you need to do is to make people happy. That is enough. I would like her to know that she made me happy. I hope that these are things she already knows.

FORTY-NINE

Her: Now

The unit manager, Louise, brings me a letter. She sits with me on the edge of the bed. Even if I didn't recognize Dr. Isherwood's elegant cursive on the front of the envelope, I would know that it was her letter because of the way Louise smiles: no teeth, eyebrows pinched inwards, eyes shining.

"Do you want me to stay while you read it?" Louise asks.

"No, thank you," I say. "I would like to be alone."

Louise squeezes my knee and gets up. She leaves the door open, because that is the rule. You are supposed to respect other people's privacy but a lot of the women here think nothing of walking in and touching everything in your room, completely uninvited.

The letter is already open because they read things before we read them. It makes me angry because I know Dr. Isherwood would want to talk to me in private and not have everyone reading her letter. But this is how it has to be, for now, while I am still here.

I have waited for the letter for a long time. At first, they wouldn't even let me write one to her. They would tell me that I wasn't allowed to contact her because of what happened. They never said I wasn't allowed to contact her because she didn't want me to. That was how I knew that she missed me, too. I knew that as soon as the police had finished investigating what happened that she would contact me.

I take out the letter, written by hand on a single, folded piece of plain white paper. It is so short, so much shorter than all the letters I wrote to her that they never let me send. How can she have so little to say to me? I almost don't want to read it because then there will be nothing left to hope for anymore but I do because I have to.

My dearest Lilly,
I hope that they are taking good care of you at the unit and that you are well. They tell me you are settling in and that your new therapist believes you are making good progress, which is good to hear.

I know you are sorry for what you did and I forgive you. Please forgive me for failing you so badly. I cared for you very deeply but this only served to cloud my professional judgment, while professional boundaries meant I couldn't give you the love you needed. As a result, you were left with neither a therapist, nor a friend.

You deserve better. Please don't let your past mistakes ruin your future.
With love,
Evelyn

They don't let me reply to Dr. Isherwood. They tell me that she didn't include her address because she didn't want me to write back but how can I tell her that she is wrong if I can't write back? That she was always the perfect friend *and* the perfect doctor. I hate to think of her being sad, thinking that I hate her because she let me down somehow.

I think of it all the time, everything I would tell her if I could just have one more chance. How is Iris? I would ask. Will she remember me?

Sometimes I think of Sean, too. I wonder where he is and what he is doing. The first days after I was arrested I worried that he would be, too. That I would have dragged him down with me again. But no one has asked me about Sean, never asked me about anyone except myself and what I was thinking. I say that if I could understand it I would tell them everything, I really would.

They let us choose classes that we take three times a week. I choose computer classes where we learn about programming and building websites. I hope that when they let me out I can use it to find Sean and Dr. Isherwood and that I won't feel lonely all the time like I do here.

Lately I have had trouble sleeping. The days are okay because there is so much to do: therapy and art sessions and my computer classes. When the lights are off at ten o'clock all the bad feelings come back. I always think of Luke's terrible eyes, of that impossibly red blood that bloomed from his skull. I think of Mr. Sampson and his loneliness, whether he had done something to deserve it, like me, or if life had always been so cruel to him, right until the end.

I try to make myself feel better by imagining that Sean is happy now. I plan my perfect day, waking up in Dr. Isherwood's house and opening the curtains to let the sun in,

having breakfast in the kitchen, Iris smiling and holding
my finger.

　　I try not to think of the worst thing. The thing I still
haven't told anyone. The thing that squirms and scratches
at the inside of my skull.

FIFTY

Her: Then

We watch Luke through the gap in the fence. He's playing with his cars and he does different voices for every toy, all high-pitched and squeaky. When Sean and I laugh we have to cover our mouths so he doesn't hear us.

Luke's mum comes outside and when she sees him she smiles like it's the first time she's ever seen him. She is hiding something behind her back and Luke strains to see it. They play like this for a while, Luke trying to see what she's hiding, Luke's mum twisting and turning so that he can't. They laugh and the more they laugh the more my eyes start to sting until I'm watching them through blurry eyes. I blink and let the tears trickle down the side of my nose, tickling like the legs of a ladybird over my skin.

Luke's mum stops and shows him she is holding an ice lolly. A Rocket. She unwraps it and hands it to Luke, kissing the top of his head and ruffling his hair. This time, Luke pulls away when she does it, like all the other kids do with their mums. For a second I can see Luke's mum's face go all hurt before she forces her smile back on and goes inside.

Even Luke is going to grow up and start being embarrassed of his mum, like the other kids. They wouldn't if they knew what it was like not to have one. If no one came out and brought them ice lollies and played silly games and ruffled their hair and kissed their heads then they would realize what they had was important.

I can feel the hole inside me burning at the edges.

"We should take Luke," I say to Sean. "We can take him and then bring him back to his mum like he ran away."

"Why?" says Sean.

I watch Luke roll a car over the patio. From the window his mum stares at him. Her face is sad and thoughtful.

"I just want to play with him," I say.

* * * * *

ACKNOWLEDGMENTS

Thank you, Selina, Luigi, Alison, Sonny, Rachel, Khan, Pippa, Catherine, Kelly, Glenn and everyone who puts their expertise and talent into these books. You are my dream team! Thank you, Richenda. Thank you, Peter!

Thank you to my amazing family, especially Jake, Megan and Oscar.

And thank you, Rhys, as always.